I0788523

HOW TO TRUST A HELLHOUND

Hellhounds of Paradise Falls
Book 4

Shannon Mae

CONTENTS

DEDICATION

For my fourteen-year-old self, and for all the people who feel like they're not enough.
You are always enough.

Copyright

ℬLURB:

Wilder

Angels, demons, hellhounds, Nephilim, and a whole host of other non-mortals—my pack of adopted hellhound sons sure knows how to pick a place. And yet somehow, the most interesting one of all is the sad, quiet human who's become friends with the pack. Helping people heal and learn to trust is a specialty of mine, but I don't see Josh as someone to adopt—my hellhound sees him as a mate. The problem? Josh doesn't believe in anything supernatural. Plus, there's the vicious and oddly hard to track ex-boyfriend, the meddling but strangely helpful sheriff, the delicate side project I'm working on, and the immortal evil rich guy running around. As I said, my boys sure know how to pick a town.

Josh

I'm the boring one. No imagination. No fun. In control. My ex-boyfriend taught me how to let loose and explore things, but then he changed... or maybe I just realized who he truly was. I want someone who cares for me, not someone who controls me, but I don't think Rick will let me go easily. Everyone is willing to help, though, including the handsome dad of my best friend's boyfriend. My inappropriate feelings for him aren't helping matters, though. Not to mention that the more I hang out with everyone, the more my writer friend's supernatural stories suddenly don't seem so far-fetched. Something is strange about Paradise Falls, and I can't help but think that Wilder is more involved than he lets on.

Tags: It's always the quiet ones (wink, wink); Josh doesn't believe in hellhounds, but they believe in him; Wilder is just the hellhound to give Josh all the comfort and healing he needs; Helene is the best therapist for someone who's been wronged; the entire pack gets involved (of course) and chaos ensues; abusive ex-boyfriends always get what's coming to them; there's torture and death (but only of really bad people); hellhounds have tails, and they know how to use them.

ACKNOWLEDGMENTS

Thank you to my daughter, Scott, Mona, Tammy B, Jennifer Cody, Avril, and Ellie Ash. You are all an integral part of my team, and I couldn't do this without your support, your friendship, your help, and your belief in me.

Thank you to my readers, especially my Patreon members. You all helped me through this book, giving me support through every chapter (and finding really silly typos lol). Your words not only kept me going, but they often gave me ideas. This story wouldn't be what it is without all your comments, likes, and messages.

I love you all! Thank you for reading!

READER WARNING

This book is intended for mature audiences. It is a dark(ish) romance that discusses torture and death (but only of very bad people). There are characters who have traumatic backstories, as well. These things occur, for the most part, off page, because I'm squeamish and can't watch horror movies without covering my eyes.

There are also some very steamy times between men. Those definitely take place on page, in full detail. All sex acts are completely consensual and fully enjoyed by everyone involved. And (as always) there's a tail, and the hellhound knows how to use it.

For a complete list of content warnings (including spoilers), please check the next page.

Content Warning

- Discussions of torture (torture occurs off page)
- Discussion of past trauma, including violence and abuse
- Abusive relationship (main character—the first chapter is rough, but then he gets out)
- Death (but only of very bad people)
- Kidnapping (but everyone will be ok—don't worry)
- Consensual biting, knotting, and tail play
- Some light elements of dominance and submission (very enjoyed by both people and totally consensual, because consent is sexy)

Chapter 1

JOSH

I sat on the kitchen floor leaning against the cabinets, tears streaming down my face, my head buried in my knees.

"I can't take this shit, Josh. I really can't. It's always something with you. It's fucking ridiculous," Rick ranted.

I couldn't even look up at him. He would see the tears, and he'd only get madder when he did. Crying always set him off.

"I'm sorry," I mumbled, and I couldn't help the hitch in my voice.

"Jesus fucking Christ, are you crying now? Fucking seriously?" he said, and I heard his voice coming closer.

Shit. He grabbed my arms, dragging me up. I winced—there would be bruises later.

"Fucking look at you. Sobbing because, what? I didn't tell you that you have a nice ass? I didn't tell you how much I love you today? I had a hard fucking day at work, and all you can think about is yourself," he yelled.

He shoved me back into the cabinets, a handle digging into my back. I winced in pain and couldn't help the little sob that escaped.

"Fucking absurd," he muttered, walking away.

"I just asked... I just needed..." I started, but Rick interrupted me.

"*I just asked, I just needed*," he mocked in a high-pitched voice. "You're *always* just needing. That's the fucking problem, Josh. I don't know anyone else who would put up with your shit."

I don't know where the anger came from, but it was just so unfair, and I was tired of it. "I just wanted something nice!" I burst out. "Is it so horrible to ask my *boyfriend* to say something nice to me? To make me feel appreciated?"

He slammed his hand against the wall, making me jump, but I didn't back down.

"I just wanted some time with you where we weren't arguing." I laughed tearily. "I guess that's too much to ask for."

"Fucking bullshit, Josh. Maybe if you didn't constantly come at me this wouldn't be a fucking argument. You *know* I'm in a bad mood. You *know* I had a rough day. I fucking told you that, and then I come home to your bullshit. You're always off galavanting with your fucking friends and ignoring me, whether or not I need you. Maybe you should ask them to say something nice, since you put them before me all the time." He stared at me, his face angry. "What about what *I* need?"

That wasn't fair. I always listened to him complain. I always tried to support him. I'd gone out less with my friends because I knew he didn't like them, but I wasn't willing to give them up, and he hated that. I only went out with Toby and Sebbie when he wasn't around.

"I always try to be there for you. If you don't think so, then why are you even with me?" I said, unable to stop the tears no matter how hard I tried.

"I have no fucking idea why I'm with you sometimes, Josh,

because I have to deal with shit like this all the fucking time! It's always you, you, you. You're whiny, boring as fuck, and an uptight control freak. You're lucky I'm with you, because no one else would deal with your issues. I sure as fuck don't get anything from this," he yelled.

"You don't seem to think that when you're fucking me or spending my money," I muttered resentfully.

I knew the moment the words were out that it was the wrong thing to say. His face went totally flat, all expression gone. He walked over and shoved me against the counters, the handle digging into my back again. I refused to look away, though.

"What did you fucking say?" he asked.

I should've dropped it. I knew money was a sore point with Rick. I *knew* it was. But I couldn't seem to help my mouth. I was crying, but I was mad, too, because I wasn't wrong this time. At least I didn't think I was. Not totally.

"It's like I'm the bank of Josh and you're just here to make withdrawals," I spat out.

The slap whipped my head to the side, and god, it hurt. I barely had time to process the sting before Rick grabbed my wrist, pressure tight, like he was grinding the bones together. He pulled me into the bedroom, pushing me toward the bed. I managed to keep my balance, just barely.

He started dragging shit out of my closet, throwing clothes at me.

"I spend too much? What about all your expensive clothes? What about your fucking hobbies—never too much to spend money on your hobbies, is it? Going out to dinner with friends— plenty of money for that, isn't there? Or maybe they're more than friends, hmm?" he ranted.

I slid down, leaning against the bed, crying as clothes were thrown at me, some landing on me, some landing next to me. I huddled down and covered my head as the barrage continued, hangers occasionally hitting me.

"And I give you *exactly* what you want in bed, so don't act like that's some kind of hardship. You're a selfish prick, Josh. I can't deal with your fucking attitude and drama," he yelled, and then the rainfall of clothes stopped, and I heard him walk out of the room. There was muttering and yelling from the other room, then the sound of things being knocked around. Something smashed, and something else fell. When the front door slammed, I jumped at the sound.

I didn't try to hold back my crying anymore, and the sobs made it hard to get a deep breath in. He'd left.

He'd left, but he'd be back. And then what?

An apology. Maybe. Maybe flowers and dinner out. Maybe make-up sex, where he gave me "exactly what I wanted." Although I didn't even know what I wanted anymore, because it was like nothing I did ever made Rick happy.

Or maybe there would be more yelling until I apologized, if it was really my fault. I couldn't even tell anymore. Yeah, I knew I wasn't the easiest person to be with, but I'd had a long day, too, and I just wanted... something. Cuddles, or a kind word, or even a fucking "I love you." I wanted more than rough sex, no matter how much I might usually like it. I wanted a connection. Closeness.

I'd known Rick was in a bad mood. I'd been able to tell the minute he'd walked into the house. I'd tried to cheer him up. I'd even playfully offered him a cheer-up blowjob, but he'd just rolled his eyes. And okay, yeah, maybe that had hurt my feelings, but nobody likes to be rejected, and he hadn't even been nice about it.

It took me another few minutes to pull myself together and stop sobbing. I was cradling my wrist, and my face hurt. There were clothes all over the floor, and I wasn't sure what kind of chaos was waiting for me in the rest of the apartment.

I was just so tired.

I couldn't do it anymore. I tried and I tried, and it was never enough. I was never enough. Maybe Rick was right and I would never find anyone who would put up with me, but at this point, I thought being alone might be better anyway.

A sob escaped me, then I clamped it down.

I got up and walked into the bathroom, splashing cold water on my face and then holding my wrist under the faucet. I looked in the mirror, and a gasp escaped me at what I saw.

There were fingerprints on my cheek. I knew my back and arms would be bruised, but Rick had never slapped me before. I laughed wetly. First time for everything, I guessed.

What the fuck did I do now?

My face was a mess, my apartment was a mess, my fucking life was a mess.

Eventually I shut off the water. I wondered vaguely if my wrist was broken. The pain only seemed to be getting worse, and I could see that it was swelling. What did I even do?

I picked up my phone, and then I stared at it. Seb was having a rough week—lots of dead bodies. He'd freak out if he saw me hurt. And Toby, well, Toby would freak out and then get his scary-ass boyfriend to go threaten Rick or something, and that was the last thing I needed. Then he'd definitely be convinced I was having an affair with one or both of them, and I couldn't deal with that.

I stared at my contact list, and there, right at the top, was the name "Amanda - Work." Aiden had put that in my phone. Aiden, who had said I could call him if I ever needed to.

I hit the call button.

⁓⟊⟊⁓

Aiden didn't show up alone—he had his big-ass dog with him, Fluffy. I was kind of thankful for that, because I didn't know when Rick was coming back or what kind of mood he'd be in. Fluffy had a cute name, but he was fucking huge, and he would intimidate anyone, including Rick.

I let them in, and as soon as Aiden saw my face, he gasped and Fluffy growled. I put my hand up to my cheek self-consciously, and then Aiden noticed my swollen wrist.

"Josh," he just said, and there was so much in that one word—sympathy, understanding, comfort, sadness.

I looked up, blinking and trying not to cry.

"Ok, then. Let's get what you need packed, and you're coming to stay with us," he said matter-of-factly, like he could tell I would break down with any more conversation.

"I can't impose on you guys," I said, looking back at them.

"You can, and you will," Aiden declared.

"No. I'll get a hotel or something. I can't stay with you guys," I reiterated.

Aside from imposing, I thought it would also be awkward. I didn't even know Aiden that well—I wasn't even sure why I'd called him, except he'd seemed like he would understand.

Fluffy sort of grumbled a bit then, bumping into Aiden's leg. Aiden looked down at Fluffy, and he seemed to be thinking. Finally, he said, "We have a spare cabin on the property that's currently empty. You'll stay there, not some hotel. And then we'll be nearby if you need anything."

I looked at him, and he seemed totally sincere in the offer. I didn't remember a cabin on the property, but I'd really only been to Toby's house, and I knew there were other houses in that area that Toby's boyfriend and his brothers owned.

"Ok," I finally agreed.

Suddenly I was just so tired. Not like have-a-nap tired, but more a bone deep weariness, like everything was just too much. Like I could just go lay in bed for a few years because I was so exhausted with life. It all seemed like too much.

Luckily, Aiden took over. He didn't comment on the broken

stuff in the apartment, and he found his way into the bedroom, not making a comment about the clothes all over, either. He managed to find bags and a suitcase in the closet, and he started emptying out drawers and picking up clothes and packing. I knew I should help, but I sat on the bed, sort of dazed, cradling my wrist.

Aiden kept up a steady stream of conversation the entire time, telling some story about Q arguing with a customer. He emptied the drawers and took some of the clothes from the floor and closet. He even went into the bedside drawers, didn't make a single comment about the sex toys, and then made his way into the bathroom, still talking loudly, this time about Jude and the sheriff and their ridiculous flirting, some of which I'd seen.

He kept up the chatter as he made his way into my home office, apparently packing everything up in there. I knew I should help, but I had very little that was actual paper—I kept everything digitally. Fluffy stayed with me, and I was comforted by his presence and by Aiden's voice talking loudly from the other room, even if I wasn't really processing what he was talking about.

By the time he had a suitcase, duffel bags, and my work laptops and stuff all packed, he was finishing a story about his boyfriend eating dog biscuits, explaining that really they were the same recipe as cookies so it wasn't a big deal. Fluffy was just patiently waiting, occasionally glancing at the door as if he was listening for Rick.

"Ok then. The guys will come get the rest of the stuff," Aiden declared, and then he ushered Fluffy out the door, dragging the bags out with him. I heard the front door open and shut, and then Aiden walked back into the bedroom. "Do you need anything else? Anything you want to bring that's important to you?"

I thought Aiden had grabbed most of what I needed, so I shook my head no.

"Let's get some ice for your wrist, okay?" he asked, and he went to the kitchen, where I could hear him rifling about. He came back with a hand towel and a ziplock bag filled with ice, and he placed them on my wrist. I gasped a little, because it really did hurt to touch, and then he helped me off the bed and out the door.

"I don't have shoes on," I muttered stupidly.

"I grabbed them. They're in the car," Aiden replied, like it was perfectly normal to walk outside in socks. Fluffy and my bags were in the backseat, and I wasn't sure when Aiden had done all that. It didn't seem to really matter, either.

He opened the passenger door, helped me into the car, and got in the driver's side, and off we went. I just leaned my head against the car window.

What was I doing?

Rick was going to come home and find me missing, and then he'd be *really* mad. I winced at the thought.

If I was lucky, maybe he'd stay out tonight. He did that sometimes when we fought and I made him really angry. I shouldn't have said the bank of Josh thing. I knew I shouldn't have. I made more than him, and it was always a sticking point.

I was such an idiot.

"Hey," Aiden said, distracting me. "Do you want to go to the ER? Or can one of the brothers take a look at your wrist? They have some... training."

Yeah, I remembered Toby saying something about Dexter maybe being in the military (after he'd decided Dexter probably wasn't a serial killer), and since the brothers all looked nothing whatsoever alike, maybe they all had that in common. Wilder seemed like he had some kind of military background, and maybe the guys followed in his footsteps. They were all incredibly well-built, handsome men.

"Yeah, they're okay," I said.

I didn't really know most of them, and they were a little intimidating, but I didn't think Toby would let any of them hurt me. Dexter was nice, if a little weird, and I knew he'd help.

Was I really gonna do this? Was I going to leave Rick?

I looked down at my wrist, red and swollen. It wasn't the first time Rick had hurt me, but this seemed different, maybe because everyone could see his marks this time. I couldn't just ignore it and pretend it hadn't happened.

I didn't think there was anything left to salvage in the relationship. Maybe there hadn't been for a long time.

Unfortunately, I didn't think Rick would agree, and I got a sick feeling in my stomach just thinking about it. I wasn't sure he would let me go easily, and I wasn't sure I was strong enough to stand up to him. It was probably why I hadn't left him already.

I was just so damn tired. My face and wrist were both throbbing, and my eyes were heavy and ached from crying.

Aiden seemed to sense it, because he said, "Just close your eyes and rest a minute. It's okay, Josh. You're safe."

Safe. I was safe. I don't know why I believed him, but I did exactly as he said, closing my eyes and letting myself rest.

CHAPTER 2

WILDER

I sipped some coffee as I walked down the steps to what had been nicknamed the "torture basement." It really was an accurate name based on what Dexter was currently doing to the... man? Woman? I wasn't sure there was enough left of them to make that call without using my hellhound senses.

Dexter was always one of the messier boys growing up. He did enjoy his work.

"Make sure to burn off the blood underneath your fingernails and in your hair before you go see Toby. And your right ear is covered in blood. Probably get inside your ear a bit, too, for cleaning up," I told Dexter.

The man—it was definitely a man—groaned when he heard my voice. I was surprised he was still alive, what with all the parts missing.

"I'm amazed you've kept him alive this long. Lovely job, son," I told him.

Dexter smiled at me, looking slightly maniacal since he was covered in blood. You could never give your kids too much praise. Yes, he had made a massive mess, but Dexter was good about cleaning things up.

I was a little surprised he'd brought someone back to the torture basement, though. Most of the boys did their work in the field since Dexter, Liam, and Atlas had human mates. This level of torture required privacy and time, however.

Humans could be squeamish about things like torture basements, although Dexter's mate Toby wrote suspense novels, so he was usually interested in the details. Liam's mate Quinton was a bloodthirsty, sassy human, so I didn't think he'd mind, either. But Atlas, the most feral of my boys, had found himself a truly sweet and lovely mate in Aiden, and I didn't think he'd enjoy knowing people were being tortured next door.

"Toby's writing a new scene, and I'm doing some research," Dexter explained. "He wants one of his characters to be tragically disfigured, and he was wondering how much people can go through without dying."

"Ah," I said, sipping my coffee. "Well, don't let me stop you. I'm not sure he'll last much longer without any treatment."

Dexter looked thoughtful at that. Shit. I could see him planning.

"I'm sure you'll get enough information for Toby without prolonging this for days. Plus, I'm not sure the mates would enjoy knowing there's a serial killer being tortured in the basement," I told Dexter.

Dexter sighed but nodded, turning back to the man. The hell-bound soul was indeed a serial killer, and he'd been quite prolific. Just sitting near him gave me a sense of his crimes, and he'd face far worse in hell than anything that Dexter did to him.

We chatted for a bit as Dexter finished the guy off, marveling at how much the human body could take. Dexter did a perfect job of cleaning up, and he gushed about his mate and Toby's newest book while cleaning up. He was truly besotted, and I was so happy for him.

We headed upstairs, and like an eager pup, Dexter raced off to fill in his mate, leaving me to my thoughts.

I finished off my coffee as I thought about our new home. Paradise Falls was an odd little town, with its eclectic mix of afterlifers and others. Usually you wouldn't find such a mix in one place—the crews from upstairs and the underworld tended to bicker—and those of us who had left heaven and hell liked to stay under the radar. After all, our dedication was no longer to our previous departments. We served Earth now, and our loyalty was to her.

But three of my boys had found mates here, and if I wasn't mistaken, the others wouldn't be far behind. It was rather miraculous.

I closed my eyes and breathed deeply, focusing on my boys. Corbin was outside with his crows, and Dexter was already with Toby at their house. Liam was on the other side in his own house with Quinton. Atlas and Aiden were... to the west, but not far away. Still in Paradise Falls.

Jude had been full of restless energy this morning, so he'd gone off to hunt. He was north, a couple hours away.

If I concentrated very hard, I could feel three other mortals—they were *almost* pack members, but they were on the fringes. Very far off in the distance, I felt another hellhound, but it was a very faint trace. Free will would determine whether any of them joined our pack. I breathed out and let my concentration fade. Finding those who weren't pack yet was difficult and a bit draining.

Being able to easily find my boys, though, had made wrangling a bunch of adolescent hellhounds a hell of a lot easier. I smiled to myself, thinking of all the mischief they'd gotten into as they'd grown up. I'd been blessed to have them all in my life.

I'd spent some quality time with most of my boys since coming to Paradise Falls, but I hadn't really had one on one time with Corbin yet. I tracked down some nuts and stuffed them in my pockets before

I made my way outside, following my senses. Corbin was a little ways into the forest, sitting cross legged on the ground. His crows announced my arrival, but Corbin already knew I was coming. He had his own sense of the pack because of his witch blood.

He nodded at me, and I sat next to him. I took out my offering, and the crow on his shoulder took a nut from my hand, and then, as if that gave the rest permission, they came down from the trees and surrounded me.

Corbin smiled fondly at them as I threw nuts out for them.

"You spoil them," he said.

"Isn't it a grandfather's job to spoil his grandchildren?" I asked.

Corbin laughed, which was my aim. He was usually too serious. Besides, the crows were like his children—his pack within the pack.

He pet the one that had returned to his shoulder, and we sat in content silence for a while, watching his crows and occasionally chuckling at their antics. I was gifted with a perfectly smooth pebble that had hues of white and blue, and I thanked the crow who brought it to me, slipping it into a pocket.

Sometimes just sitting with Corbin was enough. He was like Atlas in that way—he enjoyed quiet companionship. I could tell he had something on his mind, though.

"What have your crows been telling you? Or is it Mother Earth who is worrying you?" I asked.

Corbin hummed thoughtfully. "This town. There's something about it."

"Yes," I agreed. I sat and let him gather his thoughts. I knew sometimes it was hard to put feelings into words.

"Things are... changing. I don't think in a bad way. I think the universe wants change, and I think it helps us along." He stopped, looking into the distance. "Three of my brothers have mates," he added.

I nodded, wondering how to discuss his feelings on the matter.

He loved the new packmates—I could sense that amongst all the pack. The humans were welcomed and protected by all. Yet I could also sense a... yearning coming from Corbin.

"I scent him sometimes, I think," he said.

I looked at him, waiting for him to continue. He was staring off into the woods, and I knew that he was talking about his own mate.

"The crows... I think they know him. But for some reason, part of me is holding back," he finally said.

"You have always trusted your own judgment, and it has never led you astray. I know sometimes it's hard for you. I know your hellhound instincts and your mystical knowledge are not always in agreement. Yet you make the right choice every time. A part of you knows what side needs to be followed," I reassured him.

He hummed, but I could still sense his uncertainty.

"Do you remember the village baker?" I asked him.

Corbin looked at me then, shaking his head. I figured he'd forgotten the story, but I hadn't.

"When you were still a pup and you were brought to me, one of the first towns we went to had a rotten soul—the village baker. We were all set to take care of the man, and I thought it would be a good bonding experience for the pack. We went to his home under darkness, and as we walked towards the door, you put your hand out and grabbed onto Dexter, who was in the lead. You said, 'Not yet.' We all stared at you, and I knew some of the boys thought maybe you were feeling nervous about killing with us."

Corbin chuckled at the thought, and I smiled at him.

"I trusted my own instincts, and they said to trust yours. I could sense your hellhound yearning to bring justice to the man, but I thought perhaps you needed time to acclimate to the pack a little better. For two more nights, you said it wasn't time yet, and the boys grumbled and groaned, but I said we'd give you time. The baker wasn't going anywhere, after all, and even if he did, we could track him." I trailed off, remembering the man. He had been truly rotten down to the core.

"I don't remember a baker being our first kill as a pack," Corbin said.

"Yes, because he wasn't. The fourth night, the stench of rot was so strong in the air, and you told us all that it was time. The baker was meeting up with like-minded individuals, it turned out."

Corbin smiled. "Ah, the barn massacre. I do remember that. It was the first time I felt like I had a family since my mother had died."

I chuckled. "Yes, it was an excellent bonding experience for us all. We had many kills that night, and it was thanks to you. Your hellhound cried out to kill the man on that first night, but a part of you knew that greater justice would be served if you waited."

Corbin nodded.

"Patience has always been your virtue. Have patience, son, and your time will come. Trust in yourself. You know what's right." I placed my hand on his back.

He looked off into the distance again, clearly thinking. His crow ruffled their feathers and cawed, and there were answering caws from the trees.

Corbin looked at me. "It isn't my time, but perhaps it's yours," he stated.

We both heard the car a moment later, and Corbin smiled at me. "Time to go, old man."

I laughed at him, ruffling his hair. "Alright, pup, I'll go check it out." I stood up and started walking, calling over my shoulder, "I love you, Corbin, and your murder of crows."

I heard cawing in response, and then I made my way to Atlas and Aiden's house. I heard their voices before I saw them. Despite their attempts at whispering, they weren't very quiet.

"I can't drive to the cabin, because we don't actually have a road to the cabin. We should have thought of that!" Aiden hissed.

"He can stay here," Atlas stated, and I knew from his voice it wasn't the first time he'd said it.

"He doesn't *want* to stay here, and we need to respect what he wants," Aiden told him.

"But why not? We'll protect him," Atlas insisted.

"It's a human thing, okay? He doesn't want a lot of people around. And he doesn't even know you," Aiden insisted.

"He does so. He's met me a bunch of times," Atlas replied.

"No," Aiden said slowly, "he's met *Fluffy* a bunch of times. You're going to have to be Fluffy."

"But who will carry the stuff?" Atlas asked, obviously confused at why he couldn't be Atlas.

I almost laughed at their conversation, then I smelled him.

Josh.

The man who had been at Toby's. He smelled like cinnamon sugar and vanilla, like a tasty treat. Yet there had been something there that night that had made me stay away, despite my desire to go speak to him. There had been a faintly acidic smell of fear, like an orange gone to mold. I hadn't liked the scent, and I knew all of us hellhounds together could easily make humans nervous, so I had kept my distance and let him get used to us. After all, I knew I'd have plenty of opportunities to meet him. He was one of Toby's best friends, and he was on the fringes of the pack.

Only he wasn't near all the hellhounds now, and the tangy, rotten orange smell of fear and pain was heavy in the air. I suddenly knew that he was injured, and I began to run toward the sound of Aiden's and Atlas's voices.

CHAPTER 3

JOSH

I wasn't really asleep, but I wasn't totally awake either. I felt… kind of outside of myself. My wrist and face were throbbing in time to my heartbeat, and that felt like the only thing keeping me tethered to my body.

I was just so tired.

I could hear Aiden talking to someone I didn't recognize outside the car—probably his boyfriend. I'd never met the guy. I felt a mild curiosity to see him, but opening my eyes and turning to look at them seemed like entirely too much work. I probably did need to get out of the car, but that seemed exhausting, too.

There was a third voice, then, and I did open my eyes at that, although I couldn't manage the energy to move my head to look. I thought maybe it was Dexter's adopted dad, Wilder, who I'd seen at Toby's party. There were more muffled voices, and then my car door opened.

Aiden's voice was soft as he said, "Josh? We didn't think about the cabin not having a road to it yet. It has a trail. Do you think you can walk? It's maybe fifteen minutes. Or you can always stay with us, or with Toby."

"Of course I can walk," I said. "I'm fine."

I wasn't fine, and on some level I knew that, but I was so used to saying I was that it came out automatically.

I could hold it together for a fifteen minute walk. Then everyone would leave me alone, and I could crawl into bed, sleep for a week, and not worry about Rick coming home or Toby asking questions or anything at all.

I distractedly thought about work for a moment—I'd have to email Barb and let her know I was taking some time off. I had plenty of accrued time. Plus, I was ahead on all of my accounts because I'd been working a lot lately. Numbers and spreadsheets and organizing data helped me not to think about the mess my life had become.

"Josh?" Aiden asked gently, and I blinked, because my eyes wanted to start tearing up at the understanding tone in his voice.

Yeah, I probably needed to get out of the car.

I nodded my head, although he hadn't really asked a question, and I swung my legs out, holding my wrist close to my chest as I got out. I heard a growl from nearby when I stepped out, and I almost picked up my head to look, but I figured it must be Fluffy.

I didn't want to look at Aiden's boyfriend or the dad. I didn't want anyone to see me like this, a handprint across my face.

I felt ashamed.

Aiden must have sensed my wariness, because he said, "Wilder will bring your stuff to the cabin. Fluffy and I will walk you there and get you settled."

I nodded my head. Good. I didn't have to meet anyone right now. I felt sort of bad. Aiden had come to rescue me, and I should want to meet his boyfriend, but I just... couldn't.

"Why don't you rest your hand on Fluffy's back while we walk," Aiden suggested.

Fluffy was suddenly next to me, and he was so big that I didn't need to bend down to put my good hand on his neck. I just rested it there, and he was super warm and super soft. He started slowly walking, and I walked along with him. I wondered vaguely if he was a service dog or something—he was clearly guiding me, which I was thankful for. I didn't want to pick my head up. I didn't want to look around. It was easy to just let my legs walk, look down at the ground, and follow Fluffy's lead.

I don't know how long we walked. Aiden had said it was fifteen minutes, so it must have been that. Time was being funny, and it seemed like not long at all before Fluffy was guiding me up steps and through a door. It was like he could sense how tired I was, because he led me to a bedroom. I looked up to see a bed made up with sheets and a comforter, and it called to me.

I was so tired, but suddenly I didn't want to get into bed with these clothes on. It felt like they were somehow sullied by the fight with Rick. I wanted to be clean. Clean pajamas and bed.

"Can I shower?" I asked, sensing that Aiden was right behind us.

"Of course," Aiden said, and he guided me into the bathroom. There was a huge walk-in shower, and there was soap and shampoo and stuff inside it. "I can help you take your shirt off."

I thought about it for a minute. I could drag my pants and underwear down with one arm, no problem. I wasn't sure about the shirt, though, so I just nodded my head.

Aiden stretched it out a bit and managed to get it off my good arm first, and then he lifted it over my head, and finally down the side with my hurt wrist, barely jostling it.

"Oh, Josh," Aiden said.

I knew I was bruised. I knew I had marks on my chest and back. Some of them were consensual, I supposed, and some of them were from fights.

"They aren't... Some of them..." I started, but I trailed off, too tired to explain.

If Aiden had asked questions or showed me pity, I think it

would have been my undoing, but he just walked over and turned the shower on to let it heat up.

"Do you need help getting anything else off?" Aiden's voice was matter-of-fact and business-like, and I was thankful for it.

I shook my head no.

"Do you want me to pull out something comfy to wear? Maybe some sweatpants? And we'll have someone look at your wrist, okay?" he asked.

"I'll need a shirt," I said. I didn't want anyone else seeing my chest and back.

Aiden hummed thoughtfully then said, "I'll grab a t-shirt from the house and cut the neck a bit so it's looser and easier to get over your arm, okay?"

I nodded.

"Call if you need help." Then he left, pulling the bathroom door gently shut.

I kicked off my shoes and sat on the toilet seat to take off my socks, and then I shimmied my pants down with my good hand. I kept my head down, refusing to look in the mirror as I got into the hot spray of water and started soaping down.

I knew what I'd see. A handprint on my cheek and, based on the throbbing I felt, maybe the start of some bruising, red-rimmed eyes from crying, and a swollen wrist. I was sure there were marks on my upper arms and a large bruise in the middle of my back from today's fight. There would be older bruises, too, from being grabbed or pushed.

Then there were the.... other marks. Bruises, bites, hickeys. Once upon a time, I had enjoyed seeing my skin marked after sex— it had felt weirdly satisfying to feel like the sex had been so passionate that it had left behind marks. Now, the marks just made me feel sick. Did I even like what Rick and I did in the bedroom anymore? I used to enjoy things a little... rough. Wild. Rick and I had started out with a fantastic sex life, where I felt sexy and wanted and powerful.

Now I didn't even know what I liked. There were no soft words with a pinch or slap on the ass. Things went from being sexy and flirty to just hurting, and I never complained. Why hadn't I ever said anything? Or maybe I had, and Rick had brushed me off and made me feel dumb. That seemed to be the case when I said anything lately.

Rick made everything confusing, and there was just shame and fear when I thought about it all.

I was so fucked up.

I finished soaping myself off, probably rougher than I ought to be since I felt my skin ache. I washed my hair with the shampoo in the shower, then I turned the water even hotter to rinse off. I wanted to scald away the day. Burn off the past few months.

I gave a slight sob, and I heard rustling outside the door. I stifled my crying and turned off the water. Almost done. Almost time to just... let go. Aiden would look at my wrist, and then I'd climb into bed and just... sleep. Anything else seemed overwhelming.

I got out of the shower and there were sweatpants on the closed toilet seat. I managed to dry myself off with one arm, and then I sat down and finagled the sweatpants on one leg and then the other, standing to pull them up.

I opened the door to ask Aiden for the shirt, only it wasn't Aiden standing there. It was Wilder. I took a shaky breath when I saw him, but his eyes didn't leave mine. He didn't look down at my chest. He just held the shirt out to me without a word.

If I had seen pity or disgust in his eyes, I would have shut the door in his face. But he just looked... calm. Understanding. Like it wasn't all that bad. Like nothing was all that bad.

I took another shaky breath in, and maybe it was the start of a sob, I don't know, but Wilder opened up his arms, still staring into my eyes and not looking at my bruises.

I didn't make a conscious decision—I was just in his arms, crying onto his chest. I thought I was all cried out, but he was big and warm, and he was rumbling softly in a comforting way, making soothing sounds. Apparently I had more tears in me, because I sobbed against him.

I don't know how long I cried. It felt like ages, but it could have been two minutes. My eyes hurt. Everything hurt. Wilder was still rumbling in a soothing way. He gently guided me to the couch, leaving me tucked into his chest. He sat down and sort of pulled me into his lap as he did, like I was a little kid.

Dear god, what was wrong with me? I had soaked the man's t-shirt with tears and probably snot, and we hadn't even really been introduced. I started to pull away, but he just shushed me and held onto me. I heard a knock on the door, and Wilder draped the t-shirt over my back, covering me up, still rumbling and holding onto me with one arm.

I knew I could have pulled away—I could tell he would have let me go if I really tried—but it was just easier not to, especially now that people were here. I couldn't deal with people, and Wilder seemed to know it.

"Dry your face on my shirt, pup, and just stay here and relax while my boy takes a look at your wrist," a deep voice rumbled into my ear. Then he rested his chin on top of my head, pressing my face in a little as if encouraging me to wipe my snot on him.

I gave a little uh-uh sound, shaking my head a bit, because I didn't want to snot up the guy.

He just chuckled. "I raised five boys. Believe me, there's no mess I haven't seen."

I felt like he was talking about more than just my wet face and his ruined t-shirt, and I relaxed a little in his arms.

He picked his head up for a moment, and I knew he wasn't talking to me when he said, "Just Corbin and Aiden, I think."

"And Fluffy," I mumbled, because I wanted the big dog to come in, too.

He nodded his head against me. "Aye, Fluffy is a good emotional support animal." He seemed to be teasing, but it wasn't mean, and I didn't think it was me who was being teased, either.

I heard them come in, and Aiden asked, "Do you want me to help you get your shirt on, Josh?"

I shook my head no. I didn't want to move. I knew it was stupid and I was behaving like I couldn't take care of myself, but Wilder was warm and he smelled good and I didn't want to face anyone.

A hand reached between Wilder and me then, gently drawing my wrist out, which Wilder had been careful not to press against. I heard a caw, which sounded very close, but that didn't make sense. Fingers softly touched my wrist, there was a spark of pain, and then Wilder's smell got stronger—it almost smelled of sap and a match that had gone out.

Wilder rumbled against my ear again, only it was deeper, and it seemed to settle inside of my bones somehow. I heard another voice —maybe Corbin's?—humming or whispering or something, and then everything faded as I let my mind float away.

Chapter 4

Wilder

I could feel the moment that Josh let go and drifted into a sort of sleep. I had to resist the urge to pull him closer, but I didn't want to cause him any pain, and his body was a mass of bruises and marks.

I hadn't fully looked at all the marks, keeping my eyes on his when he opened the bathroom door. Even though I had plenty of practice schooling my expression (raising five boys will enable you to never look surprised or angry), I knew that I would do something foolish like growl if I examined the full extent of his injuries.

Josh didn't need me growling or getting all gruff and angry on his behalf. He needed comfort.

Corbin had his eyes closed and was softly humming as he felt along Josh's wrist. I wasn't sure if it was my hellhound who had caused Josh to sleep or Corbin's witch abilities, but I was thankful he could rest through this part.

"Not broken," Corbin muttered. "Bones seem okay, but the ligaments aren't. He'll need to ice and rest it, and I'll send a tincture over for him to use. Something he can use on the bruises, too."

I continued to rumble softly, a deep hellhound reverberation I felt in my soul.

Corbin looked at me. "That's helping him, too, whatever it is you're doing. If you could do that, why didn't you help us with all the broken bones we had as kids?"

I didn't tell him that sometimes I didn't even remember what I could do. Instead, I joked, "The broken bones taught you not to be so reckless. Plus, you healed them in a matter of minutes. You certainly didn't need me. Even that time Jude jumped off a roof, he was good as new in a couple hours."

Corbin snorted at that, remembering the incident. If Jude had done it in pursuit of a hellbound soul, I would have been more sympathetic. But he had just wanted to see how much damage he could deal with and how long it would take to heal. I think he'd also wanted to freak out the neighborhood kids who had been teasing Corbin about his crows (which I certainly would have handled if I'd known about).

Needless to say, we'd moved right after that. Raising hellhounds had never been dull, and I wouldn't trade it for the world.

Corbin finished humming and gently tucked Josh's hand back between us, lightly resting it on my chest. He stood up and headed toward the door without another comment, probably to start preparing some medicinal stuff for Josh.

Aiden stepped forward. "Josh doesn't know about... any of this hellhound stuff. Toby says stuff all the time, but he just thinks it's Toby being Toby."

I nodded my head, then I growled the question that had been plaguing me since I'd first smelled Josh's pain and fear. "Who did this to him?"

Aiden didn't look afraid, even though I knew my eyes were glowing flames. He looked resigned, which only made me more concerned.

"His boyfriend, I think. Only he isn't a hellbound soul, is he?" Aiden asked, looking down at Fluffy.

Fluffy growled, but he reluctantly shook his head.

Fuck. That did make things more difficult.

Fucking free will.

Usually I loved that humans had the capability to redeem themselves. It was good to know that they *could* change, that they *could* become better. It took a lot to make someone irreversibly hellbound. They were beyond saving if they were on our radar, and we were cleansing the Earth by disposing of them.

This time, though, I had the urge to kill someone who *wasn't* hellbound. Someone had done this to Josh, and I wasn't supposed to punish that person? I was supposed to wait and see if he could redeem his rotten, fucked up soul?

It was the first time I had the urge to go against the tenets of hellhounds.

"I think..." Aiden sort of trailed off, looking at Josh, then me, then Fluffy.

"What is it, son?" I asked, my voice gentle. Aiden had his own trauma, and he was pack—he didn't deserve to deal with my frustration when it had nothing to do with him.

"I think Rick has been bad for him for a long time, but I'm not sure... He said some things, and he's hinted in the past..." Aiden trailed off and blushed this time. "I'm not sure I should even say anything. He obviously didn't want his two best friends to know what was going on."

"He's pack," I said. "We take care of our own, and we don't judge."

He wasn't fully pack yet, but he would be—I would make sure of it. I could feel the stirrings of a bond, and it was nothing like the bond I had with my boys. This felt like so much more. It felt like endless possibilities, but it wasn't quite realized yet.

I didn't tell Aiden that, though. Josh had gone through a lot, never mind the fact that he didn't even know we were hellhounds. This was probably going to be a bit complicated. That was okay. I'd had my entire existence to deal with complicated situations. I was patient.

Aiden still looked hesitant, but Fluffy licked his hand, and when Aiden looked down, Fluffy nodded his head.

Aiden sighed. "He said that... Well, he was starting to explain about some of the marks, and he was embarrassed and ashamed, and I felt like I knew what he meant. Like I knew what he was talking about."

Fluffy rumbled and licked his hand again, because Aiden was obviously getting distressed. I still wasn't quite sure what he was saying, though.

"Sometimes I did things I didn't want to do to please my captor, and I felt ashamed afterwards and like it was my fault because I didn't say no. Then Josh said something about sex and trust one time when we were all hanging out..." Aiden trailed off again, blushing.

Ah. I thought I understood. I thought about the bruises. Some were clearly from being grabbed or smacked, but I thought I had seen bite marks and hickeys, too. None of that changed the fact that Josh had been abused.

"When you have to do something and feel like you can't say no, or your no won't matter, then you do what you have to in order to survive. It's still abuse, and it's wrong of the other person, but there's nothing for you—or Josh—to feel ashamed about," I assured Aiden.

He seemed comforted by that, and I saw some of his tension drain. I wondered if he thought I would judge Josh—or him.

"You can leave him with me. It's okay," I told Aiden. He was such a good soul, and I knew he wanted to take care of Josh, but I also knew this had probably brought up some difficult memories for him.

He looked at me again for a moment, then he nodded and left, Fluffy walking beside him.

I held Josh, gently rumbling and hoping that it was indeed helping the man in my arms heal. Could hellhounds heal others? As a first gen hellhound, I knew I had gifts that second gen hellhounds didn't, but even I couldn't remember them all. Sometimes the only way to live in the present and enjoy life was to let the past go, and when you'd lived since the beginning of time, you understandably forgot things. The underworld itself was a vague, distant memory—almost like more of a dream than a reality.

I didn't know if I could really heal Josh, or if Corbin had just sensed the pack bond growing and hadn't known how to describe the comfort I could provide, but I would continue to do what I could to help the man in my arms.

I sat cuddling with Josh until the sky was dark outside. Luckily, the boys had turned on the lights when they got in, because I wasn't moving and waking Josh. I was glad that he would stay in the cabin on pack lands. I knew Liam had set up cameras all over the woods, so we would be able to keep an eye on him. Perhaps his boyfriend wasn't hellbound yet, but I wasn't counting on an abusive partner just remaining slightly rotten. I'd be sure to have Liam check things out using his technology skills as soon as I was able, although perhaps Aiden had already filled him in.

Josh stirred against me, and I heard his breath quicken as his body stiffened.

"Shh. It's alright. You're safe. You're in the cabin that Aiden and Fluffy brought you to. You know me—I'm Wilder, and I helped you get ready for Corbin to look at your wrist. Luckily, you fell asleep while he was doing that," I said softly.

Josh relaxed the more I spoke, so I continued. "Your wrist isn't broken, but it *is* sprained. You'll need to rest it and ice it, and Corbin will send over some cream or something that'll help with the healing."

I felt Josh nod his head against my chest. He wasn't totally relaxed, but he wasn't as panicked as when he'd first woken up.

"Are you hungry? Would you like me to get you something to eat?" I asked him.

He shook his head no against my chest. "Just tired," he mumbled.

"Would you like me to help you to bed?" I asked.

Josh nodded, and then he gave a little exhalation of surprise when I scooped him into my arms and stood up. I carried him into the bedroom before he could protest, allowing the shirt that I had still been holding against his back to fall. I'd bring it in once he was settled in bed.

I sat him gently on the edge of the bed, then pulled the covers back, picked him back up, put him in bed, and pulled the covers over him.

I could see his eyes shining in the light from the other room, tears glistening on his eyelashes. I couldn't help it—I reached up and smoothed a hand over his head, gently petting him, and he closed his eyes, seeming to settle.

"I don't think you should go to work tomorrow. Can I send someone a message?" I asked.

"Yeah," he murmured sleepily, not even opening his eyes. "Barb —she's in my phone. I have lots of time off. Passcode is 273511."

"Ok. You just rest. I'll take care of everything." I started softly humming, and it wasn't long before Josh drifted back into sleep.

I wanted to stay and watch over him, but I had promised to take care of things. I walked into the living area and grabbed the bags I'd brought from the car. Most of it was clothes, which I quietly put in the bedroom. I didn't want to unpack that now. There was a bag of toiletries, which I placed in the bathroom. I eventually found his phone in amongst what looked like work stuff, and I set most of that in the second bedroom. It would be easy enough to get a desk delivered for Josh to work from when he was up to it.

I entered his passcode and went into the text messages, sending off a message to Barb, who was in his contacts, and saying that I was a friend of Josh's and he wasn't feeling well at all and would be out for a couple days. Despite how late it was, she responded right away, instructing me to take care of him and give him plenty of chicken soup. I wasn't sure what chicken soup would do, but I sent back a quick reply.

The most texted person in his phone was someone named Rick, and I figured this was probably the boyfriend. I opened up the texts and saw that the last one was from this afternoon.

Rick: *I'm having a shitty day. Fucking assholes at work who won't shut up. Hopefully you didn't make plans again to ditch me for your friends, because I'm not in the mood to deal with them.*

Josh had replied nicely, assuring Rick that he'd be home and asking if there was anything he could do. Rick hadn't answered.

I scrolled back through the messages, reading them. Josh was sweet, helpful, and reassuring. He stroked Rick's ego, offered to help all the time, and obviously changed plans when Rick asked him to. I saw an eager-to-please man trying his hardest to make his boyfriend happy.

Rick was a piece of work, though. He wasn't always an asshole. Sometimes there were general texts about what was for dinner or where they were going, and there was a lot of complaining from Rick about his job. He seemed like he hated everyone he worked with and everything about his job.

There were also hidden barbs throughout—subtle, yet clearly meant to undermine Josh's confidence. Rick would make backhanded comments if Josh complained, saying things like "pot meet kettle" or "you always have an issue with something," even though Rick seemed to be the one who always had an issue. Rick made comments about Josh being awkward, boring, and unsupportive, although it was always phrased in a manner like he was just helping Josh be a better person. He complained about Josh's friends, putting them down, and if Josh tried to defend them, then Rick got mean.

I got more angry and frustrated the more I read, and eventually I put the phone down. Rick was obviously physically and emotionally abusive, and I was glad that Josh had called Aiden. I knew that the scars he would have from this relationship would be far deeper than just the physical ones, and he would need time and support to build up his confidence.

That was ok—I had all the time in the world, and I would make sure Josh was taken care of in every way he needed. It was time for him to find out what it meant to have someone actually support him and care for him.

With that thought, I headed off to find Liam. It was time to find out more about this ex-boyfriend of Josh's and what exactly we could do about him. Killing him was off the table if he wasn't hellbound, but I knew he was at least somewhat rotten, and surely we could scare him a bit. Maybe some mild torture. Nothing permanent, of course. I could control myself.

Hopefully.

CHAPTER 5

JOSH

I woke up groggy and sore, but I knew where I was.

Unfortunately, I remembered everything from last night in vivid detail, and I was mortified. I was the boring one, as Rick always reminded me. I was put together and organized. I was not an emotional mess who couldn't stop crying. I guessed a slap and a break-up were enough to make anyone a mess, but I still felt embarrassed.

Then there was the fact that I had literally cried and drooled and who knew what else all over Wilder. I barely knew the man, and I had fallen asleep on him and gotten tucked in.

Sure, I kind of knew him from Toby's party, but not really. We hadn't talked, which was fine. I was plain old Josh, and he was anything but plain. I had noticed that at Toby's, even though I felt guilty at thinking how sexy the guy was. Plus, he was like Toby's father-in-law, so I shouldn't be drooling over him. Although he didn't look that much older than the guys. I wondered if he'd been super young when he'd adopted them.

I sighed again. My interest in Wilder was probably just another one of the many signs that things between Rick and I had been over for awhile now. I'd been noticing other guys a lot lately, and it wasn't even in the he's-so-hot way. I noticed how nice other guys were, and how they treated others, and I thought about how they would treat me in a relationship.

It was probably kind of pathetic when your fantasies weren't about getting bent over the nearest table and were instead about having someone make you dinner and smile at you.

Which brought me back to Rick. I was going to have to deal with him. I wondered if he'd been blowing up my phone all night. The thought of dealing with him was overwhelming. Even the thought of dealing with Toby and Sebbie made me tired. I loved them—they were my best friends—but I didn't want to explain everything, and I didn't want their sympathy and their outrage on my behalf. Usually it was wonderful knowing that you had friends who cared and had your back, but right now, I didn't know if I could deal with it.

I was surprised they hadn't come banging on the door in the middle of the night, although maybe it had been late enough that they didn't know yet. I was sure Aiden would tell Quinton, who would tell Liam, who would tell Dexter, who would tell Toby, who would call up Sebbie right away. By the end of that twisted game of telephone, I'd probably be described as near death, and Toby would decide that Rick was really a vampire or something.

Toby and Sebbie were great, but I just... I didn't want to answer questions. They were both so extroverted and full of energy, and I was boring, plain, quiet me. Usually I was grateful they had befriended me and dragged me out of my shell, but right now, I just wanted to curl up and hibernate.

I looked over at the nightstand, which did not have my phone on it. It was probably dead wherever it was, but I needed to at least text Barb about work. I sat up, and that's when I noticed my wrist. It was wrapped up in that beige bandage stuff, and it looked like the swelling had gone down a lot. There wasn't the same persistent throbbing, either. Wilder had said it was a sprain, so that was some-thing, at least.

There was a folded t-shirt on the dresser, and I managed to get it on with little trouble. My wrist really did feel better, but there was a dull ache, and I was still careful with it. I walked out into the living area and stopped when I saw Aiden sitting at the table on his phone, his big ass dog next to him, resting his head on Aiden's leg while Aiden pet him.

He looked up at me, and I braced myself for questions.

"There's orange juice in the fridge, coffee in the coffee maker, and some muffins on the counter. I brought the coffee maker over this morning at Q's insistence. Something about it being inhumane to make anyone face the day without coffee." Aiden rolled his eyes, but he smiled, too.

I walked over to the counter—the place had an open floor plan, with the kitchen, table, and living room all connected. It was nice. Cozy, but it still felt spacious. It was obviously a pretty new cabin —it smelled like new wood, and there were no decorations, just basic furniture. And a coffee maker, apparently.

"Thanks," I mumbled as I poured coffee. "I guess Toby and Sebbie will be banging down the door any minute?"

Aiden looked confused. "Why would they? Was I supposed to tell them? We didn't say anything, since you called me, not them."

I looked over, surprised. "No, you weren't supposed to tell them. I guess I'll have to at some point, but I just didn't feel up to all that..." I trailed off, unsure how to finish.

Aiden smiled. "All that Toby energy?"

I nodded my head as I finished adding cream and sugar to my coffee—both thankfully stocked in the kitchen. I grabbed a muffin and went to sit down across from Aiden at the table.

"I get it," Aiden said, still petting Fluffy.

I took a bite of the muffin. "Wow, this is delicious," I said around a mouthful.

Aiden smiled shyly. "Thanks."

He took a drink from his own coffee cup, and I waited for the awkward questions, or the staring, or the pity... but Aiden just pet Fluffy and acted like we were having a perfectly normal breakfast.

It was weird.

I finished the muffin, drank the coffee, and Aiden still didn't ask anything. He didn't look uncomfortable either, just like it was a perfectly normal day.

I finally broke under the lack of pressure. "You aren't going to ask, or say something, or... I don't know."

Aiden looked thoughtful. "Do you want me to ask something?"

I snorted a laugh. "You sound like a therapist."

"I have a really great one," he said, sipping more coffee. "I highly recommend her. Although Q wouldn't go see her. He preferred revenge over therapy."

"God, I probably do need therapy," I muttered. "I can't believe I got myself into this fucked up situation. I'm steady. I'm dependable. I'm not the one who dates the idiot boyfriend who slaps him around. I'm smarter than that."

"It's not your fault. Sometimes really fucked up things find you, no matter how steady and dependable you are," Aiden assured me. "And it has nothing to do with intelligence. You have a kind heart, and I bet Rick took advantage of that. Sometimes people can twist us up inside and make us do things we normally wouldn't."

I remembered who I was talking to, and I felt mortified. Of all the people to complain to, the guy who had been kidnapped was *not* a good choice.

"I'm sorry. I know it's nothing like—" I started, but Aiden cut me off.

"Don't minimize what you've been through. Our trauma might not be the same, but we both have trauma. Give yourself grace. That *is* something my therapist is always saying," Aiden said.

"She sounds smart. Maybe I should see her," I commented.

"Couldn't hurt. It's better to work through the fucked up things that happened to us rather than ignore them. If Q were here, he would probably tell you to torture your ex or something, but I'm a firm believer in therapy. Whatever you decide, we'll support you."

"Am I in the inner circle with you guys now?" I asked, joking. I was friendly with Aiden and Q, but only through Toby.

"Yup. It's the *fucked up things happened to me* club. Or maybe the *I have a traumatic backstory* club, if Toby had his say in naming it. We can get t-shirts made. Q would love that."

I couldn't help the laugh that burst out of me.

Aiden smiled at me, and for the first time, I thought maybe things would be okay. Yeah, something fucked up had happened, but if Aiden and Q could survive their trauma and get themselves hot boyfriends who loved them, then maybe I wasn't a totally hopeless case.

"I probably need to find my phone and charge it," I commented. I guessed in order to be okay, I needed to face the world first.

"It's on the side table by the couch. Wilder plugged it in last night," Aiden told me.

I blushed at that, and Aiden and his dog both cocked their heads at me. It was kind of comical.

"I definitely did not leave the best impression with your boyfriend's dad." I knew Aiden was dating one of the Smith brothers.

"Why would you think that? And call him Wilder. Sure, he raised them, and he *is* like a dad to them, but really, they're all just pack." Aiden paused, then added, "Like, a pack of family members."

I ignored the weird phrasing to answer his question. "Well, I was sort of a mess yesterday. I wasn't myself."

Aiden just shrugged. "I'm sure Wilder has seen worse. He raised this crew, after all," he said, making a vague gesture toward the dog. I guessed maybe the dog belonged to his boyfriend. I could totally see Wilder as having a house full of teenage boys and pets to take care of. He seemed like he'd be good with animals.

I got up and walked over to the couch, finding my phone fully charged. There were only two unread messages, which made me sigh in relief. Rick must not have come home last night. He did that sometimes, and for once I was grateful. I was sure after his work shift today my phone would start blowing up, but I at least had a few more hours before I had to deal with him.

One message was from Barb, and I saw that Wilder must have texted her about me being out sick. I vaguely remembered asking him to do that. It was just her saying I should feel better and take the rest of the week off. I typed out a quick reply, saying that I was doing better, but I would take the week off, and if she needed me to do any work from home to let me know.

The other message was from Toby, saying we needed another guy's night. I didn't know what to reply, so I just put a thumbs up emoji in response. I'd have to deal with my friends at some point, but they could wait, too.

I put the phone down, and then I just sort of stood there. What now?

"What do you do to relax?" Aiden asked from the table. "I think you should take the day and do something that is totally stress free and lets you not think. Sometimes we need that, you know?"

I blushed, thinking of Rick talking about my hobbies and how stupid and juvenile they were.

"Oh, what is it?" Aiden asked, looking intrigued. "Do you watch trash reality tv or something?"

I laughed. "No, nothing that exciting. I like documentaries.

And I like to build things. Like models and Legos and stuff. I find it soothing," I admitted.

"Ok. Do you have any at your apartment that the guys could pick up for you? I think they're planning to go there and grab the rest of your stuff later."

"No, some furniture and most of my hobby stuff is actually in a storage unit. Rick thought it was stupid, so... Yeah." I hadn't built anything or watched a documentary in ages because of Rick.

"What should they pick up?" Aiden asked.

"Umm... I guess just the rest of my clothes. And anything out of the office. Everything else they can leave. I don't want furniture or dishes or anything," I answered. I didn't want to fight with Rick over the little things, and honestly most of it was stuff he'd picked out anyway. The place was mostly his style, not mine. He didn't like my "nerdy shit" cluttering up space.

"Ok—that'll be easy," Aiden said, getting up.

"Do you think the guys could do it before five? Or maybe if someone wants to drive me, I can take care of it. I don't have a car, because I didn't need one, but I could even call a rideshare..." I trailed off, feeling bad about someone doing it for me.

"Don't be ridiculous, Josh. You're staying here and relaxing, and the guys will take care of it. They'll have it done in like ten minutes. There wasn't that much stuff left, anyway," Aiden said, heading toward the door with his dog. "I'll have them call if they have any questions about what to pack. Until then, find a good documentary to watch and just veg out on the couch or something. I put in all the streaming service info on the television already, so that's all set. I left some cookies and snacks in the pantry, and the fridge has some stuff stocked, but if you make a list we'll get more groceries."

I almost got teary again. I hadn't felt this taken care of in ages. I nodded my head, and Aiden headed out, locking the door behind him.

I went over and grabbed the remote, turning the tv on and flopping on the couch. As I scrolled through the streaming apps, I saw all sorts of new documentaries. Plane crashes, financial fraud, true crime, impersonation, major world events, medical break-throughs and scandals, history, famous families... I settled in to get lost in some drama that wasn't my life.

Chapter 6

Wilder

Despite wanting to stay with Josh, I'd left him sleeping and checked in with the boys, then grabbed a couple hours of sleep. I didn't technically need to sleep, but it had become a habit that I enjoyed. Once it was a reasonable hour, I had sought out Aiden and Atlas to see what the plan was for Josh's morning. As much as I wanted to see Josh, I had to remember that he didn't know me that well. I could be patient and give the man some space. Also, he'd called Aiden for help, so perhaps it was best if Josh saw him first thing in the morning.

Aiden had already had food and a coffee maker packed up, and he was heading to the cabin with Fluffy. I told him we'd go to Josh's to get the rest of his stuff later, so he should find out what Josh needed, then I headed off to the main house to find Quinton and Liam. They were already in their computer room, deep in a search on Aiden's grandfather, who was a bit of a problem. I stared over Liam's shoulder at one of the computer screens in his office as he talked, going over what we already knew.

"So Aiden's grandfather is a descendent of Cain, and he runs down the line of firstborns, so when he killed his younger brother in some sort of ritual, he got the mark of Cain. This protects him from dying, and it also takes him out of god's sight," Liam said.

Quinton, his mate, was sitting in an office chair next to him, tapping his foot restlessly. I didn't blame him. We knew all this, but Liam was processing information, so I just hummed in agreement. Aiden was no longer in danger since his evil brother was dead, but Liam and Quinton still worried about the missing grandfather.

"So that means that he isn't quite mortal anymore, and he's obviously evil if he told Aiden's brother that he should kill Aiden and claim eternal life as well. Plus, you know, he murdered his brother," Liam said. "So far, we can see that Aiden's grandfather withdrew all the money he set aside for his fake death, and then he seems to have disappeared. I've tried tracking deposits in large amounts within 48 hours after the withdrawal, but so far I've had no luck."

Quinton stopped tapping and looked at me. "But he won't be coming for Aiden, right? He has no reason to? Aiden is safe?"

"Yes, Aiden is safe from him," I reassured Quinton. "He has absolutely no reason to come for Aiden. My guess is that he probably doesn't know or care that his grandson is dead. It wasn't like they had plans to work together or anything. He clearly had a plan set up for after his 'death,' and it didn't involve his family."

"So how do we get the fucker?" Quinton asked.

I really did appreciate the fact that Liam's mate had a blood-thirsty and vengeful nature against those who were evil, and I felt a little bit bad at bursting their bubble. Once Liam was locked in on something, it was hard to change his focus, and I could tell Quinton was the same.

I sighed, and they both looked at me. "I'm afraid Cain's descendent isn't yours to deal with. You can't do anything against him. He's immortal. As hellhounds, we only have power over mortals."

"But... that's bullshit. He's evil!" Quinton burst out.

"We can fight with afterlifers, though," Liam reasoned. "A first gen I met a few years ago talked about facing off against a demon."

Ugh. It was probably Demetrius telling stories, although I had no idea what name that particular first gen was using now. It had been a few hundred years since I saw him, but he loved exaggerating and showing off for younger hellhounds. Sometimes first generation hellhounds were insufferable. Or maybe we'd just all known each other too long.

"Yes, it is possible to battle afterlifers, but we can't *kill* them," I answered. "We can send them back to where they came from. It's part of our allegiance to Earth. We are her protectors, and thus we have dominion here. The problem with Cain's descendent is that he originated here, so sending him back to where he came from would just relocate him on Earth."

"So, what, we just have to be like, 'Hey, you killed your brother and told your grandson to kill his brother, but go off and have a nice life now?'" Quinton asked.

I couldn't help smiling at his sass. He really was perfect for Liam. Quinton huffed at me, and Liam reached over and dragged his mate into his lap.

"I know it's difficult, but not all problems are ours to solve. I have a feeling we might have a part to play with Cain's descendent, but it's a side part only. We aren't the ones who can deal with him. I won't tell you to stop looking for him, because it would be useful to know where he is and what he's doing, but I will tell you not to engage with him. He isn't ours to dispose of."

Quinton muttered grumpily, and Liam hugged him tighter.

"We do have an issue that we *can* deal with, however, and that's Josh's ex-boyfriend," I said, ready to find out more information about the man who had hurt Josh.

"Aiden told us a few details, but not many, just that Josh was going through a hard break-up. He was heading over to the cabin this morning, and Quinton made sure he brought a coffee maker," Liam said.

Quinton slid back into his chair as Liam started to do his computer magic.

"Josh has a lot of mixed emotions right now, so I don't want this discussed with his friends. He needs to be the one to decide what to tell them. I'll just say that Rick, his ex, is an abusive piece of shit," I stated. I didn't like sharing Josh's business, but they needed to know at least that much in order to be effective in their research.

"Fuck," Quinton murmured. "I think everyone sort of knew something was up, but I'm sure Toby and Sebbie just thought Rick was a normal piece of shit, not that he was abusing Josh. Let's find and torture the fucker."

I smiled at Quinton proudly. He blushed a little at my look of approval, but I really did appreciate how well he fit in.

Liam was humming, flipping between screens and scrolling through social media accounts and emails. I put my hand on his shoulder and gave it a squeeze. He really was amazing at this type of work.

"He doesn't seem..." Liam trailed off, looking at me.

"No. He isn't hellbound... yet. Atlas was at the apartment and didn't sense that type of residue. I think we would all know if someone hellbound was in Paradise Falls, anyway. We seem to be tied to the land already. He is, however, on his way there. But he isn't within our domain yet."

"Aww, can't we still torture him a little?" Quinton whined.

I smiled, because I'd been thinking the same thing. "At the very least, we can make sure he doesn't bother Josh, and perhaps we can show him the error of his ways. Torture is probably not the best idea, though."

Quinton pouted, and Liam kissed his forehead. "Don't worry, my little hellcat, we'll still scare him a little. A few threats are fine."

"Ok, I guess," Quinton answered, giving Liam a kiss before they both turned their attention back to the computer screen.

They chatted a bit about social media and hacking the guy's cell phone, and based on Liam's tracking, it appeared he wasn't even in Paradise Falls right now, so that set my mind at ease. His job was about thirty minutes away from town, but he wasn't there, either. It appeared he was at a house about an hour away, and Liam did some digging to find out it belonged to a childhood friend of Rick's.

"Keep an eye on him, and let me know if he ends up back in town. I'm going to go over to Josh's place to get the rest of his stuff," I said.

Quinton and Liam both nodded distractedly at me, already engrossed in their research. I headed outside. Jude and Corbin were both home, and Dexter was over at Toby's. I figured I'd leave him to his mate, and I'd see if Jude or Corbin wanted to go along. I didn't really need help, but it was always nice to spend some time together.

Jude and Corbin both agreed, and we took two cars over to Josh's place. Aiden ended up texting me on the way, and Josh didn't actually need a lot, but this way we knew we'd get it done in one trip. Aiden had also said that Josh really wanted it done before his ex got home. I would've enjoyed running into the asshole, but I respected Josh's wishes.

When we got there, Jude bent down to look at the doorbell. He waved cheerily, then he stuck his tongue out at it. Corbin and I stared at him, and he said, "It's one of those camera doorbells. This way Josh knows it's us if he's watching it, and if the ex is watching it, he'll know Josh has friends."

We didn't have a key—small oversight—so we just burned through the lock; we really didn't care about the ex not having a locked door since Josh wasn't returning.

Jude whistled when we walked in, and Corbin grunted, the

crow on his shoulder fluffing up in agreement. The place was a mess—end tables were tipped over, chairs knocked down, and it looked like anything that had been sitting on the table or counters had been knocked onto the floor.

I breathed deeply, but Atlas was right. Rick was an asshole, and he was definitely on his way to rotten, but he wasn't there yet. I told the boys what we were getting, and then we split up to pack the rest of Josh's stuff.

I took the bedroom, since a part of me bristled at anyone else going through Josh's personal space. It, like the rest of the apartment, was in disarray, but I saw Aiden had packed up most of Josh's clothes. There were two closets, so it was easy enough to tell which stuff was Josh's and empty out the rest of the closet. It looked like Josh and Rick had separate dressers, as well, so I emptied out the one that contained Josh's scent. I looked around for pictures or personal items, but the room was oddly devoid of such things.

I checked the nightstand on the side of the bed that smelled most like Josh, and my eyebrows rose at what I saw. Lube, chargers, a pen and pencil and blank notepad, all neatly arranged. Behind that, however, were the toys. There was a range of dildos in various sizes, and the largest one made me think Josh would enjoy experiencing a knot. I debated whether to pack them or not, but the drawer did not smell freshly of Josh. I didn't think these were things he'd used frequently, at least not in the recent past.

Scent led me to look under the bed next, and there was a box filled with toys under there as well. There were all sorts of things— ropes, clamps, a paddle, more dildos—but this smelled even more out of use than the nightstand drawer. I was unsure whether these were items of interest to Josh or his ex, but whatever the case, the two had not used them in a long time.

I covered the box and returned it underneath the bed. The thought of Josh using something that he had used with Rick was...

upsetting. I didn't like it. The dildos seemed to be his and not mutual toys, and I opened the drawer again, memorizing what they looked like. If Josh needed toys, I would provide new ones. He didn't need ones that carried the memory of his ex. Plus, Josh was young and attractive, and he would surely be able to find a willing bed partner if he needed one.

I growled subvocally at the thought, then shook my head. I wasn't a pup to let my emotions control me, and Josh wasn't mine. I wanted to growl again at that thought. Josh wasn't mine *yet*, I amended. Apparently, I had strong feelings on the matter, and I decided if Josh needed a willing bed partner, I would be available.

I sat on the edge of the bed for a moment. I had seen Josh's soul, I had scented him, and I had held him in a vulnerable moment. He was pack, of that I had no doubt. And yet, my feelings for him were not what they were for the rest of the pack. Could it be that I had been gifted, just as my boys had been? It seemed unfair that I should come before Corbin and Jude, but I also sensed they had mates in their own futures. What did it mean, as well, that our entire pack would be mated? It was practically unheard of to find a mate—a legend hellhounds told one another to make the endless years seem less lonely—yet here we were, a growing pack. We had been blessed, and I had no idea why. The universe was... unsteady. Perhaps a time was coming when we would need our mates for some reason.

I cut my thoughts short and finished packing as I heard Corbin and Jude going in and out of the place, loading up the cars. I brought out the bedroom stuff and loaded it as well, and we made short work of emptying everything that was Josh's. I texted Aiden to make sure Josh didn't need anything else, and he told me Josh enjoyed building things but hadn't done that in a while. I thought it would be easy enough to stop at a store and pick him up something, and it pleased me to think of caring for him.

When I told Jude about my idea, he insisted on coming, and

Corbin decided to tag along. I followed their car to a large store outside of town—one of the giant box buildings that carried a little bit of everything. We made our way inside, Jude leading Corbin and I to the part of the store that mostly contained children's toys.

"I don't think..." I started, but Jude led me down an aisle filled with building sets. "Ah, yes—this is what Aiden said he liked. There are so many."

"Yep! I've built a couple in the past. They're fun," Jude said, already looking at some of the race cars. Corbin was looking closely at some of the magical buildings and castles, occasionally scoffing. He almost looked naked without a crow on his shoulder, but he knew better than to walk into a store with one.

I looked around; I hadn't expected so many choices. Some were obviously for small children, but there were many that were intricate and complicated. Some even had those human devices to prevent theft on them. When I looked at the price tag, I understood why.

"I wouldn't get him something that big yet," Jude said, noticing where I was looking. "We don't know how much of a build your guy likes. Plus, that might make him feel like he's gotta pay you back. If he's a builder, he knows how much the sets cost. Humans get weird about expensive gifts sometimes."

I ignored the flash of pleasure that went through me when Jude called him "my guy." He was right, though—I didn't think Josh was used to receiving gifts.

With that in mind, I looked at some of the smaller sets. I didn't know all his interests yet, but I was drawn to the sets of flowers and plants that could be built. Wasn't it customary for humans to give each other flowers when they were interested? I couldn't deny my interest in Josh, and the idea of courting him made me want to rumble in pleasure.

I saw a plum blossom, and I immediately thought of Josh. He was like my own mei ume—strong, resilient, and persevering despite what his ex had put him through. He might not know the meaning of the flowers, but I did, so I grabbed a set off the shelf. An old camera build caught my eye as well. I wasn't sure why, but it seemed like something Josh would appreciate. I grabbed that, although Jude gave me a slight frown when he saw me with both sets. Corbin nodded approvingly, though.

"Josh doesn't seem like he'd take gifts easily," Jude reiterated.

"All the more reason to start getting him used to it," I answered. I noticed that Jude had a few race cars in his hand, and Corbin had wandered off at some point and found a stuffed raven. I smiled indulgently and led my boys off to the cash register, happy to buy them some new toys. You were never too old to enjoy things that made you happy.

Chapter 7

JOSH

I laid around and watched a documentary on fraud, and then I watched one on an internet scammer. I played a matching game on my phone, and I stressed about texting Rick.

I probably needed to.

He'd go home, find my stuff missing, and freak out.

A tiny part of me hoped he'd be worried, but I knew he'd actually just be mad. So, the question was whether I wanted to wait to deal with his wrath, or whether I wanted to tell him before he started sending angry messages. He was probably at work, and I hated to bother him at work.

You know what? Fuck that. I wasn't at work today because my face and wrist were bruised. Why should I try and make his life easier? That was all I ever did, and look where it had gotten me.

I started writing a long text, then erased it, then started again, then erased it.

Ugh.

I paused the documentary, because I had totally lost what was going on. I couldn't even relax properly. It was so hard to turn off my brain. Work did it, because I enjoyed getting lost in numbers. But I had taken the day off, and I still felt too out of sorts to go through other people's accounts. The last thing I wanted to do was screw something up. As a financial advisor, I did a lot of different things, from bookkeeping to payroll to retirement planning. Barb was picky about who she took on as customers, so I was lucky that I got to help a lot of small businesses and individuals. I never felt like a "slimy, stuck-up wall street asshole."

Yeah, Rick had called me that once, "just joking." Which was stupid, because I didn't even work with the stock market.

I looked at my phone. I just needed to text him and get it out of the way, but I continued to stare at it. He'd probably call me. Or send a barrage of text messages back. I didn't even know what I would say, and although I knew I wasn't going back to him, I didn't know if I could handle dealing with him.

Someone knocked on the door, pulling me out of my head.

"Josh? It's Q," a voice called out.

"Come in," I called back.

Although the door was a few feet away, the thought of getting off the couch where I was wrapped in a blanket was not appealing. Plus, it was Q's boyfriend's cabin, or one of his brother's. I still didn't quite know who owned what, since they all seemed to treat everything like it belonged to everyone. It was weird, but it was also kind of nice.

Q walked in, handed me a paper bag and a cup of coffee, and stared at my face. If he'd looked sad or like he pitied me, I probably would have started crying. Q just looked pissed off, though.

"Want me to kick his ass?" he asked. "I'm small, but I'm feisty as fuck."

I couldn't help the laugh that escaped my mouth. Q quirked a smile at me and sat down next to me on the couch.

"Aiden made you some lunch, and I insisted on the coffee. They're heathens. Aiden wouldn't have even brought over a coffee maker this morning if I hadn't told him to," Q said.

"Thanks, Q." I set down my phone, pulled open the bag, and

saw a wrapped sandwich and a pouch full of cookies. I thought about eating, but my stomach cramped, thinking about the text I still needed to send.

Q was staring at me, eyebrows raised. "I'm serious about the kick-his-ass part."

"Maybe that would be easier than the break-up text I'm trying to send," I muttered.

"Ohhh, a break-up text. I can definitely get on board with that. How about 'Go fuck yourself.' Or maybe 'Eat shit and die, and don't ever contact me again, motherfucker.'"

I laughed. If only I were that bold. I probably wouldn't be in this mess if I had Q's attitude.

"Are you not sure if you want to break up?" Q asked.

I looked over at him, but I didn't see judgment.

"No. We're done. We've been done, honestly, and I don't know why it took this"—I gestured at my face with my wrapped wrist—"to make me finalize things."

"Because you're a giver," Q said. He must have seen the look on my face, because he continued, "That isn't a bad thing. You give people every opportunity and think everyone is inherently good. You have endless patience. You care about people, and you want to take care of them and make things better. I see that with your inter-actions with Toby and Sebbie. I bet you haven't even told them yet, because the idea of someone worrying over you is probably uncom-fortable to you."

I didn't know what to say.

"Rick is an asshole, and you deserve so much better. So tell him to fuck off, or let me tell him to fuck off, and then block him, because you're done taking his shit."

"Block him?" I asked.

"Yup. Block the fucker. You don't need to hear from him. Make it final. The guys are picking up all your shit. If your name is on the lease, we can totally handle that for you, and I doubt you have joint bank accounts or anything, but we can handle that, too, if necessary," Q said.

"No joint accounts," I said distractedly. "My name is on the lease. It's technically my place. I didn't even think…"

"Hey," Q said. "No worries. Liam will call the landlord and tell him you've vacated and your ex is now the resident, so he can transfer the lease or give the guy notice. Do you have a deposit you need back?"

"No, it's okay. I'm leaving without notice. He can keep the deposit. Or use it as the next month's rent. I don't care. I don't want Rick hounding me for money, so that's probably best anyway. He won't be able to afford that place, so that will give him time to find something else."

Q shook his head. "You're too fucking nice, Josh."

My cheeks heated. Maybe I *was* too nice, but I was also non-confrontational, and I didn't want to fight with Rick. I didn't want to be blamed for him not having a place to stay, because then I'd feel guilty.

Rick made me feel guilty a lot in our relationship, and I didn't need to feel guilty about us breaking up.

"I just… I don't want him to be able to blame me for anything," I answered. "I don't want to fight. I just want it over."

"Ok, so let's compose a nice, non-confrontational text and then block the fucker," Q said, and he handed me my phone.

I managed to write the text—eventually—and I even chuckled a few times, because Q was *not* good at non-confrontational. I think he suggested half the stuff he did just to make me laugh, but it felt good.

"I'm not going to tell him to dip his balls in a vat of boiling oil, Q," I said again.

"Are you sure? Maybe right between that part about not contacting you again and the information on how you're letting him stay in *your* place for another two months?" Q asked.

I snorted, then I hit send on the text, breathing out a sigh. Q put his hand on my shoulder, giving it a squeeze.

"I still can't believe you said 'we can't make each other happy.' But it was totally a nice break-up text. And very definite, at least." Q made a face when he called it nice that had me snorting again.

"Ok, so how do I block him?" I asked. I mean, I knew, but somehow it was just easier to give my phone over to Q so he could do all the work.

Q pressed a few buttons, then looked at me. "He's blocked on texts and calls. I'm going to block him everywhere. What socials do you have? What's his email address? I'll block that, too."

I told Q, and he went to work. I kind of just sat there feeling a little numb. Would it really be so easy to get Rick out of my life? Somehow, I didn't think so. I *had* been final and decisive in the text, but Rick was used to getting his way. I didn't think he even really cared about me anymore, but he *would* care about being broken up with. He'd once told me he'd never been broken up with before and that he always chose his boyfriends carefully. I think I was supposed to feel honored or something.

Q eventually handed my phone back, patted my shoulder, and said, "Done. You let us know if the fucker finds some way to contact you. Liam is good with computer shit. We'll handle the lease and the landlord—you have nothing to worry about. The guys will bring your stuff over later. Do you want me to stick around?"

"Nah, I'm okay. Thanks a lot, Q. I really do appreciate all this. You guys have been... I mean, I don't even know why you guys are helping me so much."

Q smiled, and it didn't even look snarky. "We've been there, Josh, in some way or another. Sometimes we all need help, and we all *deserve* help." He paused, then added, "God, I sound like Aiden. Don't tell him I got sappy. That's his job. If you want anyone's dick cut off, you let me know."

I laughed, which I'm sure was Q's intention, and then he wandered off and left me to watch more documentaries. I wasted most of the day on the couch, and eventually I got up to go shower. If the "guys" were bringing my stuff over, I didn't want to look like a mess. I'd already embarrassed myself enough yesterday.

I grabbed some underwear, khakis, and a polo from my stuff—yes, my clothes were boring, too—and headed into the bathroom. I unwrapped my wrist, and I was amazed at how much better it looked. I'd need to wrap it again, and I could probably manage, but... Well, Toby would be pissed. I'd been here overnight and all day, and I hadn't even told him yet. Shower first, I decided, then a message to Toby, because I was sure he'd be knocking on my door five seconds after I texted him.

The hot water felt amazing, and I took my time. Getting undressed and dressed was slow work, but I managed. Once I was dressed and brushed my teeth, I texted Toby.

I'm in the cabin on your property. Stop by if you can and I'll explain.

It was short, but I didn't want to text the whole story, especially since Toby would just need all the details in person anyway. When I walked out of the bathroom, I stopped. There was a takeout container and a bag on the table. When I walked over, I saw a note, too.

Dear Josh,

We got the rest of the stuff from your place. We put it in the bedroom for now, since Aiden told us we shouldn't unpack for you. I also picked you up some pasta from the little place in town. The sets in the bag are for you—I hope you enjoy them.

I'll see you soon. Call if you need anything.

. . .

It was signed by Wilder, and his phone number was below that. I blushed a little looking at it. He was just being helpful, that was all. I still took the note into my bedroom and grabbed my phone to enter his number in my contacts.

I walked back out and opened the bag, and inside were two building sets—a plum blossom and a polaroid camera. I felt tears gather in my eyes, and I blinked to try and clear them. How long had it been since I'd done a build? Even more than that, how long since I'd done one and hadn't hidden it or taken apart the end product because it was "stupid looking"?

Now I could build it and leave it out, since Rick wasn't here to talk about my shitty taste. Not that this was my place, and I needed to remember that, too. God, I'd have to figure out where I was gonna stay. I couldn't take advantage of the Smith family forever.

I still couldn't believe Wilder had got me building sets and brought me dinner. I was almost glad he wasn't here. I wouldn't have known how to react, and I probably would've made a fool of myself somehow or another. I didn't remember the last time I'd gotten a gift, aside from special occasions. Of course, Toby and Sebbie and I all exchanged presents for birthdays and stuff. This felt weirdly intimate, though, and I wondered if Wilder felt sorry for me. Or maybe he was just that much of a nice guy.

A knock at the door interrupted my thoughts, and I went over to open it. Both Toby and Sebbie were in the doorway, and they both gasped a bit when they saw my face.

I put a hand up to my cheek where it had bruised, covering it. "Yeah, it's been a rough day. I have to wrap my wrist—it's sprained—if you guys can help me."

That seemed to spur them into motion, because Toby and Sebbie both bustled in, and Sebbie grabbed the wrapping off the table where I'd put it and maneuvered me into a chair. He looked at my wrist critically, gently prodding it, and Toby just stared at me. They didn't say anything.

"Don't make this weird, you guys. I'm not dead or anything," I joked.

"I'll kill him. No, I'll have Dexter kill him," Toby started, and I could tell he was really upset. "He can make it look like an accident, and he can make sure his body is never found. He can burn him to ash so there's no trace left. He can even torture him first. Maybe remove his fingers, although maybe his dick would be better…"

Sebbie just looked at me and smiled softly as Toby ranted. This was more like it. Toby was a bloodthirsty paranormal romance writer, and the situation wouldn't be complete without some plotting.

"You okay?" Sebbie asked softly, finishing up the wrapping on my wrist.

I nodded my head. Toby was pacing and discussing torture methods for when they murdered "Rick the Dick." I chuckled at the nickname, but Toby just kept ranting. Sebbie put a hand on my shoulder.

"I'm sorry we didn't do anything," he said softly, and Toby heard him.

"Fuck. We knew something was off, but we didn't want to push, and we should have pushed. We should have asked more questions. We should have gotten more involved." Toby wiped at his eyes.

I stood up. "Please don't do that. You couldn't have done anything. I wasn't ready to face the situation. I knew you'd be there for me, and that helped more than you know. I'm okay. I broke up with Rick, and for now I'm staying here. I'll have to figure something permanent out, but I'm sure I have time. Right now, I'm just really glad to have my friends here, and I kind of just want to hang out and *not* talk about all that stuff, if that's okay with you."

"Of course it is," Sebbie said, standing up next to me. "And it looks like you have takeout waiting to be eaten, and we can order more food."

Toby looked petulant for a minute. "We can still have him tortured and killed." Sebbie gave him a look, and he put his hands up. "Ok, ok—food first. Ohhh, is that from that little Italian place? It smells amazing! You gotta let us try some!"

I smiled and grabbed the bag from the table, putting it off to the side and going to grab forks and plates for the food. For some reason, I didn't tell them about the building sets, and I didn't tell them who'd brought dinner. It felt nice that Wilder had taken care of me, and I kind of didn't want to share that, even if it was silly.

"So, talk to me about normal stuff," I said, coming back to the table where we all sat down. "How's the hospital?" I asked Sebbie, "And what book are you working on now?" I asked Toby.

They started chatting, and we all ate. They occasionally glanced at my face for a little too long or looked at my wrist, but overall they acted like it was a typical evening. Yeah, there was a lot to deal with, and I'd have to tell them more, but we had time for that. I was glad to pretend that life was normal for a little while.

Chapter 8

Wilder

As hard as it was to keep my distance from Josh, I didn't stay when we dropped off dinner, the stuff from his place, and my gift. Q had apparently checked in on him, and his advice was to let the human have some time to himself. I wasn't sure if it was the best advice, and I probably wouldn't have been able to resist checking on him anyway, but shortly after we left I saw Toby and his friend Sebbie walking to the cabin, so I knew Josh would have company.

I spent a restless night and did a little driving to check for hellbound souls, but I didn't venture far, and I didn't sense rot in close vicinity to Paradise Falls. We'd keep checking the neighboring towns, but it was reassuring to know that no one truly evil was in the town or those nearby. I knew I could hunt in the city about an hour away, but I had no desire to travel that far. My instincts were keeping me close, and I had long ago learned to trust my feelings.

The next morning I checked in with Dexter, Jude, and Corbin, and then I headed over to see Liam and Quinton. They told me they'd blocked Josh's ex on all social media, and the guy was at work today, so apparently it was back to normal life for him. It was hard to resist the urge to pay him a visit and exact some revenge, but that was outside our scope. I almost wished he would harass Josh so that we could teach him a lesson, but I knew that was petty.

I had been around a long time, and torturing souls that weren't hellbound didn't generally accomplish much. Still, it would have been satisfying.

When I walked out of Liam's place, my eyes turned toward the path to the cabin. It was mid-morning, and we had stocked some food in the place, but I still had the urge to make sure Josh was fed.

I stopped by Aiden's and Atlas's little house, even though I knew Aiden was at the shop. Atlas opened the door to me—he was always intuitive, and he'd sensed I was coming.

"I was hoping Aiden had some treats I could bring to Josh."

Atlas just shrugged and grunted, but he was in his human form, and he even had clothes on, which was rather surprising.

We walked in and he gestured toward the counter, where there were muffins, croissants, and some kind of other baked thing that smelled delicious. Atlas reached into a jar, took out a cookie shaped like a dog biscuit, and took a bite of it, leaning against the counter. I helped myself to one of each of the baked goods, and Atlas handed me a container to put them all in.

Then we both looked at the coffee machine.

I looked at Atlas and raised an eyebrow. He grunted at me and shrugged.

I knew how to make coffee. Of course I knew how to make coffee. I was a first gen hellhound, and I'd been on this earth since its inception. I could make fucking coffee.

Just not with this... thing.

"What the fuck is that?" I asked Atlas. It had coffee beans on the top in a little clear thing, and then... it was just all gleaming surfaces and wands and buttons and screens. "Is it a computer or a coffee machine?"

Atlas shrugged again. "Quinton wanted it, and Liam bought it, so probably it's both. Aiden seems to know how to use it."

Atlas walked over and pushed a button, and the thing lit up and started making noise.

"Is it supposed to do that?" I asked.

Atlas nodded.

"Now what?" I asked, and Atlas just looked at me.

Yeah, I figured he hadn't taken much interest in the coffee maker.

"Ok. We can figure this out. We're hellhounds. We can make coffee. It'll be easy."

⁓⁓⁓

A half hour later, after I'd changed my shirt, mopped up the spilled coffee, and Liam and Quinton had come to fix the "espresso machine," I finally made my way to the cabin.

Quinton had ended up making the coffee, and there had been only a little hissing about us almost breaking "his baby." There'd been quite a bit of muttering, too, but that was just Quinton, and Liam had stared adoringly at his mate while the man cursed under his breath.

I hadn't baked the snacks or made the drink, but I was still providing for Josh, and that was what mattered. Quinton had offered to stop in to see Josh, and he'd only looked a little pissed at my insistence that I do it. Luckily, Liam had started sniffing his neck, distracting him, and I suspected that they were going to have a fun morning.

I could smell Josh inside the cabin. He smelled like sunshine and warmth, and the tangy, citrusy smell of fear and pain was much more faint than it had been two days ago.

I knocked, and Josh's footsteps came closer as he opened the door. His face turned a pretty pink color when he saw me, and he stepped back, clearing his throat.

"Ah, hi. Come in. I mean, obviously, since this is your place and all," he said.

I handed him the container of baked goods and the coffee, saying, "I brought you over some treats from Aiden and Quinton."

He blushed again, murmuring a soft thank you, and I let him walk ahead as I came in and shut the door behind me. Josh set the stuff on the small island that separated the kitchen area from the living room, turning to look at me.

"Can I offer you some? Or something else? There's eggs and bacon and sausage, and I could make you some breakfast. Or I could make a sandwich for lunch, since it's later," Josh offered.

I smiled at him. "No, I'm good—I wanted to make sure you had something, though."

He got even pinker, which was adorable, and looked down at the container to fiddle with it. It was terribly sweet that he wanted to provide for me, and I thought I might have my work cut out for me in being the one to provide for him. I was up for the challenge, though.

He finally looked up, and he drew in a breath as he walked around to the other side of the kitchen island. It was clear he wanted to say something, and I wondered if he even realized he'd put a barrier between us. I wanted to growl about his ex, but I just put a pleasant smile on my face and sat in a stool, my body loose and open.

Josh took out plates and a cup, then he cut the pastries in half, arranging them on the plates neatly before sort of pushing one in my direction. I could sense that Josh had a giving and kind nature, but I felt like it was fear driving him to share his food. There was a hesitance to him that I felt wasn't natural, but I wouldn't upset him by turning down his offering.

Josh backed up a step when he looked up. I knew my face was calm and placid, but he still looked nervous and unsure.

"Thank you, Josh. I love that you want to share your food with me," I said, pulling the plate closer to me and taking a bite of the muffin. I groaned in approval, and Josh looked down, fiddling with his own food before taking a bite.

He finished chewing before speaking, still looking down at his plate. "I want to thank you. For everything. I'm sorry I was a bit of a mess, and I really appreciate being able to stay here and you guys getting my stuff."

"No apology is necessary, Josh," I said softly.

He looked up and cleared his throat, seeming to straighten up. I could see him putting on his organized, take-charge persona. Not that it was an act, but it wasn't all there was to Josh, despite what he wanted others to think.

"Yes, well, I wanted to thank you all for letting me stay here for now."

"You're welcome to stay here for as long as you want, Josh," I told him. I didn't like the "for now" part. "This cabin is empty, and we're happy to have you here. In fact, I think your friends would probably insist on it." I didn't add that I would also insist on it.

"Oh. Well. Thank you," Josh said, looking down at his food again and picking at it. He seemed to be bracing himself. "I'd like to discuss rent, and I'll pay you back for the stocked food and the Legos—"

I cut him off. "Josh." I waited until he looked up at me before continuing. "Those were a gift. Do you like them?"

"Of course! Thank you! I didn't meant to imply—"

I cut him off again. My poor Mei Ume was flustered and nervous at my question, which was not my intention. "You didn't imply anything. I'm glad you like them. There are so many options that it was hard to decide."

"Oh, yes, there really are," Josh said, getting animated. "I haven't built anything in ages, and I spent the evening working on the plum blossom after Toby and Sebbie left. It's really beautiful."

"Did you finish it? Can I see it?" I asked.

Josh seemed flustered but still excited. He blushed, turned toward the bedroom, turned back, then seemed to come to a decision and practically marched into the bedroom. He came out with the plum blossom tree, placed it in the center of the table, and looked at me with a hint of defiance in his face. I quite enjoyed the look.

"It looks lovely on the table. It fits in nicely with the cabin's look," I commented.

That seemed to take some of the stiffness out of Josh, and he looked at it. "Thank you. It was a lot of fun. I still have the camera to do, and I'm looking forward to it."

"That would look great on the television stand. Or any of the tables, really," I commented, looking around the room.

When my gaze came back to Josh, he was staring at me. "You don't think it's... stupid? Having Legos as decorations?"

"Why would it be stupid? They look amazingly well crafted, and you've created them. I think it's unique and fun and fits your personality."

"Unique and fun isn't my personality," Josh muttered.

"Josh, look at me," I insisted, waiting until his eyes came up to mine. "You're unique and fun. You're also intelligent, kind, and giving. Never doubt it."

He held my gaze for a moment and then shrugged. I could tell he wasn't quite convinced, but I had time to work on building him back up. It made me want to go and torture his ex, though. Still, I let none of that show on my face. Josh didn't need anger. He was understandably skittish, and I would not have him afraid of me because I acted like a pup.

"As for rent, we don't need to worry about that," I added.

That was apparently *not* the right thing to say.

Josh looked angry, and he went back behind the kitchen island, placing space between us again before he spoke. "If I'm going to stay here, I insist on paying rent. I'm more than capable of doing so."

"Ok," I agreed easily. If it was important to him, I would obviously respect that.

He stuttered a little bit. I didn't think he'd expected easy acceptance.

"I have no idea what the rates would be—that would be Liam's area of expertise. Although I'm sure he and Quinton will also argue that you shouldn't pay rent, so be prepared for that. Quinton can be feisty when he has his mind set on something."

Josh leaned back against the counter, smiling. "Yes, he really can."

"I have no doubt you'll be able to handle him, though," I added.

Josh looked surprised at that. "Really?"

"Yes. He may be a hellcat, but you're like your plum blossom," I said, motioning to the table. "Resilient and able to thrive in even the harshest conditions. A cat is no match for a tree, Mei Ume. You may get scratched up and battered by storms, but your roots are strong."

Josh looked a little surprised, a little disbelieving, and a little embarrassed at that.

"Oh," he said. He was endearingly flustered again.

He looked at me and I smiled, then I smelled the faintest tint of arousal in the air. He looked down again, obviously uncomfortable. I had to remind myself to go slow. I was patient. Raising so many second generation hellhounds through adolescence had taught me all the patience I'd ever need.

"I'll tell Liam you'll talk to him," I said. I picked up my now empty plate and walked slowly around the island to put it in the sink. I gave Josh plenty of time to move away, but he didn't. He just stared at me, biting his lower lip nervously.

Patience, I reminded myself. I had patience.

I headed toward the door, calling over my shoulder, "You relax and enjoy your documentaries and Legos today. I'll see you later for dinner." Perhaps it was cheating to not give him time to respond, but I left, firmly shutting the door behind me.

My Mei Ume was persistent and resilient, but he was also stubborn, and I had my work cut out for me in spoiling him. I knew just how to start, though, even if it might require another trip to the store to pick up some more builds. I thought perhaps I should stock up so I had one to give him whenever he finished what he had. Liam could probably find all sorts of interesting ones online as well.

I smiled to myself, excited to start spoiling Josh. Somehow I thought it might be a bit of a battle, but I was up for the challenge. I was, after all, a first gen hellhound.

CHAPTER 9

JOSH

The next few days passed in a sort of haze. Toby insisted I come over for dinner each night, and it was never just him and Dex—Q, Aiden, or a couple of Dex's brothers seemed to stop over all the time, too. And Wilder—he always seemed to be there as well, although I could admit to sort of avoiding him. I didn't want to make a fool of myself with the man again.

Aiden or Q stopped by the cabin each morning or afternoon, depending on their shifts at the coffee shop, and I might have forgotten to eat if they weren't constantly bringing over food. They didn't pressure me to talk, which was good, because I couldn't seem to muster the energy. Mostly I watched documentaries and built Legos, because new sets kept appearing on my doorstep as soon as I finished the one I had. And I slept. I felt like I had never been so tired. I slept all night, and I took naps, dozing on the couch, and sometimes I was amazed to look up and see that the day was gone.

By the weekend, I was no longer wearing the wrapping on my wrist, and my bruises were faded and almost gone, which was quick for a bruise to fade. It occurred to me how sad it was that I knew how long bruises usually lasted, but I pushed that thought out of my head.

My phone had rung a few times—numbers I didn't recognize—and I told myself it was just telemarketers. Probably it was. They never left messages. I talked to work, and Barb assured me I didn't need to do anything until next week, so I didn't. I just... existed.

It was a little like being wrapped up in blankets and half asleep. Everything was warm and muffled and seemed far away. Occasionally Toby would send me concerned glances at dinner, but I didn't want to talk about it. If I thought that Wilder was sending glances my way, too, well, he was a dad. He cared about people. That was all.

I was pretty sure he was leaving me the Lego sets, although he didn't leave a note. I should have thanked him, but instead, I was avoiding him. I knew it was childish and stupid, and he probably thought I was an ungrateful brat. I *was* an ungrateful brat. He had been nothing but kind to me, and I couldn't even muster up a thank you. But if I talked to him, I might just end up a blubbering mess again. I remembered too clearly what it felt like to be wrapped in his arms while I broke down.

The thought of his visit embarrassed me, too. I had acted weird, and I knew it. I'd gotten mad over the rent thing, because I didn't want his pity. I also thought I'd probably offended him. He noticed when I put space between us and when I stepped back. I *knew* he wouldn't hurt me. I really did, but I guessed old habits died hard. It wasn't even really a conscious decision, but as soon as I did it, I realized that he was aware of it—he seemed to get a bit stiffer before he relaxed and smiled at me. It made me feel like a stray dog, afraid of any hand that reached out to me.

Who was I kidding—I *was* like a stray dog. I did think that an outstretched hand was just as likely to hit as to pet. I was just ashamed that Wilder knew it. Which was also ridiculous, because the man could be my dad. What did it matter what he thought?

Was I so pathetic that I found the smallest act of kindness attractive and wanted to attach myself to that person? He probably wasn't even gay, for goodness sake.

Mostly, though, I let thoughts like that float away. I let everything float away. I thought about serial killers, nuclear accidents, internet fraud, money laundering and whatever other documentaries I got my hands on. It was probably weird as hell to have documentaries be my way to relax, but if I was thinking about the horrors of people dying from radiation poisoning and looking up Chernobyl facts on my phone, then I wasn't thinking about my life. My problems paled in comparison to a nuclear disaster.

The week and weekend passed, and I was looking forward to going back to work and getting lost in numbers, so it was quite a shock to wake up at five in the morning on Monday in a panic, gasping for breath with my heart racing. I looked at my phone for the time, and I took it with me as I got up to look around the cabin, thinking something had startled me awake.

There was nothing. Everything was as it should be, and there were no alerts or messages on my phone. So why did I feel this way? I took a deep breath, trying to calm myself. I was okay. Everything was fine. I wanted to go in to work, or I could work from home if I felt like it today, so there was no reason to panic over that.

I felt like something awful was going to happen. I didn't often feel that way, only when... No, I wasn't going to think about Rick. I hadn't done anything wrong. I hadn't made anyone mad. He wasn't around anymore to get mad at me. There was no reason to feel dread.

I sat down on the couch, letting my head fall between my knees, trying to calm my gasping breaths. I'd been living in a bubble for the last week, not facing anything, not thinking about anything, but now I had to go back to real life. I had to leave this cabin and this property—I couldn't stay hidden forever.

What if I ran into Rick? He knew my schedule and my

patterns. He knew where I worked, where I got coffee, where I liked to go for lunch. I'd just ignored everything that had happened, putting it all out of my head. I'd pretended that Q had taken care of everything, but I knew Rick wouldn't just let it go.

He never let anything go.

I thought I heard a knock at the door, and I lifted my feet up onto the couch, huddling into a ball. It couldn't be Rick—he didn't know where I was staying. I hadn't conjured him up just by thinking about him. I'd imagined the sound. No one would be up this early. I was all alone.

I was all alone.

I stifled a sob. I thought I heard a noise and curled myself in tighter, unable to help the tears.

"I'm here. It's okay," I heard, and then strong arms were wrapping around me, drawing my head into a warm chest.

I knew it was Wilder without even looking up. His voice flowed over me like warm honey. His shirt smelled of evergreens, forest, and outdoor air. The logical part of my brain realized he must have been out walking and heard me. I tried to pull away, ashamed at being caught crying again, but he only pulled me closer.

"You're okay. I'm here for you, Mei Ume. Let it out," he murmured, and I felt a kiss on the top of my head.

It was the kiss that did it. When had I last felt such casual affection? I wrapped my arms around Wilder and sobbed, unable to hold back. He gripped me tightly, and I felt like I might fly apart if he let me go. He murmured soft words to me—I wasn't even sure what, and it didn't matter. His voice was gentle and calming, and he held me and let me cry, not trying to shush me or make me talk. He just let me cry.

By the time I was calmer, the cabin was softly lit with the rising sun. I unwrapped my arms from around him and went to pull away again, but Wilder just held me tight, leaning us over a bit and handing me a tissue from the side table.

I wiped my face and my nose, small hitches in my breath still coming out every now and then.

"Talk to me, Mei Ume," Wilder said.

I was struck by that phrase—Mei Ume. It made me feel warm inside. It probably meant something like "son" or "little child," but I wasn't going to ask and ruin the cozy feeling it gave me that Wilder had a nickname for me. People didn't usually give me nicknames.

"Rick never gave me a nickname," I said.

I felt stupid as soon as it was out of my mouth, but Wilder just squeezed me a bit and made a sound that I knew meant I should go on.

"He wasn't always like that. I know that's what they all say, but it's true. When we started dating, he was charming. He was so impressed with me. We got along and had fun. Rick had a lot of friends, and we liked to go out. I felt exciting when I was with him.

"After we moved in together, he wasn't so impressed with me anymore. He hated his job. He didn't care for my friends. He didn't make enough money. I was boring, dull, and lacked imagination. He had to 'put up with' so many things from me. I started to feel bad about myself, like I just wasn't good enough for him.

"I thought maybe we should break up, but he talked about how much he loved me. He talked about how perfect we were together, how we couldn't give up on all our time together, and he..."

I trailed off. I knew now what he'd done. He'd persuaded me with sex. He'd distracted me physically, and I'd thought there was emotion behind it. I'd thought he really loved me.

"Go on, Mei Ume. It's ok—you can tell me," Wilder murmured.

"He made me feel... attractive. We were... physically compatible." I blushed stupidly. Some people could talk about sex easily, but I found it awkward.

Wilder didn't laugh or mock me, though. He just hummed in encouragement and kept holding me.

"It was exciting, what we did in the bedroom. Or it started that way, anyway. Then I don't even know. I just wanted to make him happy, and I thought I was making him happy there, and sometimes he seemed so loving when we were together like that. I don't know. I think for him it was all just playacting, but it had me all muddled inside," I admitted.

Wilder's voice was calm and reassuring when he spoke. "What happened wasn't your fault, Josh. He manipulated you, and he abused you. He took advantage of everything good inside you. That isn't your shame—it's his."

The words made me cry again, and I wrapped my arms around Wilder while he held onto me.

Yes, I had been manipulated. I had been abused. I couldn't believe I hadn't admitted that to myself. I'd always made excuses for Rick—he'd had a bad day at work, he'd just been taking out his anger on me because I was safe, he hadn't meant it, he'd been drinking, I'd done something wrong. But really, none of that mattered. He'd hurt me, emotionally and physically.

I wasn't even sure when it all started. There was no defining moment, like in the movies. There was no beating that took place out of the blue. I couldn't even remember the first time he'd gotten physical with me, shoving me or grabbing me. It hadn't seemed like a big deal at the time, I was sure. Then it had gotten progressively worse, and somehow I hadn't really noticed.

And there was the sex. That definitely confused things. I had enjoyed when Rick got a little rough, because it was always accompanied by praise and him talking about how good I was for him. And it felt good—I liked it. I hadn't known that about myself. I hadn't known that playful slaps on the ass, bites and scratches, or a rough blow job where he took control could make me feel so good.

Eventually the sex wasn't always like that. Sometimes—maybe

more often than not—I was left feeling used and vaguely cheap, but Rick would call me selfish and say every time didn't have to be some big production. And then there were the times where he made me come apart with pleasure and whispered sweet words to me the whole time. I held on for the times where it was still good. I'd thought they meant something to him. I'd thought I meant something to him.

I'd been a fool.

I cried for a bit longer, and I basked in the warmth of Wilder's arms. When I was done, he gently maneuvered me so my head was in his lap, his arms still on me, and he gently caressed my hair. It was soothing, and I really didn't want to sit up and face the man. The embarrassment didn't last, though, because a wave of exhaustion overtook me.

I closed my eyes and gave in to the urge to sleep.

<hr>

When I woke up, the cabin was brightly lit by the sun, and I was still snuggled on Wilder's lap. He pressed his arm against me, almost as if he knew I was awake and he was reassuring me.

I still felt kind of stupid, though.

I sat up, avoiding glancing at the man. "Um, thank you. I'm sorry. I must have disturbed your morning walk."

He waited, and finally I looked at him. His gaze was soft and affectionate, and he was smiling at me. "Josh, you could never disturb me."

I blushed, and I got off the couch, starting to babble. "I have to get in to work. Well, not that I have to get in to work, because I could work from home, but I think it would be good if I went to work, because I think I've kind of been hiding out, which is okay I guess, but I'm ready to get back to the real world. So, yeah, umm... thank you. And sorry. And thank you for... everything."

I kind of wanted to thank him for the Lego sets, but I wasn't actually sure it was him, and what if it was Toby or Aiden or Q and I thanked him and he had no idea what I was talking about? I would feel really stupid then. And wasn't it more likely that it was Toby or Aiden? Just because Wilder had gotten me sets once didn't mean he was going to keep on giving me gifts. I felt kind of dumb for even assuming that.

"Can I bring you some breakfast?" Wilder asked.

I looked at the clock in the kitchen. Shit. It was almost eight in the morning, and I liked to be into work by nine. "I have to shower and get ready if I want to be on time. Not that Barb will care if I'm late, but I like to be in by nine."

"Ok. I'll grab some coffee and breakfast pastries from Aiden's and drop them off while you're getting ready," Wilder said, and he got up.

I was still avoiding looking at the man, but he came over and wrapped me in his arms anyway, giving me another kiss on top of the head and squeezing me. I breathed in the scent that was Wilder, feeling his strong muscles holding me tight. I was torn between wanting to cuddle in and wanting to pull away, because if I cuddled in I might make a fool of myself. Again.

He seemed to sense my hesitance, because he let me go and headed toward the door. "I'll leave food and coffee on the table if you're in the shower. I'll see you later, Mei Ume," he said, and it sounded like a promise more than a parting comment.

With that, he went out the door, and I stood there for just a moment trying to gain my bearings.

What the hell was it with me and that man? He was old enough to be my dad. He *was* Dexter's dad. He probably thought of me as a son. I was sure he was comforting me just like he would any of his kids.

I breathed out a sigh. Maybe if I kept telling myself that, I could squash the totally inappropriate attraction that was forming. Who was I kidding—that had already formed.

I went into the bedroom and gathered my clothes before heading to the bathroom to shower. My thoughts strayed to Wilder again while I was getting undressed. He was sexy; there was no denying it. It wasn't just his physical appearance, although the entire Smith family seemed to have cornered the market on being insanely attractive and well-built.

He *was* gorgeous, but it wasn't just that. He was kind and caring; he really listened to people. He was patient and understanding. Those were things that Rick had definitely not been.

And, yes, he was all muscles and strength, and the man even freaking smelled good. Rick and I had been fighting a lot for months, and it had been awhile since I'd had any sort of physical intimacy. I tried to think back to when I'd last had sex...

I soaped up and shampooed my hair, my mind searching. I thought it had been a quick blow job I'd given Rick where I'd then jerked myself off afterwards. It had probably been two months ago, at least. When Rick finished, he had little interest in my pleasure. I mean, he'd explained to me many times that after he came he just wasn't in the mood anymore, and that was okay, but sometimes it left me feeling disappointed. But if I said anything then I was selfish, and... yeah, I guess that's why our sex life had dwindled. I'd gotten sick of quickies where I got Rick off and took care of myself, and he was always complaining how he was just too tired after work to put in effort for some 'big sex session.' He preferred blow jobs, and I loved giving them, but I also liked to be touched or talked to or *something*, and it seemed like that had dwindled in recent months.

I snorted as I rinsed off. I was so much better without him. I realized as I had the thought that it was true, not just something I was telling myself.

I'd known I had to leave him when he slapped me. I wasn't sure why that was a defining moment when all the shoves, the bruises, and the grabbing and pressing hands had somehow been excusable in my mind. I guessed because I could write those off as being sort of accidental, even if I knew that wasn't true. Rick had seen the bruises he'd given me. He always played it off as accidental, but he was never less rough.

I didn't know why the slap had been different, but in calling Aiden, I'd been admitting to myself that something was seriously wrong. There were no more excuses when I told someone else.

I had known the relationship was over, but I'd still wondered if Rick loved me, or if he'd really meant the slap. Or if it had been my fault somehow.

I realized now that he didn't love me. I liked to think that once upon a time he did. I know I'd loved him, but somewhere in the past few months, or maybe even the past year, that love had died. We hadn't even liked talking to each other anymore. He never wanted to hear what I had to say, and I'd grown sick of his constant complaining. The sex had fizzled out as time wore on, and I'd been holding onto memories more than reality.

I'd gotten passion and love all mixed up in my head, but what Rick did when we fought wasn't passion—it was abuse.

I finished up in the shower and dried off, getting dressed.

I was better without Rick. I didn't need him in my life. I had friends, a good job, and he hadn't made me happy in a long time. I didn't love him anymore, and he didn't love me either.

It felt freeing to realize that. I would go to work, and I would tell everyone I had been out because I'd broken up with Rick. I was officially done with him, and I was ready to move on.

When I got out of the bathroom, there was coffee and a muffin on the table, and I tried not to read too much into it. I called a rideshare to go into work, and I ate while I walked up to the main road.

I'd have to figure something out for transportation if I stayed here, and I did want to stay here. The cabin was really nice, and it was close to Toby and Aiden and Q. It was good to have friends nearby. Yup. It definitely wasn't also because Wilder was nearby. I snorted at myself. I'd definitely have to get a handle on my attraction before I made a fool of myself.

I distracted myself by thinking about getting a car. I could certainly afford one, and I could drive. I hadn't needed one since Rick had a car, never mind the fact that I'd actually made the down payment on it and usually paid the car payments. He could keep it. It had been in his name, anyway.

I was ready to move on. As the rideshare pulled up and I climbed in (after checking the license plate and driver, of course), I felt calm. If Rick *did* show up, I would handle it. We were done, and he wouldn't be able to convince me otherwise. Rick wasn't crazy or anything, either. He was volatile, but it wasn't like he was a killer or anything. My fear of him was overblown. I was a grown man, and I could handle him.

I was done being afraid.

Chapter 10

As much as I wanted to stay and have breakfast with Josh, I knew he had to get ready for work. Still, my hellhound pushed me to go back and cuddle the man and not let him go. It was a hard impulse to fight, but I left the food on the counter and headed out, strolling back towards the main houses.

I had been awake earlier when I sensed that Josh needed me. When I'd walked into the cabin (after knocking and not getting an answer), I was glad to see that he wasn't in any danger, but it still broke my heart to see him huddled up, the smell of fear and sadness thick in the air. I was just glad he'd let me hold and comfort him.

I sighed as I walked, thinking about the last week. Josh had been avoiding me. He'd been avoiding everyone, though, so I'd let him have his space. Perhaps that needed to end, though.

I knew he was avoiding talking about it with anyone, even Toby (much to Toby's concern). He'd seemed content enough, getting visits from Aiden and Q, building Lego sets, and watching documentaries. I felt like that had been a waiting period, though. Josh hadn't dealt with his emotions, and maybe it was time for him to do so. Hopefully this morning had helped purge some of the bad feelings.

I had the urge to do something, to fix things, even though I logically knew that wasn't possible. Josh needed to work through his trauma, and being there for him was what I needed to do. Sitting back and waiting was not my forte, though.

There was still an itch under my skin. I had comforted Josh, and that was what had started the feeling of needing to act this morning, but I felt like there was something else that needed my attention.

Sometimes being a first generation hellhound was a pain in the ass. We'd forgotten a lot over time, and I often ran on instinct more than anything else.

With that thought, I headed to Liam's. He was, as usual, ensconced in his technology den, although Quinton was at work, so he was alone.

"We might have a problem," he said when I walked in.

Ah, there it was. Nothing urgent, but Liam had an issue. Sometimes my boys needed me to listen and let them figure things out on their own. It was frustrating when my instincts told me to back off and not take care of everything for them. I expected that was a curse parents everywhere faced. We couldn't solve all our children's problems, no matter how much we wanted to. Hopefully this was something I could help with, however, so I sat in the chair and nodded for him to go ahead.

"There have been some discreet inquiries into the whereabouts of Aiden's brother. Unfortunately, it isn't that hard to trace him to this area. Nothing is going through official channels, and I was able to do a bit of backtracking to find where the inquiries are coming from," Liam said.

"I didn't think he would take any interest in Aiden," I said, aggravated at myself that I had gotten it wrong.

"No, he doesn't seem to be. There's absolutely no mention of Aiden anywhere, and no one appears to be looking for him. The search is only for his brother, who vanished. We know he's dead, of course, but there's no body, so..." Liam shrugged.

"So people think he's still alive. Why is that a problem?" I asked.

"You know how I've been trying to track the cursed grandfather through a money trail? Well, I haven't found much, but I did find that the brother had a large amount of money transferred into his own accounts right after the grandfather supposedly died."

"You've got to be kidding me," I muttered. "Could he really have been stupid enough to steal money from his immortal grandfather?"

"Looks like it," Liam sighed.

Humans. The evil ones never ceased to amaze me with their stupidity.

"Ok," I said. "Maybe I'm being shortsighted, but I don't see an impact on Aiden. He didn't get the bulk of the inheritance."

"No, I don't think the grandfather gives a shit about Aiden. He does care about the money, though, and he's started making inquiries into this area. If you know what to look for, it isn't hard to find out that Paradise Falls has a lot of afterlifers. I'm not sure what conclusions he'll draw about anything or if he'll be a problem for the area."

I sighed. "We'll keep an eye on things. We're already grounded here, and I think we'll sense a descendent of Cain in town."

"Well, that's the other thing..."

I raised an eyebrow when Liam looked over at me.

Liam breathed out a sigh before continuing. "I can't find his exact whereabouts, but I think he may be in league with a cult. I'm not sure if he restarted the cult, if it's something that runs down his family line, or if he just happened into it and he's now taking advantage of them, but there are clear ties between the cult and the person searching for Aiden's brother."

"Shit," I muttered. "I hate cults. Nothing but trouble. Rotten to the core souls taking advantage of the innocent. Despicable."

"Is there an afterlifer in charge of that territory? I usually wouldn't think to deal with other afterlifers, but this town has quite a few, and they're all willing to help," Liam said.

I shook my head. "Cults were the creation of humans. Free will and all that. No afterlifer is in charge, and the humans being sacrificed even get all the power now after a memo went out a few centuries ago. It curbed some of the cult activity, but not all of it. Cults are an earthly creation, and thus they fall under our domain. Cain does not, but if he's in league with a cult, then it has become somewhat our problem."

Liam nodded, looking back at his screens. "I'll keep digging and find out what I can. I'll get in touch with other hellhounds, too, to see if there's any info on the cult."

I clapped him on the back as I got up. "Good job, son. Keep me posted. I know you'll protect our pack, and we'll sense if anyone evil is nearby. Perhaps for now, a hellhound should go with a human packmate whenever they leave town."

Liam turned to smile at me. "Already being done. You don't think any of us would let our mates out there without a hellhound for protection, do you?"

I laughed. My boys were always overprotective of each other, so yes, I imagined they were even more protective of mortal packmates. Not that their mates were quite mortal anymore, but I knew it was no use arguing that.

I made it to the doorway before I turned around and asked, "Which cult?" They were all awful, but it helped to know if it was one I'd run into before.

"The Order of Asterphagia. Aster is a plant, and phagia means to eat, so I'm not sure what that has to do with anything. Are they eating plants or something ridiculous like that? I can't find much on them at all. They don't have an online footprint."

"Aster means star in old Greek. It's a cult with ancient roots." I sighed. A pain in the ass, that's what they were. They'd been dealt with a dozen times over the centuries, but they just kept coming back.

"The star eaters?" Liam asked, turning to look at me.

"The devourers of the stars—they seek to end the universe as we know it. They seem to have an uncanny knowledge of afterlifers, as well. I'm not sure who fucked up on giving someone too many details, but it's been passed down through generations. They're trouble."

Liam blew out a breath. "And Aiden's grandfather is in league with them."

I walked over and rested my hand on his shoulder. "You'll dig deeper and find out what you can. Our boys will be safe, Liam. We'll all make sure of it."

Liam nodded, and then he turned back to his computers, effectively dismissing me. I didn't mind. He was heading into the zone, and he'd be focused on unearthing every scrap of knowledge about the cult that he could.

I wandered out, following my instincts and grabbing some nuts from the kitchen on my way out the back door. I guessed I was going to see Corbin.

He was in the forest, sitting cross-legged on the ground, crows surrounding him. I sat by him, taking a moment to feed and pet the crows. We chuckled over the antics of his friends, and then we sat in comfortable silence. I wasn't surprised when Atlas, in his wolf-like form, came and laid down beside us. The crows didn't pay him any mind, and we all basked in the sunlight filtering through the trees.

I felt my tension fade as the warmth seeped into my skin. I hadn't realized how agitated I'd been. The last week had been harder than I'd acknowledged, even to myself.

"It's in your nature to help," Corbin said, as if he'd read my mind. It wasn't out of the realm of possibilities. I don't think Corbin himself even knew how he knew things.

"It is," I admitted, "but it's more than that."

"I still remember when Atlas came to us," Corbin said, gesturing toward him. "Or should I say Fluffy?" he joked.

"Fluffy in this form, I think." I smiled, ruffling his fur when he leaned into me.

"He was feral. He wouldn't change into a human. He barely even changed into a hellhound. I think it broke your heart every day," Corbin said softly.

Atlas whined next to me.

"I was fine," I reassured him. "You needed time to feel safe, to get acclimated. I knew that, and the best thing I could do was show you that I loved you and be there when you were ready to accept that love."

"You did that for all of us, in whatever way we needed," Corbin mused. "You were so patient, so understanding, but I think you suffered for us. Worried about us. Sacrificed for each of us."

"It was no sacrifice," I rumbled gruffly. "You're my boys, and every one of you is worth everything to me. You're pieces of my soul walking around outside of this vessel, and I wouldn't have it any other way. You have all been a gift."

Corbin nodded. "Yes, but that doesn't mean it wasn't hard. I don't think any of us ever got how hard it was." Corbin smiled then. "None of us were ever the best at being patient and not taking action."

I chuckled, thinking back to some of their antics as pups. Corbin was probably the most patient of all of them, but they had all favored action.

"You were never any trouble. None of you were," I reassured them both.

Atlas changed into his human form, and Corbin raised an

eyebrow, obviously shocked at the transition. I just put my arm around his shoulders where he sat next to me.

"You're worried about Josh," Atlas murmured quietly.

I sighed. "I know that sometimes waiting is necessary. It's hard, and it's a struggle, but I can't force things. Hellhound or human, each being must come to their own place of self-discovery. Josh is on his way, and I can't rush him. I wouldn't want to rush him. He's beginning to trust me, and I cherish each moment I get to spend with him."

"He already trusts you," Atlas rumbled.

Corbin hummed in agreement.

"He avoids me," I murmured. "I understand why, and I respect the space he needs."

"He might have needed space before, but is that what your instinct tells you he needs now?" Corbin asked.

I thought that over. I *did* have a hard time leaving Josh this morning. I hadn't wanted to let him go, but I'd thought that had been my own neediness.

"He is human," Atlas grunted. "Sometimes they need 'therapy.'"

Corbin nodded, adding, "It's more than him being human, though. You treat Aiden and Toby and Quinton just like you treat us. We're all your children. He isn't your child, though."

I smirked. "Do you think I'm so unaware of myself that I don't know that? What I feel for Josh isn't fatherly." My smile faded. "But he still needs to heal."

"Mates help each other heal," Atlas said. "He needs to be needed, too."

Corbin and I both looked at him, and Corbin smirked. "Well, looks like Fluffy has some good advice."

Atlas reached over to smack Corbin on the head, and Corbin smacked back at him. I ignored their mild squabbling as they started to roll around and wrestle.

Josh *had* needed space—I was sure of that. But perhaps I was ignoring my instincts and the time to give him space was over. I understood the point my boys were making. Partnerships were equal, and Josh couldn't feel like I was treating him like a child.

Maybe I needed to make my interest in him known. I wasn't sure if he was ready for that... but I trusted my instincts, and my instincts were telling me that I needed to see Josh before this evening.

The crows were scrabbling about and cawing as Atlas and Corbin continued to roughhouse. I winced as Corbin elbowed Atlas in the face, then Atlas kneed him in the stomach. Some things really never changed. Corbin was usually so sedate, but I could always count on Atlas to bring out the playfulness in him.

"Boys," I said, and they both stopped and looked up at me. They were covered in dirt and grass, and there was a wee bit of blood—I wasn't sure whose. "Perhaps you should both head out for a hunt? Get rid of some excess energy?"

They looked at one another, and then they both got up. Corbin brushed himself off, then Atlas shook himself off, flinging some dirt and grass back onto Corbin. I tried not to laugh as Corbin shot Atlas a dirty look.

They managed to stalk off without any more fighting, the crows following.

I sat for a moment longer. I 'd been in fatherly mode for so long, but Corbin was right. Josh wasn't a child, and I couldn't treat him like one. With that thought, I headed back through the house to grab my cell phone and keys. When I picked the phone up, I noticed a missed call. That itch under my skin started again. I hit redial.

"Wilder?" a female voice asked. She didn't wait for me to answer, though. "Wilder—I turned into a fucking fiery dog. What the fuck, Wilder."

Well, then—never a dull moment.

CHAPTER 11

JOSH

Barb was glad to have me in the office, and she was *thrilled* when I told her I'd broken up with Rick. No one had really liked him, and that should have been another sign. Of course, Rick didn't like any of my friends, either. It was always more important to him to hang out with his friends.

After that, I tried to put Rick out of my mind. The morning flew by catching up with work and discussing any new accounts and what needed to be done for the upcoming month. Our office wasn't huge, but I wasn't the only financial advisor, and Barb had an estate planner, a lawyer, a couple brokers, a CPA, and some personal assistants on payroll. I was the most senior financial advisor, though, and Barb depended on me for a lot of the accounts. In some ways she made me feel like a partner as opposed to just someone who worked for her.

It felt good to be back in work mode and focused on the numbers, making a to-do list of what needed to happen and who needed attention. Before I knew it, it was afternoon. I checked with everyone else to see if they wanted some lunch before I headed out to grab something.

"We have a new client calling to talk to you sometime this afternoon," Barb informed me. "They didn't give a definite time, since their shop is busy in the afternoons, and I told them that was fine."

"Yeah, that's okay. I'll be on the lookout for the call. Anything else before I head to lunch? You want anything?" I asked her.

"No, I brought a sandwich." Barb made a face at that, and I laughed. She preferred to bring leftovers when her wife cooked. I didn't blame her—Sally was a damn good cook.

I headed out, thinking about Barb and Sally. Sally always packed Barb something for lunch, even if there weren't leftovers. Relationship goals, I thought. Rick had *never* made me lunch. It wouldn't have occurred to him.

I was going to do better for myself next time.

I knew it was soon to be thinking about next time, and I probably needed to take some time to myself. At the same time, though, I felt a bit like I'd been alone for the past six months. Rick and I had grown more and more distant; we'd been more like roommates than partners.

I had distanced myself from my friends, too. Part of it had been because Rick didn't like them and I didn't want to fight, and part of it had been because I didn't want to admit what was happening in my relationship. I hadn't wanted to look too closely at my life. It was easier to just carry on, even if I was miserable.

As I walked the sidewalks of the downtown area, I decided to head to Cass's shop. I did have friends, and I was done isolating myself. Yes, some of them were nosy and exuberant and could be overwhelming, but they also loved me just as I was, and I loved them.

The little bell chimed above the door as I walked in, and I saw Q behind the counter scowling at a customer. I almost laughed out loud. Some things never changed, and I was glad of it.

"Are you *sure* you want pumpkin spice? It isn't even fall, for fuck's sake," Q was asking the woman.

She was smiling at him, and I thought I recognized her as a regular. "Yup. I just *love* pumpkin spice. It's *so* delicious."

I thought everyone in the shop was staring at Q and the woman, and half the shop was smiling. I wondered if Q realized that the woman was baiting him.

"No, pumpkin spice is not delicious. It's a fucking abomination. Okay, fine, I'll give you that *some* pumpkin spice isn't bad, but that's because most 'pumpkin spice' doesn't even have fucking pumpkin in it." Q was ranting now and even using air quotes, and everyone in the shop was staring at him with amusement.

"You want a coffee with cinnamon and cloves and nutmeg and allspice, then go for it. That's a good fall blend, even though it isn't *fucking fall*. But Cass doesn't do shit half-assed here, so our pumpkin spice actually has fucking pumpkin in it. And who wants pumpkin in their coffee? Pumpkin tastes like old socks and regret," Q ranted.

"Regret?" the woman asked, trying not to laugh.

"Yeah, like the morning after Halloween when a bunch of kids smashed your beautifully carved pumpkin because they're fucking assholes, and there's stinky orange pumpkin guts just scattered everywhere like a slaughterhouse. Who puts pumpkin in coffee, anyway? Why not have squash coffee? Or sweet potato coffee? It's fucking absurd. Get a nice spring flavor. We've got coconut and mixed berries. We even have fucking lavendar, although why anyone would want *that* in coffee, I have no fucking idea. It smells like grandmothers."

"There's nothing wrong with grandmothers!" an elderly woman called out from one of the nearby tables.

At that moment Cass came out of the kitchen, glared at Q, and pushed him out of the way, smiling at the customer. Q just kept grumbling as he walked into the kitchen. Cass took the orders and another barista made coffees, moving the line along.

When I got up to Cass, I was smiling. "You know your customers were baiting Q, right?"

He glared over my shoulder at the woman who was sitting at a table. "Oh, I know. They seem to find his grumpy-as-hell attitude endearing. Which is fine until he insults someone who isn't a regular."

"I can't imagine someone getting bent out of shape over his opinions about coffee flavors," I said.

Cass rolled his eyes. "You have no idea."

I laughed at that, and Cass looked more closely at me.

"You look good, Josh. I'm glad," he said.

I figured one of the guys probably told him about Rick, or at least about the break up. Rick and I had come in before, and he had kind of been a dick when we ordered. I hadn't brought him here again.

I ordered a coffee and some lunch, thinking about just how much Rick had made my life miserable. I hadn't even realized all the things I'd stopped doing because he didn't like them, or all the places I didn't want to take him. Looking back, it was almost like I was waking up from a dream. Or maybe a nightmare.

I took my coffee and lunch over to a table by the window and ate, alternating between looking at emails on my phone and people watching out the window. I heard a chair scrape and looked up to see Aiden sitting down.

"Hey! The ham and cheese croissant is amazing, and you totally outdid yourself with the cranberry brie bites. I haven't tried the lavender cupcake yet, but after Q's rant, I couldn't help buying one," I laughed.

"Yeah, I heard him from the kitchen," Aiden admitted. "Cass was out back taking a delivery, or he would have intervened sooner. The cupcake has a very light lavender flavor, and it's mixed with vanilla and has a cream cheese frosting, so it's really subtle."

"I'm sure it's delicious. You made it, and I don't think I've had anything I didn't like that you made," I reassured him.

Aiden beamed at me, and then he got a serious look on his face. "How are you?" he asked.

I knew he was asking about everything that happened, but he was also giving me an out to not talk about it. Aiden was good like that.

"I'm okay, I guess. Still processing, I think. Really glad it's over, and really unsure why I stayed so long," I admitted.

Aiden nodded his head. "Sometimes it's easier not to make a change, even if you're in a really bad situation. Change is scary, and sometimes what you know seems safer, even if it totally isn't."

"Yeah, our brains are funny like that, huh?" I asked. "I keep looking back and kind of wondering what was wrong with me."

Aiden reached out and patted my hand. It surprised me, but it was nice at the same time. Other than Wilder holding me while I cried, I really hadn't had much physical contact lately. Another thing that had been wrong in my life that I just hadn't seen.

"Don't beat yourself up, Josh. Hindsight lets you see a lot of things, but when you're in something, you can't see the whole picture. Give yourself grace."

"Yeah, I guess that's true," I admitted. "I still feel kind of... I don't know... stupid or something."

"Don't. No negative self-talk. Helene would tell you that if you wouldn't say it to your friends, then you shouldn't say it to yourself. I'm not sure that advice would work on Q, but you're really nice to your friends," Aiden added.

I laughed, just like he meant for me to. He was also right, though. "Helene? She's your therapist, right?" I asked, voice low.

Aiden smiled at my lowered voice. "It's okay. I don't mind everyone knowing about therapy. I think everyone could probably use someone to talk to."

"Yeah. Maybe I should get her number from you," I said.

Before I could think twice about it, Aiden pulled out a little pad of paper and a pen from a pocket, jotted something down, and then handed me the paper. "Tell her Aiden recommended you. She's really fantastic."

I took the paper and nodded. Aiden smiled and took his leave, heading back into the kitchen. I finished up lunch—the cupcake was light, fluffy, and just the right level of sweet—and headed back to the office. I wasn't totally sold on making an appointment with Helene, but it was something to consider.

I got back to work, and I was lost in a spreadsheet—this particular business was a hot mess with regards to keeping track of expenses and categorizing anything at all—when my phone rang. It was a number I didn't recognize, and I figured it was the new client.

"Good afternoon, this is Josh. How can I help you?" I answered.

"Babe! Thank goodness you're okay!"

I just sat there, frozen. It was Rick's voice on the line, and he sounded relieved and happy to hear me.

"I'm so sorry, babe. I know you're upset with me. I was really worried when I couldn't get a hold of you. I thought something had happened to you." His voice was vaguely reproachful at the last comment.

"Rick?" I asked stupidly.

"Of course, babe. What happened to you?" he asked.

I took a deep breath. "What happened to me? I had a bruised face and a sprained wrist."

"Baby, I'm so sorry—I'm not sure how your wrist got sprained, and I know it was wrong to slap you. I was just so upset and hurt by what you said, and I lashed out. You know I don't normally do anything like that."

I made a sound of disbelief.

"It's not like I ever slapped you before, Josh. Passions were high, and I was worried about us. I was scared of losing you. I love you, babe. You mean the world to me." Rick sounded so sure and so passionate. I almost wanted to believe him.

Almost.

"Rick." I sighed. Shit. I didn't want to have to do this. "I meant what I said. I don't think we're good for one another."

"Baby, how can you say that?" He lowered his voice. "We're a perfect match, and I've missed being with you."

"We haven't had sex in ages, Rick. You weren't interested," I answered, and I was sure the hurt could be heard in my voice.

"Is that what this is about? Come on home, baby, and I'll treat you right. We'll have a marathon in the bedroom, and I'll make everything up to you. I know exactly what you like," Rick purred.

I couldn't believe I had thought that voice was sexy. Now I just felt vaguely ill thinking about being with him.

"Rick, it isn't about sex. We're done. We've been done," I said.

"I know you're mad—" he started.

I cut him off. "It's not about being mad. Or about being hurt. You hit me, Rick. You talk down to me and make me feel like shit about myself. You hate my friends, and we barely talk or have sex anymore. I don't love you anymore, and I don't think you love me. I'd like to think you did once, but I don't even know. We are *done*. There is *nothing* that could make me change my mind."

I was shaking a little, but I had gotten all that out. I should have hung up the phone, but I didn't.

Rick laughed meanly. "Is this about the assholes that were on the front camera?" he asked, his voice nasty.

"What?" I asked, having no clue what he was talking about.

"I'll find out who they are. Waving and winking at the camera before taking all your shit. Are you cheating on me?" Rick accused.

"Oh my god, Rick. When would I have been cheating on you?" I demanded. "I hardly ever went out anymore because it wasn't worth dealing with your shit."

"Dealing with *my* shit? What about *your* shit, Josh? You're so fucking dramatic. *You hit me, Rick*," he mocked. "I barely fucking tapped you, and you make it like I'm some abusive asshole. You make everything such a big fucking deal."

I blinked, my eyes getting watery. I was not going to let him hear me cry. I was not going to give him the satisfaction.

"Then you have some assholes move your stuff out of our place without even a fucking word," he ranted.

"I sent a text," I started, but he cut me off.

"*I sent a text*," he mocked. "Do you even fucking hear yourself? We've spent years together, and you think sending a fucking text is a good way to deal with our relationship? What the fuck, Josh? How heartless and cruel are you? Do you have no feelings at all?"

"I—" I started, not even sure what I was going to say.

"No, because you're selfish, only thinking about yourself. It's always what you need, what you want, how you feel. You leave me without a word because we had one little argument, and you don't even have the decency to talk it out with me," Rick continued.

"Because there is no talking with you!" I yelled. I *never* yelled, and it surprised Rick into silence. "This is what talking to you is. You berating me. You ranting about all my faults. I'm *done*, Rick. It's *over*. And part of it being over means I don't have to listen to you anymore. Don't call me again. Don't come looking for me. I have proof of the bruises, and I'll get a restraining order. Leave me alone, and get on with your life."

He started to answer, but I hung up the phone, going into settings and blocking the number he'd called from before he could call back.

I was done. I would get a new phone number. I would do whatever I needed to. I didn't have to deal with him anymore. I wouldn't deal with him anymore.

Barb stuck her head into my office. "You okay, honey?"

I nodded my head, my lips pursed.

"Oh, hon—why don't you take the rest of the day off? It's late afternoon anyway. Head home," she said.

"The new client," I said halfheartedly. I really was done for the day, but I didn't want to let her down.

"I'll call and reschedule. They were saying today was a busy day for them anyway—I'm sure they won't mind. And I'll send you their contact info and nail down a time, so you can call them," she answered.

I looked at her. There was pity in her eyes, and I couldn't deal with that. I looked down and started to gather my stuff. "Ok, I'm gonna head out. Send me the info."

"Do you need more time off?" she asked gently.

"No," I answered sharply. I looked up then. Barb was kind and sweet, and I loved her as a boss. She didn't deserve my ire. "No," I said more softly. "I want to work."

"Ok, hon. Maybe the rest of this week you can work from home. We can do daily calls to catch up."

I just nodded, focusing on packing up whatever I would need for the rest of the week. She closed the door of my office as she left, and I breathed out a sigh. I pulled up the rideshare app. I'd need to figure out a car, but not now. I ordered a ride, heading outside to wait for it.

I felt restless and jittery, and I paced up and down the sidewalk, my arms full of folders and my computer bag slung over my shoulder. I needed to do something. I couldn't live in fear of Rick calling me again, or, god forbid, coming to my office at some point.

I'd talk to Q. He'd handled things with blocking Rick, and I was sure he could help get my phone number changed. I breathed out a sigh. Yes, I was sure Q could help.

When the car pulled up, I checked it was my driver and got in. Once we were headed to the cabin, I stuck my hand in my pocket, feeling the paper from Aiden. Maybe I'd call his therapist, too. I couldn't be stuck in my head like this.

Before I could second guess myself, I sent a text off to Q, letting him know what had happened and asking him about changing my phone number. Then I looked at the number Aiden had given me, thinking about making an appointment.

I was done feeling like this. I was going to change things, even if it was scary.

CHAPTER 12

WILDER

I sat on the front porch drinking some sweet tea and waiting for Josh to get home. I could sense that he was on the way, and I was feeling impatient to see him.

It had been an interesting morning.

I hoped I'd managed to convince Thea to come to Paradise Falls, although I wasn't quite sure. She was a spunky, fiery young woman who grew up thinking she was human, and I wasn't sure how she hadn't changed forms for the first thirty something years of her life. She had been taking care of rotten souls, but she'd just assumed she was a sociopath.

Needless to say, when I'd found her and told her that she was a hellhound, she had been... Well, disbelieving might have been an understatement. Convincing her to let me guide her hadn't been very successful, thus my break from that project. I already thought of her as one of mine, though, so I was worried about her, and I was glad she'd reached out.

I hadn't told the boys about her yet, and I figured I'd wait until they were all here. Corbin had left after our chat to do some hunting, and Atlas and Liam had headed out a few minutes ago without a word. They had that sneaky, suspicious look I knew from when they were young, but they were grown hellhounds. Hopefully they wouldn't get into too much trouble.

I snorted at that thought. My boys could always find trouble, but usually they did a decent job of covering up their mayhem.

I heard a car pulling up the road to the houses, and I casually stood up on the porch. It was a rideshare, and Josh got out carrying a computer bag, a messenger bag, and some folders balanced on top of a computer he was carrying. I made a mental note to have a drivable road cleared to the cabin and to look into lending Josh a car.

I casually walked down the steps, calling out, "You need some help carrying stuff to the cabin?"

Josh blushed, which was adorable, and mumbled, "Uh, no thanks."

Just as he said it, he sort of tripped a little, and I rushed forward to grab some of the files before they hit the ground. He looked at me, slightly shocked. Oops. Had I been too fast? Probably too fast.

"It's fine. I could use a little walk," I said, taking the rest of the stuff from his hands. I noticed he looked a little troubled, although I didn't smell pain or fear. "You're home early," I said, hoping he would open up.

He sighed. "Yeah. I took a call at work, and it was my asshole ex."

I stopped walking, holding in the growl that wanted to erupt. Josh stopped, too, turning to look at me.

"I'm fine," he reassured me. "I actually yelled at him." He smiled a bit at that, and we both started walking again.

"Can I do something to help? What do you need?" I asked.

"No, I'm really okay. I'm glad I got to have a final conversation with him and let him know how I felt. It was upsetting, but it also had to be done. It also reminded me that he's a dick, and I really am better off without him. It made me realize I can stand up for myself, too."

Josh told me all about the conversation, and although I wanted to growl about Rick, I was glad Josh had gotten some closure.

"I'm proud of you. I'm sure that took courage," I said.

Josh blushed and looked down. I replayed my words in my head. I *was* proud of Josh, but had that come across as fatherly? I didn't want him to think of me as a dad. My brain scrambled for some way to switch gears, but it wasn't like I could just burst out and say I thought he was cute and sexy. That would be awkward. Probably.

Yes, that would be awkward. He was talking about dealing with his ex, so it was not the time to talk about me finding him sexy.

I suddenly felt a bit more empathy for my boys and what they'd gone through with their mates. Dealing with humans wasn't as easy as dealing with other hellhounds. My conversation with Corbin and Atlas came to mind. Mates helped each other. Perhaps I needed to open up to Josh like he had opened up to me.

I sighed, letting the day's stress out in a long exhale.

Josh looked over, brow furrowed. "Are *you* okay?" he asked.

"Yeah. I'm okay, although today was a bit interesting."

"What happened? Are all the guys okay?" Josh asked.

I smiled at him. I loved how concerned he already was for our family. "Yes, the boys are fine. And all their mates, too."

Josh snorted. "You've been hanging around Toby too much if you're using the phrase mates."

I paused for a moment, then kept walking before Josh could notice. This brought up another issue—Josh had no idea that we were really hellhounds. I would have to explain things without giving away too much.

It wasn't that I had an issue with telling Josh about us. I would happily fill him in on everything and show him my hellhound form. The problem was that the guys had been talking about it all rather openly in front of Josh for quite some time, and he absolutely refused to accept it. He blew everything off as being about

Toby's writing or the boys joking around. At some point, he would realize that everything was real, but I didn't think now needed to be that time. He'd had quite a bit of stress recently, and he didn't need afterlifers shoved in his face on top of it all.

How would I even explain Thea? I didn't even understand it all myself. I remained lost in my thoughts, and next thing I knew we were at the cabin. Josh opened the door and ushered me inside, carrying his folders. I walked in and placed them on the table.

"The Lego centerpiece looks great here," I told him, turning to face him.

"Thanks." He blushed a bit and sort of looked around before adding, "Do you want some coffee?"

I sat at the table. "That would be great, Josh. Thank you."

He bustled about, getting out cups and cream and sugar, saying, "I'm a good listener if you want to talk about it. Whatever made today interesting, I mean. Although it's fine if you don't want to talk."

I smiled, although Josh's back was to me so he couldn't see it. He really was the sweetest man. "I would love to have your thoughts on it, but it's all rather complicated. I'm not even sure how to explain it."

Josh brought over the cups, and I noticed that he had fixed my coffee. I wasn't sure when he'd noticed how I took it, but it was such a Josh thing. He really was a caretaker. He also needed someone to take care of him, though, and I was happy to take that role.

I took a sip and groaned in approval, smiling at Josh. He smiled back before answering me.

"It's okay. Sometimes we just need to talk, even if it doesn't seem to make sense." He laughed a little then. "I'm used to that from Toby. He works out a lot of his plot ideas by talking through them. Believe me, nothing is as weird as trying to decide the logistics of how often a vampire would need to drink blood, or whether a crossroads demon actually lives at a particular crossroads or visits many different crossroads."

"Depends on the demon. Some like to settle down at one crossroads, but some like to travel," I answered.

Josh laughed. "I see Toby got to you with that one, too."

I gave a noncommittal smile. Yeah, today was not the day to fill Josh in on afterlifers. I shifted gears, trying my best to describe the situation with Thea. "So, a while ago I got a message from... Well, a sort of friend. They were letting me know that someone was in trouble. They'd been the one to guide me to some of the boys, so of course I wanted to check on the person they mentioned."

"Of course," Josh agreed.

"Obviously, in the past I've adopted boys. It isn't because I wouldn't take a girl in, but it just seems like trouble making, rambunctious boys are far more the norm, and I was willing to take them in when others wouldn't." Yes, I thought trouble making and rambunctious was a reasonable way to describe hellhound pups.

Josh reached across the table and patted my hand. "It's amazing, what you've done for them. I know they love and appreciate you."

I flipped my hand over and held onto his. He startled a little at the gesture, but he didn't pull away. I kept talking, enjoying the sensation of his skin against mine. "So, this time I was directed to a young woman named Thea. She's... Well, she's a female version of the boys."

Josh smiled. "Does that mean she's a little wild, a little rough around the edges, and maybe a bit socially awkward?"

I breathed out a chuckle. "Yep. That pretty much sums up Thea. She clearly needs guidance, just like the boys did."

"So is she moving here, or are you moving to wherever she is?" Josh asked.

He sounded sad when he said the last part of his sentence, but I loved the fact that he didn't even question whether or not I would take Thea in.

"I'm not going anywhere," I reassured him, squeezing his hand. "You can count on me staying right here."

Josh gave a small smile before asking, "Are you afraid of how the guys will react if you adopt a daughter?"

"No, the problem is that she had no interest in being helped. She doesn't trust easily, and she's old enough that she can get by on her own. She's been doing it for quite awhile, so she doesn't think she needs help. But she called me this morning, and she's run into a bit of trouble. Nothing major or anything, but enough that maybe she'll finally be open to letting me help her."

Josh squeezed my hand this time. "I'm sure you'll help her if you can, and I know you'd welcome her into your family. She has to be ready, though. Sometimes it takes a while to realize you need help."

"It does, and that only makes it more admirable to reach out. No one can go it alone, and no one needs to." I knew we were talking about more than Thea now, and I almost expected Josh to clam up. I should have known better, though.

"That includes you, you know," he told me. "You raised all these great guys, but you don't need to do things alone, either." He blushed a bit as he added, "I'm always willing to listen and help however I can."

"Thank you, Mei Ume. That means more than you can possibly know. And I can *always* use help reining in my troublesome pack of boys. They only egg each other on to more chaos."

He laughed at the last part, just like I intended, but I hoped he also saw that I thought of him as an equal. Atlas and Corbin had been right—I was always willing to support Josh and be there for him, but he needed to know that I wanted him to be there for me, as well.

My phone dinged at that moment, and Josh let go of my hand,

motioning to my pocket. I would have ignored it and continued our moment, but I guessed that would be awkward now.

When I looked at the phone, the message was from Quinton, and I stared at it, puzzled.

"What is it?" Josh asked.

"Quinton messaged me, but I don't know what he's talking about. He said, 'It isn't my fault that they went all hellhound on the dick.' I have no idea what that means." I looked up as Josh groaned.

"Ugh. Hellhounds are good guys who take care of bad people in Toby's books, and Q calls my ex Rick the Dick. I told Q about the phone call from him because I was asking about changing my number. My guess is that Liam said something or did something to Rick." Josh stood up, suddenly looking a little nervous. "I hope Rick didn't hurt him."

I stood up as well, giving him a smile. "Trust me, Liam can hold his own. Not only that, but I saw him looking mischievous earlier, and he had Atlas with him. I'm sure they meant well, but..." I trailed off.

Yeah, there was really nothing else to say. They always meant well, but that didn't mean they didn't occasionally fuck things up. I just hoped the fallout didn't come back on Josh.

I was also a little miffed. After all, if anyone got to threaten Josh's ex, I really felt like it should have been me.

"Let's go see what trouble they got into," I told Josh, and we both walked up toward the main house.

⁓⁓⁓

We all sat in Liam and Quinton's living room—the main house, not the one they shared with Aiden—and listened to Liam describe their little field trip. Quinton looked pissed off, as usual, but he was also throwing concerned glances at Josh. Atlas was still in his human form, but he mostly just sat there looking menacing while Aiden sat on his lap.

Josh had introduced himself to Atlas and said it was nice to meet him, which had made Atlas look puzzled since they'd met a dozen times already. A subtle elbow from Aiden had him grunting and nodding. He'd apparently forgotten that he'd been Fluffy every time Josh had met him in the past.

Dexter, Toby, and Jude had come over as well, because everyone wanted to hear about their escapades. Corbin was the only one missing because he was out hunting for a few days.

"...so then, Atlas put his face close enough to kiss the guy—not that he would ever kiss anyone but you, Aiden—and he growled. And that's when Rick actually peed his pants, and Atlas just looked down as the wet patch continued to grow, and then he dropped Rick right into the puddle," Liam boasted.

"You're both fucking morons," Quinton muttered. "Go ahead and tell them the part where the dickhead threatened to call the cops on everyone."

"Hey, I'm sure he wasn't *really* serious about calling the cops," Liam reassured Quinton. "After all, what's he gonna say? We didn't leave a bruise on him, and nothing is on camera anywhere."

Toby was frantically writing in a notebook, and he distractedly said, "You did threaten him, and if a person feels bodily harm or death could result from the threat, that's illegal. Plus, I'm sure you guys were all scary and... stuff." Toby looked up at Josh for the last part.

We all knew what he meant, though. The boys had more than likely gone all fire and glowing eyes on Rick. Not that I blamed them.

"Eh, so he was ranting a little bit about us being psychopath killers." Liam shrugged, and they all continued to chatter about their visit to threaten Josh's ex.

I looked over at Josh, but he looked surprisingly calm. "Are you okay?" I asked him.

He didn't look at me—instead he continued to stare at Liam. Liam and Atlas sensed it, because eventually everyone stopped talking, and they all looked at Josh, who was still staring down Liam.

"I must have given you the impression that I'm incapable of taking care of myself," Josh said, and I could hear the fire behind his words.

Liam, Atlas, and Quinton all rushed to reassure him that wasn't true, but he just put a hand up, and they all stopped talking. It was rather impressive, and to be honest, it was also a turn-on. My Mei Ume was feisty and ready to take charge.

"I understand why you might think that, but I can assure you, I am an *adult* who can make *logical* decisions." The unstated part was that perhaps Liam and Atlas were not capable of making logical decisions. Q snorted in response, and Jude quietly slipped out the front door. I could hear a car in the distance, so my guess was that he was going to investigate. He also probably wanted to avoid getting yelled at since everyone looked a little shamed by Josh.

"Uh, yeah, of course we know you're an adult, Josh," Liam assured him, looking at me for help.

"Don't look at me. None of this was discussed with me, after all," I chastised. "I certainly wouldn't have condoned it. If Josh wanted something done about his ex, all he had to do was ask, which I'm sure he knows, since he did ask Quinton for some assistance."

"Yup. I did ask Q for assistance in changing my phone number, but I don't recall asking anyone to track down Rick and threaten him. Not that I have any sympathy for the man, but don't you think it's my right, as the one who was wronged here, to have a say in what happens? But you took that away from me, didn't you?" Josh was looking from Atlas to Liam and back again. "Worse than that, you stooped to his level of pettiness. I expected better from friends."

They both looked guilty as hell at that. I almost laughed, but I managed to hold my grin in. Josh was going to be the perfect mate—he had successfully put both boys in their place, and he hadn't even raised his voice to do it.

A moment later the sound of a car coming up the driveway became audible to the humans in the room, and we all heard Jude shout, "Walrus!"

Josh got up. "And this will be the sheriff dropping in, because I can assure you that Rick would be someone to call the cops on you. So now there's something else for me to deal with, because you two didn't think this through or ask my opinion." Josh sighed before adding, "Let me handle this. I'll make sure no one gets arrested."

Josh walked toward the front door, and I sidled up next to him, putting my hand on his shoulder and giving it a squeeze. I heard everyone else following behind us.

Of course, we walked outside to mayhem.

I sighed, Toby started mumbling to himself and writing in his notebook, and Quinton cursed under his breath.

Jude really needed to get a handle on dealing with his crush on the sheriff, because although he looked quite happy with himself, being handcuffed and pressed against a police car was probably not a good thing.

CHAPTER 13

JOSH

I may have laid it on a little thick with Atlas and Liam, but I was *mad*. I was mad at Rick for being an asshole, and I was mad that the guys had stooped to his level of petty threats and bad behavior. Most of all, I was mad that they did it without talking to me. I wasn't a child. Yes, staying with Rick had been bad, but I'd gotten out. I knew I should have left earlier, but Q was right —sometimes you couldn't see the whole picture when you were in the middle of it.

So, yes, I'd made a bad decision. Maybe a string of bad decisions when it came to Rick, but overall I was level-headed and smart, and I thought things through. Which was why I would have told them not to go near Rick. The man was petty and entitled. I didn't think he'd always been that way, or he'd at least hid it well for most of our relationship.

But I couldn't really think about that, because Jude was handcuffed and leaning against the sheriff's car, and he was...

"Jude, I swear to god, stop shaking your ass at the sheriff and wipe that smile off your face. I'm about to be mad at you, too," I yelled, walking down the steps.

Both the sheriff and Jude looked slightly chastised at that.

"Sheriff Paul, I'm sure he deserved to be handcuffed"—all the guys hooted in laughter behind me, but I turned around and gave them a glare—"but please tell me we aren't going to have to bail him out or anything," I said.

The sheriff undid the handcuffs, muttering at Jude the whole time. Jude just blew him a kiss and whispered something that made the sheriff blush.

I wasn't touching that with a ten-foot pole. I was pretty sure the two of them liked each other, although why they had to act like grade schoolers about it was beyond me.

"Josh, you're okay," the sheriff said, and he shot a look at Jude.

I walked over to the sheriff, and I heard everyone else following behind me. Jude walked past me towards the house to join them. It looked like I would have an audience for whatever Rick had done now.

"I'm fine. I'm sure Rick called the cops, and I'm sorry he dragged you into this, but I'm *really* sorry if he somehow blamed the Smiths or dragged them into things. They've done nothing other than show me kindness and support," I said.

Wilder put his hand on my shoulder, and it seemed like I could feel the heat of his body against my back.

"Boys, why don't you go inside while we chat with the sheriff," Wilder suggested, and I was thankful that he was giving us a little privacy. He seemed to know I was uncomfortable.

"Actually, I need Liam, Jude, and Atlas here as well," the sheriff said.

No one seemed surprised by that, and Q ushered Aiden, Dexter, and Toby back toward the house, despite Toby's mild protests about really wanting to see a police interrogation for research purposes. They didn't go far—they sat up on the porch, but it was at least far enough to give me the semblance of privacy.

"Rick reported that you were being held against your will and that these guys had stolen things from your apartment. He had a photo of this one"—the sheriff pointed at Jude—"from your door-bell camera."

Jude started to say something, but one of the other guys must have elbowed him, because he was cut off.

I turned around and shot them all a glare before I turned back to the sheriff. "I can assure you I am *not* being held against my will, and they didn't do anything but move *my stuff*, which I asked them to do because I didn't want to see Rick. In fact, they left things there that were also mine, and I can show you receipts for all the expensive items if you doubt that."

"No, that's not necessary. That makes sense considering there were still some expensive items in the place. Unfortunately, Rick also made some accusations of assault," the sheriff said. He looked at Jude when he added, "Although I doubt Rick is in the trunk of Jude's car, since I just came from talking to him."

Jude pushed forward. "Aww, Walrus, you knew he was fine. You just couldn't wait to get me in handcuffs, spread against your car." He actually winked after he said it.

"You cannot do things like that to a police officer, Jude. One of my deputies would have tasered you and brought you in," the sheriff grumbled.

"Don't worry, I would never grab anyone else's... weapon—only yours. And tasers—don't promise me a good time," Jude said, his voice low and raspy.

"Jude, you aren't helping," I murmured. "Go up to the porch."

"Awww, but Josh," he whined.

Wilder smacked him on the back of the head, and Jude looked at me, slightly chagrined. I just raised my eyebrows, because he totally deserved it. He turned and sulked his way back up to the porch. I swear the sheriff was staring at his ass as he went, although maybe he was just making sure Jude actually listened.

Liam cleared his throat, saying, "Atlas and I did visit Rick, but we..."

I cut him off. "Rick hit me and sprained my wrist."

The sheriff had a good poker face, because he gave nothing away. I knew Atlas and Liam would lie for me, but I was tired of lies. I was tired of covering up for Rick.

"I have photos," I added. "I can produce various medical reports of injuries over the time I've been with Rick, if it's necessary. The Smiths moved my stuff out because I didn't feel safe going back. Rick called today to threaten me, and though I certainly didn't suggest they go speak with him, Atlas and Liam were defending me and asking Rick to leave me alone. Rick is very angry that I'm staying here."

I knew my face was red. I felt embarrassed admitting that I'd ever gotten into that situation, even though I saw no judgment in the sheriff's eyes.

I was also starting to feel really angry about it, and I wanted the sheriff to know what an asshole Rick was. Wilder squeezed my shoulder, and I leaned back a tiny bit, feeling him against my back. Somehow it made this a little easier.

Wilder asked, "Did Rick have any bruises or marks from this supposed assault?"

The sheriff glanced at Liam and Atlas. I knew what he'd see; both guys looked totally fine. Not a hair out of place, no bruised knuckles—nothing to imply any sort of fight. The sheriff looked back at me.

"Would you like to file for a restraining order?" he asked me.

I was surprised he took me at my word so easily. A restraining order wasn't a bad idea, but.... "I'm changing my phone number, and I'm staying here right now. I think this was Rick's dying attempt to cause trouble, and as long as the police don't give in to his lies, I don't think he'll be any more of a hassle."

The sheriff grimaced at my last statement, and my stomach dropped. He'd believed me rather easily, and he hadn't even asked to see pictures of the bruises. What exactly had Rick said to him?

I probably would have turned and walked away, because I really didn't want to know what trouble Rick was up to, but Wilder was a warm, solid presence against my back.

"What did he do?" I asked, my voice shaking a bit in anger.

"As far as I'm aware, nothing, but, Josh..." The sheriff sighed, looking at Liam and Atlas. "Did he seem... lucid when you spoke to him?"

Lucid? What was the sheriff getting at? I must have looked as confused as I felt.

"Rick claimed that these two threatened him and set him on fire with their glowing red eyes. He was ranting about it, alternating between extreme anger and what seemed like genuine fear," the sheriff said. "There were no marks on him, but he seemed convinced of his story. To be honest, I was worried about your safety because of his behavior. However, he didn't pose a threat to himself or others as far as I could tell, and he said he had no intention of driving anywhere. I didn't smell alcohol on him or see any drug paraphernalia, either. I wasn't sure if there was a history of mental illness..."

I leaned further into Wilder as the anger drained out of me. "Rick doesn't use drugs, at least not to my knowledge. He drinks on occasion, but he doesn't usually imagine things." I paused, still trying to process everything he'd said. "He really said they set him on fire? I could see him making up that one of them hit him or that they threatened him, because he's very manipulative, but saying they had laser eyes or whatever seems kind of far-fetched even for Rick. Do you think my breaking up with him caused some sort of psychotic break?" I couldn't keep the worry out of my voice. Rick was an asshole, but I didn't want to be responsible for something like that.

Wilder's arm wrapped around me, basically hugging me from behind, and I couldn't find it in me to complain or think how weird everyone probably thought that was.

"This isn't your fault, Josh," Wilder murmured. "You take care of others all the time, but you aren't responsible for them when they don't take care of themselves or make bad decisions."

The sheriff stared at us for a moment, and I felt like I should pull out of Wilder's embrace, but I couldn't bring myself to do it.

Eventually the sheriff spoke. "Ok. I see no indication that you did anything wrong, but I'd advise you all to stay away from Rick. Josh, I can file an Emergency Protective Order, which will keep Rick away from you until you can file for a restraining order with the courts. I can go back to the station and work on that, maybe give Rick a little time to cool off, then go and inform him of it and check in on his mental state."

I nodded my head. "Ok. He's an asshole, and I'm angry at him, but I really don't wish him ill. Will you keep me posted about what happens? He has family in the area as well. He isn't super close to his mom and dad, but they'd certainly step in if there was something wrong. I'm not sure if you're allowed to call them by law or whatever, but I can if he isn't doing well. Like I said, I don't wish him ill, despite what happened between us."

The sheriff nodded again. "You're a good person, Josh. I'll keep you posted."

With that, he got into his car, and we all watched as he drove off.

It was silent for a minute after the car was gone from sight, and then I heard Jude quietly sing-song, "Josh and Wilder sitting in a tree..."

Someone must have elbowed him again because he stopped with an oomph. I pulled away from Wilder and turned around to look at him, but he was grinning at me. Liam and Atlas didn't look upset, either, just sort of curious. I did not need them thinking I was crushing on their dad, though, so I deflected.

I pointed at Liam and Atlas first. "You two. Stay away from Rick. I appreciate the sentiment, but I do not need any more trouble. Whatever the hell you did, you upset him enough that he's either hallucinating or making up crazy stories." I snorted. "Laser eyes and fire. Completely absurd."

Atlas and Liam both looked a little guilty at that, and I narrowed my eyes at them, suddenly suspicious. "You guys didn't drug him or something, did you?"

"Or something!" Jude giggled, and I watched as his eyes flashed red. He blinked, and the color was gone.

"Seriously? Colored contacts? You guys are about as mature as middle school boys. What would make you think it was a good idea to threaten and try to scare Rick?"

Liam and Atlas continued to look vaguely guilty, and Jude said, "Ohhhh, you guys are in trouble with step-dad!"

I turned on him, pointing my finger. "And you! You haven't even reached middle school age maturity yet! You're like an elementary school kid on the playground pulling the hair of the person they like! Just ask out the freaking sheriff before we all get arrested!"

Atlas and Liam turned on Jude, smirking. "Yeah, Jude, just ask out the sheriff," Liam taunted.

"Ugh! You guys are freaking ridiculous! Act your age!" I yelled, and I turned and stalked off towards my cabin. I wasn't going to deal with them, and I certainly didn't want to think too much about what Jude had said.

I got to the front door in record time, stalked inside, and started pacing across the living room. I knew I wasn't really angry at Liam and Atlas and Jude, and I probably owed them an apology. Although, really, the whole thing with Jude and the sheriff was ridiculous. And Liam and Atlas had been pretty juvenile with Rick, wearing colored contacts to scare him. They'd said something about grabbing him around the neck, too, and I just hoped they hadn't given him brain damage or something crazy because they cut off his oxygen supply.

I would feel bad if Rick were hurt, but I have to admit I'd feel even worse if the guys got into legal trouble and ended up in jail. Maybe that made me a bad person, but I was done worrying about Rick. I didn't love him anymore, and I knew he didn't love me. I wasn't going to hold onto the memory of love, if he'd even been capable of loving me to begin with. The asshole was probably too self-centered to really care about anyone else.

Ugh. I was just so *angry*. I didn't even know what to do with myself.

I heard the door open, and Wilder walked into the cabin, looking calm and unruffled, as usual. God, he was probably here to tell me he didn't like me *that way,* since Jude had implied we were a thing or something. How freaking embarrassing. He just stood and stared at me, though.

"I'm sorry," I said. "I shouldn't have yelled at them."

"Oh, you totally should have," Wilder answered, walking further into the room until he was near me. "They shouldn't have done that, and it's good for them to get called out on bad behavior."

I paced away, still angry about Rick, and also angry that Jude had put me in this awkward situation with Wilder. I tried to keep my mouth shut, but Wilder was just staring at me, and I felt like I needed to say something.

"And the fact that Jude implied that we were... that you and I... Well, obviously that's absurd. Not that I'm not super grateful for all the support you've given me, and if you've been leaving me Lego sets I've been a total asshole because I never said 'thank you,' so thank you for those, and for caring for me, and I'm sure you just see me like a kid or whatever, obviously, because you're obviously older than me, and the idea that Jude thinks that I think that you might like me *like that* when obviously you wouldn't be interested in someone who is your son's age is obviously absurd. Obviously."

I was babbling. I was not a babbler. I think I'd said obviously about twelve times, and when I turned around, Wilder was just staring at me.

This would be so much easier if he wasn't so sexy and so freaking nice and so darn supportive, because being able to lean against him with his arm around me had felt amazing.

I breathed out, my anger leaving me, and I leaned against the wall of the cabin, closing my eyes.

I really was an idiot, because I had to admit to myself that I actually had kind of hoped that Wilder was interested in me. But why on earth would he be? I was boring Josh. Works with numbers, no imagination Josh.

"I'm sorry," I said, leaving my eyes closed. I was not going to start crying now. Wilder probably already thought I was an emotional basket case. "You should go check on the guys. I'm fine. I was just mad. I'm sorry."

I heard the creak of a floor board, and I breathed out in disappointment, because I really didn't want to be alone. Only then I felt Wilder's hand on my face, lightly holding my cheek. My eyes flew open, and I was staring into Wilder's eyes, because his face was really close to mine.

"Josh, if it's okay, I'm going to kiss you now," he said softly.

I just stared at him. He was going to... What?

Then he did. His lips brushed against mine ever so softly. Once, twice—gentle kisses. The third time, I wrapped my arms around him and opened my mouth.

It seemed like that was all he was waiting for, because his tongue explored my mouth, tasting me. He pressed his body fully up against me, the wall at my back supporting me. It was like he was a dying man in the desert and I was water. I don't think I'd ever felt so wanted from a kiss.

His body was hard and firm against mine, and I felt totally caged in and surrounded by him. I groaned as his lips slanted over mine again and again, until I was panting for breath while trying to still kiss him back.

I was hard and aching in my pants, and I rubbed up against him, feeling his own hardness and making us both groan.

He bit my bottom lip, the sting sending sparks through my whole body. "Wilder," I moaned.

Only rather than encouraging him, this made him slow the kiss down, easing back to soft, gentle pecks before he rested his forehead against mine, both of us breathing heavily in the silent cabin.

"Mei Ume, we need to talk," he said.

Of course we did. I sighed, pulling away. Wilder reluctantly let me go, and I walked over to the kitchen to grab two mugs. If we were gonna have the whole *we can have sex but don't let my kids know* conversation, then I needed coffee. Even worse, maybe I was about to be offered a pity fuck. I mentally winced at even using the term in my head, and I'm sure Wilder would never think of it like that, because he was simply too nice.

If I were practical, I should tell him to forget the whole thing and that we should pretend this never happened.

"Do you want some coffee?" I asked, and Wilder nodded his head as he slid onto a stool. Maybe we would just ignore the whole kiss, which at this point might be for the best. As much as I wanted to get on my knees in front of Wilder and get my mouth on him, I *was* practical. There were too many complications. I knew that. It was best we'd cut things off when we had.

Yep, definitely for the best.

Being an adult sucked.

CHAPTER 14

Pulling away from Josh was one of the hardest things I'd ever done, but I knew today had been a lot, and the last thing I wanted to do was take advantage of him.

I had to admit that when he put the boys in their place, it was a turn-on. It just reaffirmed what a strong and caring man he was, and what a perfect mate he'd make. Of course Jude had needed to go and be juvenile about it, which had probably embarrassed Josh. He'd still handled Jude beautifully, though. My jokester needed someone to rein him in sometimes.

After Jude's joke, I'd been worried for a moment that Josh wasn't interested, but his talking had seemed to focus on the idea that *I* wasn't interested in *him*. Kissing him had seemed the easiest way to correct that assumption, and based on his response, he returned my interest.

He did not seem pleased at the notion of talking, however. I wasn't sure what to make of that. I thought communication was important, and at some point Josh needed to know that we were hellhounds. I thought it was probably good manners to let him know before I mated him.

Because that was definitely what I wanted with Josh—a permanent relationship.

Josh set a cup of coffee in front of me and took his own cup, sipping it. He did not come over to sit next to me. He stayed on the other side of the kitchen island. I opened my mouth, but he cut in before I could speak.

"We can just pretend that never happened," he said, sounding like he was reassuring me.

I looked at him, tilting my head. "Why would we do that?"

"Well, I don't really do one night stands, especially not with someone I'll see all the time. It would make things really awkward. And anything more than that would probably get noticed by your boys, which I'm sure you wouldn't want." He took a sip of his coffee when he was done speaking.

"Why wouldn't I want that?" I asked, rather confused.

I wasn't sure what Josh was thinking. I once again felt more sympathy for my boys in trying to navigate a relationship with a human. They had some odd ideas. Why wouldn't I want my sons to know we were together? Hells, Jude had already insinuated it. At the very least, the boys would be able to smell our scents on each other once we got more involved. There wasn't really any hiding a relationship amongst hellhounds.

"Well, I'm not actually your age," Josh answered.

I huffed a laugh. He had no idea how true that was. It then occurred to me... "Josh, are you embarrassed that I'm older than you? Are you not comfortable with that? I just assumed..."

That hadn't occurred to me, and I rubbed at my chest with my free hand, feeling the ache there. As much as Josh might want me physically, that didn't mean he wanted to actually form any sort of bond with me. I wasn't sure why that hadn't occurred to me.

"What? No!" Josh said, putting down his coffee cup and coming over to me.

"I realize that I may be... old-fashioned about some things. I'm not up to date on lots of things, and maybe I have a bit of a stodgy personality," I said.

I was going to continue and start listing my positive traits, because I had plenty to offer Josh. I wasn't going to give up without a fight, but he walked over and kissed me, his hands running through my hair. I couldn't help hauling him forward until he was standing between my legs.

The taste of Josh swept some of my worries away, and I growled low in my throat. He quickly let me take over the kiss, and I sensed a submissive streak in Josh. I nipped at his lip, and he groaned.

"Damnit," he muttered, pulling back.

He was right. "Yes. We need to talk," I reiterated before we could get lost in the physical again.

He glared at me, a little of his fire coming back. "Will you stop saying that! You can't kiss me like that and then say that!"

I was utterly perplexed. I couldn't say we should talk? "Do you not enjoy talking during intimate moments?" I asked. There were some people who liked silence when they were having sex, although I wasn't one of them.

Josh stepped away and rolled his eyes. "We aren't having sex. We're 'talking.'"

"I like talking to you, Mei Ume. I'd like to talk to you during sex, too. I think you would enjoy that," I murmured.

Josh huffed out a groan. "So what do we need to talk about? I already said I'm not going to do a one night stand, and I don't want to be some secret from your kids. I just... I can't do that."

"Mei Ume," I said, standing up and pulling him into a hug. He leaned against me, even though I could sense his confusion and a bit of hurt. I wasn't sure how I had caused him to hurt, but I needed to fix it. "I don't want to have one night with you. I want many nights with you. And I wouldn't keep you secret from the boys. They already know I'm interested in you."

"They what?" Josh asked, trying to pull back.

I didn't let him go. He was getting into a panic for some reason that I didn't understand, and we would work through this.

"They know I'm interested in you. I'm sorry Jude was teasing, and I can speak to him about it—"

Josh cut in. "Jude's an idiot." He pulled out of the hug, looking at me in horror. "I'm sorry! I know he's your son, and he's great, but..."

"But he's a bit of an idiot," I agreed, smiling.

Josh huffed a laugh, then he leaned back into me. I wrapped my arms around him.

"Why the breakup talk, then? Not that we're dating or anything," Josh hastily added.

"Breakup talk?" I asked. "Josh, I would like to date you. I care about you, and I'm attracted to you, and I don't want to hide you from the boys. I don't want you uncomfortable, either, so if you'd rather not discuss it with the boys, I can tell them not to mention it or tease."

"But you said we had to talk," Josh mumbled into my shirt. "You stopped kissing me so we could talk."

"Well, yes, you've had a lot happen today, and I don't want to take advantage of you," I began.

"Please take advantage," he murmured under his breath, but of course I heard him.

I smiled and continued. "I thought communication was important when starting a relationship, and we do need to talk about me and the boys. I don't think you're really aware of... everything. I want you to have all the information before we become physical with one another."

I let Josh process that. He didn't let go of me, and I gently rubbed his back.

"Does this have to do with what Toby is always talking about?" he asked softly.

"Yes," I answered. Perhaps Josh wasn't as unaware as I assumed he was.

"He isn't making it all up?" he asked.

"No, he isn't," I gently replied.

"But you don't..." He paused, clearly thinking. "Your work doesn't harm innocent people, right?"

I thought his choice of calling it work was interesting, but I supposed it fit. It was our job, after all, and perhaps that made Josh more comfortable. "No, we'd never harm anyone innocent. We work for the greater good."

He nodded his head. "Sort of like the military, I guess. Is that how you ended up all becoming a family? You were all in the same line of work? I guess you sensed the... umm, the necessary skills in the boys as teenagers?"

"Yes," I answered. Josh was obviously more comfortable talking around us being hellhounds, and that was okay. I didn't need to hit him over the head with it.

Josh pulled back, his face horrified. "Oh my god. Jude really is going to get himself arrested! He can't be messing with the sheriff like that when you guys do that kind of work." He paused, adding, "Although I'm guessing it's sanctioned or something from some of what Toby has hinted, and if it came down to it, maybe he wouldn't end up in jail because higher powers would intercede?"

I nodded. "Yes, exactly. We're all perfectly safe. There's no concern there. Although Jude is a bit ridiculous with the sheriff. He isn't always comfortable showing his feelings, which is probably why he's acting the way he is."

Josh nodded his head, pressing back against me. "So now what?" he asked.

"Well, now we either start a relationship or you tell me to get lost," I joked. I ignored the nerves in my stomach. I *knew* Josh was interested, but I was still nervous. It was an entirely new sensation for me.

"Yes," he said.

That was all, and then he leaned up to kiss me, the warm softness of his lips pressing against mine. I was so tempted to take the kiss deeper and further, but I kept it gentle and light, and Josh followed my lead. When I pulled back the slightest bit, he leaned down and pressed his head against my chest.

I kissed the top of his head, wrapping him in my arms.

"Do you want..." he asked, but he trailed off, waiting for me to fill in what exactly I might want. My Mei Ume had a giving nature, and he was clearly looking at me to take the lead.

"I want us to cuddle on the couch, watch one of the documentaries that you like so much, and talk to each other," I answered.

Josh breathed out, but he didn't protest. He'd dealt with a lot of emotions today, and although sex might be a good release for those emotions, I needed to know more about what he wanted.

We moved together and settled on the couch. I sat down and pulled Josh up against me. He lifted his legs, laying across the couch, and snuggled into my chest.

"I missed this," he murmured. "Cuddling, I mean. I can't even remember the last time I was just held. When I wasn't crying, that is," he joked, looking up at me and smiling.

"You can always cry with me, Mei Ume," I answered.

He laughed a bit, then tucked his head back into my chest. We were silent for a few moments, but he made no motion to grab the television remote.

"I think I might go see Aiden's therapist," he said quietly.

I hummed in agreement. "Aiden likes her very much, and if you would feel comfortable doing that, then I agree. You can always tell me anything, too, although I certainly don't have the same expertise as her." She was, after all, a fury, and I was a hellhound. I didn't add that, though, since I wasn't sure Josh was up for the full afterlifer explanation.

"I just... I feel stupid for what happened with Rick. But I'm also so angry at the same time."

I hugged Josh tighter. "You are *not* stupid, and I do not want to hear you call yourself that. You're strong, brave, and resilient. You have a giving nature. You want to please others and take care of them. Rick took advantage of that, and your goodness kept you from seeing what he was doing."

Josh snorted, and I could tell he didn't agree.

I squeezed him tightly for a moment, adding, "Hey, no disagreeing over your good nature."

"It isn't that." He sighed. "I mean, maybe I do have a giving nature or whatever, but that isn't what attracted me to Rick."

"What attracted you to him?"

Josh seemed uncomfortable, and he shifted in my grip a bit. I pulled him tight again, and that seemed to settle him. I made a mental note that he seemed to enjoy being held tightly.

"We, uhh... Rick was into... Well..." Josh seemed unable to get out his thoughts.

"The stuff under your bed?" I asked.

Josh burrowed into my chest even more, and I could smell his embarrassment.

"Oh my god, you saw that stuff?" he asked.

"Did you enjoy the toys? Or was that something Rick enjoyed that you just went along with?" I asked.

The distinction was important, and I needed to know. I wanted nothing more than to give Josh whatever pleasure I could, and I wanted to know what he liked.

"I, um, well, I liked them, I guess," he murmured.

"What did you like?" I asked.

Josh sighed. "You're not gonna let me out of answering, are you?"

"Nope," I answered, kissing his head again. "I've enjoyed all types of things during sex, and I don't have a problem with anything I saw in your toy collection. I want you to get pleasure from whatever we do, and I have to know what you enjoy in order to do that. I have a feeling that if you think I'm enjoying it, you might not speak up about it. It would ruin my pleasure if I realized you didn't like something and were just doing it because you thought I liked it."

He pulled away and looked at me. "But I like giving my partner pleasure and doing things they like. That's what gives me pleasure."

I hummed in agreement. Josh was definitely submissive. I wasn't sure if he even realized how submissive he was when it came to sex, because he wasn't submissive in his friendships. I had seen that time and time again, and I had thoroughly enjoyed him putting the boys in their place. He had done that because he was a caretaker, though, and he wanted what was best for people.

"Documentary?" he asked, changing the subject.

I nodded my head. Josh had obviously had enough heavy conversation today, and we had plenty of time to figure out the physical. The trick would be to figure out what my mate enjoyed in his submission. I already knew he liked a little sting when we were kissing—he had loved when I'd bit his lip. It definitely wouldn't be a hardship to explore, and if he couldn't talk about it now, then I'd see if he was more open to answering questions during sex. I really did enjoy talking to my partner.

That could wait, though. Josh needed to relax, and I was happy to cuddle and watch something with him. I reached over and grabbed the remote off the side table, handing it to him.

"Any particular documentary you're interested in?" he asked, turning on the television.

"Show me some that interest you, and we'll pick one together," I said.

He happily settled in and clicked on a streaming service. We went through documentaries, discussing ones that he liked and didn't. We finally settled on one about an evil human who was hunted down by other humans that looked interesting. Humans dealing with evil in the world on their own was always admirable and interesting.

Unfortunately, before we could get too far into the program, my phone rang.

"It's Thea," I said, recognizing the ring tone I had set for her. I was loath to break the moment between Josh and I, even if it was my delicate side project.

"You said she's like the boys, and that she had some trouble. You're thinking of bringing her into your work with the guys, aren't you?" he asked.

I nodded. She was already a hellhound, but yes, I would feel better if she learned from our guidance.

"Then you better take the call," he said, pausing the show.

I picked up the phone. "Yeah."

Josh laughed at my greeting.

"Who's with you?" Thea asked suspiciously.

Josh must have heard her, because he whispered, "Do you want me to go?"

He didn't realize Thea would be able to hear a whisper.

I shook my head no, putting the phone on speaker. "Thea, this is Josh. He's my mate."

Josh laughed again. "He's using Toby-speak. Toby is my friend, and he's a paranormal suspense writer, so he phrases things in an interesting manner. I'm Wilder's boyfriend."

He blushed when he said it, looking at me, and I smiled at him reassuringly.

"You a hellhound, too?" she asked.

"Um, no. I'm a financial advisor," Josh answered.

"Huh. I figured you'd all be…" she trailed off.

"In the same line of work?" Josh asked. "No. I mean, I guess the Smiths are, but the boyfriends aren't."

"Boyfriends? What, is it some kind of reverse harem thing there?" she asked.

I didn't sense any judgement, but Josh turned red.

"No! We all date different Smith men. I mean, I'm dating Wilder. Aiden is a pastry chef, and he's dating Atlas, and Q works in the same coffee shop, and he's dating Liam. Dexter is dating Toby—he's the paranormal writer, so don't mind some of the crazy stuff he says," Josh answered. "So, we're all pretty normal. Well, Q is snarky as hell, and Aiden was actually held captive for a year by a stalker, and Toby gets lost in plotlines... Okay, maybe we're not *normal* normal, but we're normally abnormal."

Thea laughed, and I looked at the phone, surprised. I don't think I'd ever set her at ease enough to get a laugh out of her.

"Are you coming to visit the Smiths? Wilder said you're kind of in the same line of work as him, and I'm sure he'd be a great mentor. He's really kind and understanding," Josh said, looking at me.

I grunted. I wasn't sure if I was agreeing or disagreeing, but I felt a bit odd having him praise me to Thea.

"I don't know, Josh." She sighed.

"You should. Our town is great, and it's also totally normal," Josh said. "A pretty boring town, just the way we like it."

"I might make my way there, then. It was nice talking to you, Josh."

She hung up before Josh or I could answer.

"Yeah, she's got the same manners as the guys," he laughed. Then he picked up the remote and looked at me. I nodded my head, cuddling him back in as he unpaused the show.

Somehow, Josh seemed to have convinced Thea to come here when I hadn't been able to. Of course, he'd also said Paradise Falls was boring and normal, and really, it was probably the furthest thing from either of those.

I'd explain all the afterlifers in town later, though. After all, we had a documentary to watch together.

CHAPTER 15

JOSH

"So you know how Toby is always going on about them being hellhounds? Well, apparently that's what they're named," I said into the phone.

Sebbie had called, and he'd barely gotten a hello out before I'd burst out with my news.

"Josh, did you hit your head? You're the rational one," Sebbie answered.

I laughed. "Not hellhounds like Toby is always saying. You know how he is—everything gets a little twisted. No, apparently it's their job. They're like special forces or something, or hitmen, and they're called The Hellhounds. But they work for the government or something, and they really do only go after bad people."

"Huh. Like a motorcycle club? The Hellhounds?" Seb asked.

"Yeah, except without the motorcycles," I said. "I didn't ask too many questions, because I don't know if I really want to know, but Wilder told me last night."

"Ohhhh. Wilder told you last night?" Sebbie said, drawing it out.

I smiled. "Yeah. He kind of asked me to date him."

Seb gasped. "Josh! That's so exciting! I could tell you were totally interested in him, even when you were still with the dickbag."

I laughed at Sebbie's name for Rick. "Yeah, I was. I just hope I'm not jumping into something too soon. Seb, he's really amazing, and I don't want to ruin this because I have so much baggage from Rick. And it *is* soon."

"You and Rick have been done for a while," Seb stated. "You stayed because he was a manipulative asshole, and now you've had some time to process everything that happened. I think you and Wilder are a great idea."

I was glad to have Seb's support, but I was still worried. "A week or two after a break up is not a lot of processing time. I'm thinking of maybe going to see Aiden's therapist."

"That's a good idea. It sure can't hurt." Seb paused, adding, "Just be careful of your heart, Josh. Wilder seems like a great guy, and I'm sure he wouldn't hurt you, but once you invest in someone, you give them your all. Sometimes more than your all."

"Eh," I answered.

"It's true! Josh, you are, like, the most supportive guy I know. You have *always* been there for Toby and me, and you give every relationship you've ever been in so much attention. You remember that guy in college, don't you?"

I groaned. Yes, I remembered Mike. He was a sweet guy, and we really didn't match up well, but we'd ended up dating for almost a year because neither of us wanted to hurt the other one. It was kind of comical when we'd actually had the break-up talk, and we'd stayed friends until he started dating someone new who thought it was weird he still talked to an ex.

"Exactly. So just... I don't know, Josh, maybe try to put yourself first for once," Seb said. "And call the therapist. I think it would be good."

"Yeah, I will. But how are you?" I asked. I didn't want to monopolize the conversation.

"I'm good. Nothing on the dating front, unless you count the birds," he answered.

I chuckled. Seb had befriended the local crows, and he was sort of fascinated with them. "What did they do now? Still leaving you shiny rocks?"

"Yeah, and other shiny things. Plus, and this is really wild—they left me a stuffed crow. How funny is that? It's small and light, so it wouldn't have been hard for one of them to carry, but it's so funny that they would give that to me. And it's kind of hysterical to think of a crow carrying a stuffed crow and someone seeing that."

I laughed. "You have to tell Toby. He'll totally put that in one of his books."

"Oh, he definitely will!" Seb agreed. "I have to call and check in with him next. You should go make that appointment. And when are you seeing Wilder next?"

"I'll call the office as soon as we get off the phone," I answered, feeling determined. "And Wilder is coming by when I'm done with work today. I'm working from home for a couple days. Which reminds me that I need to talk to Liam about paying rent. I'd like to stay here, although not having a road to the cabin is a pain. Wilder said they're having that done soon, though. The Smith property is really pretty, though."

Seb agreed, and we made small talk for a few more minutes before he got off the phone to call Toby, promising not to give away my news about Wilder. Not that I minded if he did—Toby, Seb, and I shared pretty much everything and had since college.

That thought made me feel bad for shutting them out when everything was happening with Rick. They were the best, though, and I knew they didn't hold it against me.

I called Aiden's therapist, Helene, and made an appointment with her. She seemed really nice on the phone, and she ended up having a few moments to talk. She asked me what was bringing me to therapy, and next thing I knew, I was pouring out my story about Rick. She was very easy to talk to, and I felt really good about going to see her. It was also nice that I'd given her some of the backstory before we met in person. It felt good to know she didn't judge me for what happened, and she was reassuring about it not being my fault. I could see why Aiden liked her.

I passed the rest of the afternoon with numbers and spreadsheets, and time dragged while I waited for the work day to end so Wilder could come over. Maybe things with him were all kinds of fast, but Wilder was just such a good person.

I'd always known that Rick was kind of an asshole. He had plenty of red flags, but the sex had been really good at first, and I had kept making excuses for his bad behavior. I always wanted to believe the best of people, and I guess sometimes that didn't work out in my favor. Next thing I knew, we were living together because Rick had hinted that he needed a cheaper place to stay, and I, of course, had been helpful. Then it had just seemed really complicated to break things off.

I sighed, finishing up the last spreadsheet for the day. Enough thinking about Rick. I had Wilder to look forward to. He was sweet and kind, and it didn't hurt that he was also sexy as sin. Who knew that an older guy was my type? The bit of gray in his hair really did it for me. He was in amazing shape and built just like his sons, too, which made sense considering he was in some secret military organization or something.

And yeah, that was a little worrisome. What if he got hurt? What if something happened to him? Did he get, like, deployed on jobs or anything? I guess those were things we would need to talk about.

Mostly, though, I hoped there was more kissing. And maybe more than that. It had been a long time since I'd had intimacy, and I was craving it.

As if that thought conjured him up, I heard a knock on the door, and I knew it was Wilder. I yelled for him to come in as I closed my laptop and got up, stretching.

Wilder came into the living room where I'd been working for the last hour (I alternated between the kitchen table and couch—I didn't have an office set up yet), and he made a sound of appreciation. I felt my face get warm, but I didn't stop stretching. It was nice to think he thought I was sexy.

I also wasn't sure what to do next. Did I go over and kiss him hello? Hug him? Do an awkward Toby wave? Luckily he walked right in and pulled me into a hug. I wrapped my arms around him, sighing at the contact. Being in Wilder's arms made me feel safe.

He smelled so good, like the outdoors and man. His arms and chest were firm and muscled, and I couldn't help thinking about the kiss yesterday. I was getting turned on just from being in his arms, and it would have been embarrassing if I didn't know he returned my interest. He growled low in this throat, which was crazy hot, and then his lips were on mine.

Thank god. The man was a freaking amazing kisser. He led the kiss, licking at my lips until I opened up, his tongue playing with mine and licking into my mouth. When he nipped at my bottom lip, drawing it between his teeth, I couldn't help the sound that escaped me.

Wilder put his hands under my ass and lifted me up. Holy shit, that was fucking hot, and I instinctively wrapped my legs around his waist. He continued to kiss me, our mouths slanting together, his teeth lightly nibbling on my lips between kisses. He walked with me and rested my ass on something, and I vaguely realized from the height it had to be the kitchen table, because we were pretty even.

Wilder bit down onto my lip hard, and the zing went through my entire body, making me gasp. I jerked my hips into his, desperate for some friction, and I felt his hardness against mine. I leaned my head back and groaned at the contact.

"Do you like that? Do you like a little bite with your pleasure?" he rumbled, and he kissed his way down my neck, lightly nibbling.

His light nibbles felt like a tease, and I wanted more.

"Answer me, Mei Ume," he growled.

"Yes!" I gasped.

In reward his teeth sunk into the space between my shoulder and my neck, the feel of it making my entire body jerk. He pulled off and licked at the spot, and I hoped he'd left a mark. The idea of it was such a turn on.

"What do you want, Mei Ume?" Wilder asked.

"I want to make you come," I answered. "I want to please you." I wanted to show Wilder I could bring him pleasure, too. I wanted to make him happy.

"Mmm, you do please me. All your beautiful sounds please me."

He reached down and squeezed my nipple beneath my shirt, and I pushed into him as he increased the pressure. I couldn't help grinding against him as he squeezed tighter, sending waves of pleasure through me, and I let myself groan loudly, wanting Wilder to hear me.

"What do you want to do to me?" he asked.

I tried to think about what he might like, but he switched over and pulled at my other nipple, biting on my neck at the same time. I could barely think, and I couldn't process what to say.

"What do you like doing, Mei Ume? Be good and tell me," he rasped, pulling at my nipple again as he ground our hips together.

I couldn't think, couldn't process, but I thought of Wilder's dick. "I want to suck you."

"Good boy for telling me," he murmured, biting my ear after

he said it. I mewled again, and Wilder's lips were back on mine, kissing me.

He lifted me off the table and peeled off our shirts between kisses until we were skin to skin. I ran my hands over his chest, which was firm and hairy, and I went to drop to my knees, but his hands grabbed onto my elbows, stopping me.

"Naked, Mei Ume. I want to see you," he ordered.

Fuck. I stripped off my pants and underwear in a rush, and Wilder dropped his own pants. I paused, staring at his dick. It was long and thick—I loved a thick dick, and I would have dropped down to suck him in, except he was holding my shoulders again, looking at me. I didn't have time to be worried or embarrassed, though.

"Such a pretty cock," he said, reaching down and giving me a squeeze. "So hard for me."

I groaned, leaning against his chest. "Please," I murmured, not even sure what I was asking for.

He hummed and let me go, walking us over toward the couch. If he wanted to sit, that was fine with me. Only he didn't sit; instead, he threw one of the couch pillows on the floor in front of him for me to kneel on. His thoughtfulness made me want to pleasure him even more. I knelt on the pillow, placed my hands on his hips, and licked at his dick.

He was leaking precum, and he tasted like salted caramel— both sweet and salty at once. I groaned at the taste.

"Mmm, yes, put your mouth on me, Mei Ume," he told me.

I swallowed him down at the command, happy to have directions. I let him deep into my throat, gagging, but that only made me harder. I loved feeling my mouth and throat full, and the inability to breathe for just a moment only made it all sharper and more pleasurable. I held myself there for a moment, listening to him moan, and then pulled back, licking at the head, swirling my tongue around. I looked up, and he was staring down at me, his eyes seeming to glow.

Fuck, I needed... something, and I moaned around him.

His hand went to my hair, and I groaned. I pulled against him to feel the sting against my scalp, my sounds getting louder. I wanted to taste his come. I wanted him to use me for his pleasure. I was moaning steadily, my dick hard, my tongue swirling, my hands gripping his thighs, but it almost felt like I was outside myself. I pulled against his hand again, and he tightened it in my hair, making me groan even louder. Yes, that was what I needed. The sting. The pressure. Someone else taking control.

"Does my Mei Ume want me to use his mouth?" he rumbled.

I looked up, and he was staring down at me. I could only mumble "Mmmhmmm" around his dick, trying to nod my head but still keep him in my mouth.

He took over, using both hands to hold my head still, pulling my hair and sending sparks through me as he began moving his hips back and forth. God, yes. I loved the sounds he was making. I loved that I was doing this to him.

He thrust deep into my throat, making me gag, and he went to pull off, but I reached around and grabbed onto his ass, holding him there.

"You like that, Mei Ume? You like choking on my cock? Such a good boy, taking me so deep." He pulled back and thrust in again as he spoke.

Fuck. I was so fucking hard I ached, and I knew if I touched myself I'd probably come. I wanted Wilder to come first, though, and I continued to moan as he thrust into my mouth.

He was murmuring words of praise, and I felt myself go fuzzy around the edges as he continued to thrust into my mouth. I didn't need to do anything, just focus on the dick in my mouth, sucking and licking as he thrust. I was doing so good for Wilder—he kept telling me so—and I couldn't help pushing my hips into the air, seeking pressure against my hard length.

He pulled my head down onto his cock, holding himself deep in my throat, and I held on, everything light in my head.

"Such a good boy," he murmured. "Look at you swallowing my cock down. So beautiful. You're going to make me come, Mei Ume. Is that what you want?"

I moaned again, the word "please" trying to come out. Yes, I wanted to make him come. Please, yes.

He picked up the pace, fucking my mouth and groaning until he was spurting down my throat. I eagerly swallowed, humming in happiness, wishing the moment could last forever.

He gentled his hands, but he didn't pull me off, even after he was done coming. He let me gently suckle his cock, which hadn't gone all the way soft. I felt light and drained, like I was the one who had come. My cock was still hard, but it felt distant, and I just enjoyed suckling gently on Wilder, barely realizing how much I was leaning into him.

Eventually he gently withdrew from my mouth. I made a sound of protest, but he helped me up and kissed me passionately, his tongue licking into my mouth. He could probably taste himself, and that made me moan again.

"That was so good, Mei Ume. You made me feel so good," he whispered as he broke the kiss. "You want to keep making me feel good, don't you?" he asked.

"Yes," I groaned. "Whatever you want, Wilder. Please."

"I want to play with that pretty cock of yours. Can I do that?" he asked.

I nodded my head. Yes, he could touch me. Please.

He backed me up until I was somehow against the couch, and he gently pushed me down so I sprawled across it.

"You going to keep making those pretty sounds for me?" he asked.

I could only groan again as his hand reached down and gripped my cock. I bucked my hips up, and he squeezed tighter. There was a flash of pain that was pleasurable, and I moaned even louder.

"You like that? You like a little pain with your pleasure?" he asked.

I could only nod, and then he was stroking me, his grip so tight that the pleasure was almost painful, or maybe the pain was pleasurable. I didn't know, but it felt amazing. He leaned down and bit my nipple, and my entire body shuddered, gasps erupting from my mouth.

"So pretty. You want me to leave a bruise on your nipple, Mei Ume?" he asked.

I jerked again, because the thought of being marked by him was hot as fuck.

He leaned down and nibbled my nipple. I mewled as he stroked me steadily and sucked at my skin. It was both too much and not enough at the same time, and I was moaning and wriggling, trying to get more somehow.

As if he could read my mind, he bit down on my nipple, the feeling of his teeth in my flesh my undoing. My body spasmed and stiffened as my orgasm crashed into me. I was yelling as he jerked me through it, not stopping or letting up, and that only made the orgasm more intense. It felt like it went on and on, and eventually the line between pleasure and pain got more distinct. As if sensing it, Wilder loosened his grip and picked his head up from my chest.

He stared into my eyes, and I watched blurrily as he lifted his hand up and licked my cum off it. My dick twitched at the sight, but it was too soon. Holy shit, was that hot, though.

"You taste so good, Mei Ume, just like I knew you would. And you were so good to give me your pleasure. So beautiful," he murmured.

I felt boneless and exhausted, and I was unsure what to do next. Wilder stood up, gently shifted me and lifted my head, and slid onto the couch with me leaning against him. He pulled me so I was snuggled against him, and he murmured sweet things that all blended together. Words like "beautiful" and "good boy" and how good I made him feel. It made me feel soft and blurry as exhaustion pulled me under.

"Yes, Mei Ume, rest now. Close your eyes and rest. I have you," he whispered.

So I did.

Chapter 16

Wilder

Josh was snoozing against me, and I reveled in his skin pressed against mine.

He was so beautiful.

I hadn't meant to take things physical right away, but when I'd hugged him, I'd smelled his arousal, and I apparently didn't have as much self-control as I'd thought. Josh clearly wanted to please me, and I couldn't say no. I'd seen him relax and let go, and I wanted to keep him in that beautiful, carefree space he'd found.

Josh liked things a little rough, but he also adored praise—the combination had made his eyes glaze over even as his cock leaked precum. I thought he would probably be uncomfortable being the center of my attention during sex—he'd worry about what I was getting out of it—but when I was telling him how much he pleased me, he seemed to lose his inhibitions.

I could imagine sliding into his ass, telling him how good he felt, and hitting his prostate over and over until he was spasming around me. I wanted to taste him, and I wondered if he'd let me, or if he'd be too concerned with what I was getting out of it. Perhaps if he were tied down he wouldn't worry about that. Something to talk to him about.

He stirred against me, and I brushed my hand through his hair. "You were beautiful, Mei Ume."

"What's it mean?" he murmured, still half asleep.

"What does what mean?" I asked, confused.

"Mei Ume," he murmured.

"Ahh. It means plum blossom. They're a symbol of resilience and renewal, and the flowers smell both sweet and spicy," I answered.

"The first building set you gave me," he murmured, gently petting my chest with his hand.

"Yes. It reminded me of you. Strong and starting anew, and you're certainly both sweet and spicy." I ran my hand through his hair again.

"Mmm," he murmured, obviously pleased.

I sighed as I heard voices in the distance. The light was fading and it was near dinner time, and I could sense Liam and Quinton both coming toward the cabin.

"Mei Ume, we're going to have company," I told him.

He sat up. "Shit! We aren't dressed!" he hissed, getting up and grabbing our clothes, thrusting mine at me as he pulled on his own.

I smiled at his urgency, but I knew Liam would wait respectfully outside until we were ready.

"Get dressed!" he whisper-yelled at me.

I complied, amused to be ordered about. He saw my smile, and he paused, pants undone, to come over and give me a peck on the lips.

We finished dressing, and Josh straightened his hair before he turned his attention to me, brushing out some wrinkles on my shirt and running his hands through my hair.

"There. I don't think we look like we had sex, right?" he asked.

Liam would be able to smell it on us, but I thought perhaps I shouldn't mention that, so I simply nodded my head. He looked very put together.

Liam and Quinton were patiently waiting outside the door, and after Josh's statement, Liam knocked on the door, calling out, "It's Liam and Quinton," for Josh's benefit.

Josh breathed out, taking a moment to collect himself, then called, "Come in!"

They did, and Quinton's smirk meant he was probably about to say something inappropriate, but Josh must have known him well enough, because he didn't let him talk before he started.

"I'd like to rent the cabin, if it's amenable to you guys. I understand if it isn't, but if it is, I'd like to know what you'd want for a security deposit, monthly rent, and what you'd like to do about utilities. If you'd prefer to keep them in the family name, I'll happily pay you the additional cost." Josh sat on the couch as he spoke, and I slid down next to him.

Quinton and Liam just stood there, looking vaguely confused and off kilter.

"Rent the cabin?" Liam asked. "What for?"

"To live here," Josh said, raising his eyebrows only slightly.

"But... you already live here. You don't have to rent it." Liam looked at me, as if for backup. I just smiled at him.

"Of course I have to pay you rent," Josh answered. "And sign a lease. Unless you don't want me staying longer than the month."

"Don't be an ass, Josh. Of course we want you staying," Quinton said, finally chiming in.

Although Liam looked confused, Quinton was looking a little fiery. I sat back, eager to see the drama unfold. Somehow, I had no doubt that Josh would win this battle in some way.

Josh nodded. "Good. Then I'll need the amounts. Of course, I understand if you need some time to discuss all the details with family. I'm sure your brothers will want to be consulted."

Liam looked even more confused. "Why would they want to be consulted? I don't understand. You just said you're staying."

"How much to charge me for rent, Liam," Josh stated slowly, as if he were talking to a child.

"We aren't charging you rent, you dumbass," Quinton cut in. "You're, like, family and shit. Duh."

"Of course you're charging me rent. And being family is no excuse not to let me contribute. Families contribute, too," Josh reasoned.

"Aiden and I don't pay rent, so are you saying we're slackers?" Quinton demanded.

Ah, point for Quinton.

"Of course not, Q. But you know perfectly well that your situation is far different from mine." Quinton sputtered, but Josh just kept talking. "Besides, not all contributions are monetary. You both contribute in numerous other ways."

I nodded. Definite point for Josh on that one. It was probably a two-pointer.

Quinton snorted. "What, is snark and assholery now a contribution? Never mind that we both work now, so implying that our tragic backstories would keep us from financially contributing to the pack is frankly insulting. So if you pay rent, then I guess Aiden and I need to pay rent, too, or get the fuck out."

Hmm. Maybe two points to Quinton on that one, and he'd backed Josh into quite the corner. Josh seemed entirely unruffled, however. I knew Liam would never accept money from Aiden and Quinton, but he remained quiet. He seemed to have given up his place in the fight, even though technically the property belonged to us. His head just volleyed back and forth between the two mortals.

Josh held up his index finger. "First of all, you work with Liam doing all his computer stuff, so you contribute that way to his work. He doesn't pay you, I'm sure, but he ought to be paying you."

Liam looked pleased and opened his mouth, as if he was now going to insist on giving Quinton money for his help, but one glare from Quinton had him shutting it quickly before he could utter a word.

Another finger popped up on Josh's hand. "Second of all, Aiden bakes for *everyone*. He cooks dinner, too. I *know* that you know how much those pastries sell for. We're all eating your rent payments, and let me tell you, I'm sure that none of the Smith family is complaining about that trade."

Quinton opened his mouth this time, but Josh wasn't done, and a third finger popped up.

"Next, you haven't mentioned Toby, who *owns* one of the houses in this family grouping. So he obviously contributes quite a bit financially. And it doesn't matter that he owned his house first. Dexter lives there, and I'm *sure* he doesn't pay rent, does he?" Josh stared at Liam and Quinton, waiting for an answer.

Liam shook his head no, and Quinton shot him a dirty look. Three points for Josh then. I was losing track of the score, but it was still anyone's guess who was gonna win this argument.

"Finally," Josh added, putting his hand down, "you and Aiden moved into an existing structure on the land that the guys bought. This is a new structure, and Wilder said a road is being added, and that will be an additional expense. How could I justify them footing the bill for that without contributing anything?"

Quinton opened his mouth, but Josh added, "Never mind the fact that you, Toby, and Aiden are all in relationships with Smith brothers, so that alone gives you rights to live rent free. Plus, I know Aiden takes care of training the guard dog, and probably you both take care of a million other household activities for the Smiths."

Huh. I turned and stared at Josh. He obviously didn't realize that Atlas was the "guard dog," and I supposed I hadn't really mentioned that when I explained hellhounds. That was something I would need to rectify.

Liam obviously found that funny, because he laughed, adding, "Getting Fluffy housebroken and friendly is something we couldn't pay enough for."

"Not helping our argument, Liam," Quinton muttered.

Liam seemed to realize his mistake, because he added, "But if you use that argument, you're in a relationship with Wilder, so that means you shouldn't pay rent either."

Josh and Quinton both stared at Liam, their mouths slightly agape, and they looked like a united front of outrage. Liam looked at me, but I just shrugged. He wasn't wrong, so I had no idea why both humans seemed so shocked by his statement.

Quinton smacked Liam's arm. "What the fuck, Sexy Stalker! I swear to god, if you put fucking cameras in here, I will be extremely pissed."

Liam was shaking his head no to that, hands held up in supplication.

"Fine, but you're *still* not off the hook, because you're my boyfriend, and if there is fucking gossip to be shared, I am the *first* one who is supposed to hear it, so the fact that you knew this and didn't tell me is a *problem*."

"I just found out now, my hellcat," Liam swore. "Of course I would tell you first. I forgot you couldn't hear them."

"Oh. My. God." Josh enunciated. "You heard us? Liam, what the hell! And you can't go making assumptions about people and then spewing them out for the whole world to hear!" Josh threw his arms out, like Liam had told the entire world, when really it was just the four of us in the cabin.

Quinton seemed to agree with him, however, because he was nodding his head. "You can't just say shit like that to people. We don't even know what their status is, and now you've gone and made it fucking awkward and shit."

I decided not to let Liam flounder through this alone. "Josh and I are in a relationship, but I don't think Josh is ready for everyone to know."

Ah, perhaps not the wisest course of action. Now both humans were glaring at me. Luckily, Josh put aside his ire first, sighing.

"I don't mind if the guys know," Josh reassured me. He looked at Liam then. "I just... Listen, it's too soon to move in together. We just decided to start seeing each other today."

Liam and I both glanced at each other. Too soon? Huh. I didn't sense any displeasure from Josh at the thought, so I wasn't sure why it was too soon. Perhaps a human thing. Also, I had been courting Josh for a while, but I knew sometimes humans didn't count things as actually happening until they spoke about it.

Quinton sighed as well. "Fine, I'll give you that. But you're still not paying rent. I'm sure you'll contribute in other ways, just like Aiden and I do. And Aiden would agree with me," he said, taking out his phone and typing.

Josh ignored that and snorted. "How else will I contribute? I don't bake, I don't do computer shit, and I don't make a killer cup of coffee, either. I know money, so I'll pay."

Quinton finished whatever message he was sending off and looked thoughtful. "You know money. You're like... into finances and shit, right?"

"I'm a financial advisor. I don't really deal with the stock market. I go over books and payroll, and I give advice and get people sorted when it comes to money," Josh answered.

"So, if you were given financial information, could you follow a money trail? Find out where the money was originating? Maybe figure out if there's some way to shut it down?" Liam asked.

"Uh, well, theoretically... Maybe?" Josh rubbed the back of his neck. "You're talking about financial crime investigation, and that's not my specialty."

Quinton looked at Liam, and they seemed to have a silent conversation between mates. Then Quinton turned to Josh. "Good. That's settled then."

"No, nothing is settled," Josh huffed.

"You'll do some investigative work for computer shit that Liam needs help with, because we don't know finances as well as you, and that will be your contribution to rent." Quinton was smirking like he won, but I knew Josh wouldn't go down without a fight.

"And if I'm no help? What then? We need to agree on a price. I would think 2k a month would be reasonable for all the utilities and monthly rent."

Q snorted. "Fuck that. Are you insane? Don't high-ball me. Think more like a hundred a month."

It was Josh's turn to snort. "A hundred won't even cover the electricity and gas. Nineteen hundred."

Qunton's eyes narrowed. "It's not prime property location, and that would detract from its value. You don't even have a road. Two hundred."

Josh smiled. "Exactly, and putting in a road is an added expense. I ought to up it to twenty-one hundred just for that. But I'll go as low as eighteen."

Liam seemed unsure, but he bravely stepped between Josh and Quinton. "Um, I think negotiations are supposed to go in the other direction?"

"Shush, Sexy Stalker. Let me work." Quinton pushed him out of the way, staring at Josh. "Two-fifty."

Josh snorted. "Still absurd. Do you take me for a chump? That isn't even remotely reasonable."

Quinton narrowed his eyes. "You're lucky we'll let you pay at all, so I suggest you take what you can get. You're the one who's throwing out outrageous numbers. I make a barista's salary, and there's no way I could afford it, and if I couldn't afford it, we sure as fuck aren't charging you it."

Josh paused, thinking. "Fair point. I'll go as low as a thousand."

"Five hundred," Quinton countered.

"We'll meet in the middle at seven-fifty. That's my final offer, or I can always go find something else and pay an actual rent."

Quinton snorted. "We have connections. Try it. We'll make sure no one charges you above what we say."

Josh's eyes narrowed, and Liam must have sensed things going further off the rails, because he grabbed Quinton into a hug, saying, "That's acceptable, but *only* if you are of zero assistance in our computer investigations."

"Fine," Josh conceded. "Although don't you guys have connections to look into financial stuff? I'd think with your backing, you would."

I wasn't sure what he meant, and Liam looked confused as well.

Quinton had no problem asking, though. "What the fuck are you talking about?"

Josh looked at me, raising his eyebrows, and I nodded. Yes, Quinton knew about us.

"The Hellhounds," Josh answered.

Quinton still looked perplexed. "Why would they have someone who's good with financial shit? They're lucky Liam is a hacker. Most of them are pretty old-fashioned about things."

"I just thought with, like, a military operation, or whatever this is, that they might have outside connections or resources," Josh answered.

We all stared at him.

Well, shit. Apparently he hadn't taken the news about us being hellhounds quite the way I'd thought he had.

Liam, Quinton, and I looked at each other. I wasn't sure what to say. I took hold of Josh's hand and turned to face him, causing him to look at me.

"Mei Ume, we aren't a military operation."

Josh chuckled. "Well, yeah, I mean, I kind of figured it wasn't anything officially sanctioned. It still doesn't change that you guys hunt down bad guys and have the blessing or permission or whatever of someone in a position of authority. Right?"

"Well, yes..." I answered. He wasn't wrong, but... "There's more to us than that. We aren't like you, Quinton, Aiden, or Toby."

Josh chuckled again. "Of course not. You guys are all in crazy good shape and probably know all sorts of things about weapons and self-defense and whatever super-humans who kill bad people know."

"Josh," Quinton cut in, "they're, like, actual hellhounds."

"Yes, I know," Josh answered.

"No, you really don't," Quinton sighed.

At that moment, there was a knock at the door from Aiden. I had sensed them getting closer but didn't know if this was their destination or if they were just walking by on their evening walk.

"Come in!" Quinton called, adding, "Good thing I texted Aiden for back-up."

Aiden and Fluffy walked in at that moment, and Aiden called out a greeting.

Josh smiled at them both. "Hey guys!" He looked at Quinton. "We figured out rent already, and there's no take-backs just because you have back-up now."

"Oh good, the rent thing you texted me about is settled?" Aiden asked.

"Oh yeah, we're on to the hellhound thing now." Quinton gestured at Josh, rolling his eyes.

Aiden looked at Josh, raising his eyebrows.

"Yeah, I know they're some super secret organization that hunts down bad guys. It's okay. I'm okay with it," Josh assured Aiden.

"They're *actual* hellhounds, Josh," Quinton cut in. "Like, fire and flame and living forever and shit."

Josh smiled, holding up his hands. "I don't need any details on how they do things, and I sincerely hope they do all live forever. I don't want anyone getting hurt, and I'm sure their line of work is dangerous."

Quinton looked at Aiden, as if for help.

"They turn into fiery dogs, Josh," Aiden added.

Josh just laughed again, and Liam and I stared at each other, at a total loss.

Atlas obviously felt the need to weigh in on the conversation, though, because Fluffy was gone, and Atlas was standing in his place.

We all stared at him for a moment, waiting to see what he had to say. Only he didn't say anything, just stared at Josh.

"Aiden," Josh said, and I could hear him swallow. He wasn't afraid, exactly, but he wasn't calm either. "Aiden, why is your boyfriend naked?"

We all looked at Atlas. He was, indeed, naked. Oops.

I hoped Josh wasn't shy about that sort of thing.

CHAPTER 17

JOSH

Aiden's boyfriend was naked in the living room, and no one thought that was weird. And Fluffy... Nope, not thinking about that. Nope.

Aiden's boyfriend was naked in the living room.

I tried really hard not to stare at his dick, because, you know, it was just *there*. And that was definitely enough for my mind to focus on. Or not focus on. Or whatever. Dear god, would no one give the man some pants?

"Atlas, you can't go walking around naked," I said. I thought my voice was quite reasonable considering... you know, *everything*.

"Clothes are itchy," he answered.

"Yes, well, that's neither here nor there. You still have to wear them, especially when you're with company." My god, I sounded like someone's mother. Maybe I could lecture him about washing behind his ears next.

Atlas just grunted, though, and then he was gone.

Fluffy was back. He grinned a doggy grin at me and sat down.

Nope. Not thinking about that. Nope.

"Is Atlas going to get pants on?" I asked, and yeah, I knew it was stupid even while I asked it, but Atlas was gone.

Q dragged his hands down his face then gestured to Fluffy. "Actual hellhounds, Josh."

"That's not a hellhound. That's Fluffy," I answered.

Except Fluffy was on fire. I stared. Yes, that was fire, dancing all along Fluffy's body. He seemed fine, but the cabin was brand new. New wood everywhere. Did they even have a fire extinguisher in here? I kind of doubted it, and I was going to live here, and now it was going to burn down before I ever got the chance.

Everyone was staring at me. I could feel it, but I was staring at Fluffy as the flames seemed to reach a little higher, and he wasn't standing *that* far from a small, wooden side table.

"Fluffy, we do not go around all..." I paused and gestured toward him. "Flamy. It's rude. This is a brand new cabin, and I will *not* be happy if anything catches fire."

Fluffy was no longer on fire, but he huffed at me in displeasure.

Liam chuckled, and using a typical *you got in trouble and I didn't* voice said, "Yeah, Fluffy, no flames in the house. First the naked thing, then this. What, were you raised by wolves?"

Q elbowed Liam in the side, and Fluffy narrowed his eyes and growled.

"Boys," Wilder said mildly, and everyone settled down and looked at him. And at me. At us. Wilder was still holding my hand.

"Not my fault he's mad he offended step-dad," Liam muttered.

Well, that seemed to be the point where reality checked out, because Fluffy was once again Atlas, and he was *still* naked, and Atlas lunged at Liam, and the two of them were rolling around on the floor smacking each other and wrestling.

I must have been the only one having a break with reality, because Quinton just muttered, "idiots," under his breath, and Aiden just backed up. Wilder heaved out a sigh of exasperation.

"I think I need a CAT scan," I murmured. "Unless it's a CT scan. Never can remember which is which. Or if they're the same."

Q snorted, but I ignored him. I was too busy watching the grown men—the hallucinations—rolling around on my floor.

They seemed to be mainly playing, although they were coming awfully close to the wooden side table that had my Lego camera on it.

As if manifesting the chaos, which is probably what I did, because they were my hallucinations, after all, the two rolled into the table. The Lego camera fell off and broke into pieces.

Both of them stopped, staring at me guiltily. Atlas was still naked, but my hallucination at least kept Liam clothed. They literally had their hands around each other's necks, although they didn't appear to be choking each other at the moment.

I stood up, staring at them. I wasn't really sure what I was going to do, but then I saw the broken Lego camera again and sighed.

"And *this* is why we don't roughhouse inside," I said, going over and picking up some of the camera pieces. "Stand up, for goodness sake. And put some clothes on, Atlas. Or a towel. Or something."

Atlas grabbed a dish towel to hold in front of himself. Yeah, that was definitely going in the wash. Because apparently I was just going to embrace my mental breakdown.

Why not? Wilder was here, and when I looked over, he just looked pleasantly amused. He winked at me, and my insides felt a little warm and fluttery. He didn't seem bothered in the least.

I turned back to Liam and Atlas. "You're grown ass men, and you should not be rolling around on my floor fighting each other."

Aiden and Q looked amused, and Liam and Atlas looked like sulky little boys. I swear they weren't normally like this, especially Liam, and I wondered if Wilder being here gave them an opportunity to let loose and be kids again. Well, my mind must have thought so, because they were my hallucinations, after all.

"He started it," Liam mumbled.

"Excuse me? What did you say?" I asked, staring at Liam. And yes, I was totally using some kind of angry parent voice I didn't even know I had.

Liam looked at me, opened his mouth, and then wisely shut it.

"Mmhmm. Because I thought I heard you making fun of your brother and saying he was raised by wolves."

"But he *was* raised by—" Liam started, but I cut him off.

"You were being a smartass, and don't even tell me you weren't. I expect that of Jude, but not of you, Liam."

Aiden giggled. "Oh, Liam, you got compared to Jude."

I glared at Aiden, who put his hands up. "I didn't break your camera!!" he said.

"Who came to my apartment the night I called you?" I asked, and Aiden looked a little guilty.

"Uh, Fluffy and I did," he answered.

"Mmmhmmm. Who came to my apartment the night I called you?" I asked again.

Because I was just going with the chaos at this point, and the flamy dog was Aiden's boyfriend. Aiden had brought his boyfriend to my house as a dog. And I think I'd *cried* on him. And cuddled him. And stroked his fur. And that was just... nope.

I turned to Atlas. "Would you care to answer the question?"

Atlas looked at Aiden and then back at me, and he looked nervous and absolutely ridiculous—this big, muscled guy holding a dish towel in front of his junk. The only thing that kept me from breaking into hysterical laughter was my mortification.

"I *cuddled* with you," I said accusingly.

"He's really good at cuddles," Aiden said, and I shot my glare over to him. "Uh, I mean, sorry? We went over to help, and Atlas prefers to be Fluffy, because he *was* raised by wolves, but it still isn't nice that Liam was being a jerk to him. But anyway, you were upset, and he would have given you cuddles whether he was Fluffy or Atlas."

I stared at Atlas, and the big man just shrugged his shoulders.

I'd had enough. I was done. Flamy dogs and naked men and a broken Lego camera—I had reached my limit.

"Out," I said, pointing to the door.

"Would you like us to put your camera back together?" Liam asked.

"Nope. I would like you all to leave for now. I'm obviously having a stroke or a brain bleed, or maybe it's a brain tumor? At any rate, I'd like to have my mental breakdown in private, please. So off you go."

They shuffled out, although Q definitely looked like he wanted to argue. For once, he kept his snark contained.

I walked them to the door. "You can bring the finance stuff over tomorrow for me to look at." As I ushered them out, I added, "And no more fighting!"

Did I maybe slam the door? Yes, I did. But... Well...

I walked back into the living room, where Wilder was sitting on the couch. He was leaning forward on his elbows, and he opened his mouth to say something.

I didn't want to know what.

"Nope! I am having some type of break from reality, and they broke my Lego camera, which, fine, that really isn't a big deal, because it'll probably take me five minutes to put it back together, but Fluffy was all flamy! The cabin could've burned down!" I sat down next to Wilder as I finished.

Wilder pulled me into his arms. "Hellhound fire only destroys what we choose for it to destroy. Well, mostly, anyway. The boys are pretty good at controlling things now. Not so much when they were younger."

I didn't answer. He pulled me tighter, and I snuggled into his chest.

"Josh, you know..." he began, but I reached up to put my hand against his mouth.

"Not now. Let's just... bask in the weirdness of my hallucinations and cuddle a bit. It's been a long day. Maybe we can finish that documentary on the giant music festival gone wrong?" I asked.

I could feel Wilder's stare, but eventually, he grabbed the remote and switched the television on.

We passed the night watching documentaries, and someone—I didn't ask who—dropped dinner off for us. If Wilder seemed to know about it before it happened, even though I didn't see him on his phone, that was fine.

We ate, and he helped me put the Lego camera back together, although I certainly didn't need help. Seeing his thick fingers handle the Lego pieces was weirdly sexy, though.

And we chatted about mundane stuff—jobs and different places in the country we'd visited and music. Wilder asked about me growing up, and he shared stories about when he was raising the boys. If some of the stories seemed a little odd, that was fine. As was the comment that Wilder didn't have parents, since "first gens" just came into being.

Totally fine. Not everyone liked their parents, after all.

We had a really nice evening together, and the cuddles and chatting were amazing. If Wilder occasionally threw a concerned look my way when he said something weird, well... It was fine.

Everything was fine. Totally normal.

Really. Fine.

⁘

I woke up the next morning feeling like a bus had hit me. I knew I'd fallen asleep on the couch in Wilder's lap while binging documentaries, and my body didn't thank me for that. Luckily, I was in my own bed.

Wilder must have moved me here.

I could see my phone resting on the night table, and when I picked it up, I saw text alerts. The multiple dings was probably what had woken me.

Wilder had texted me, letting me know that he'd gone to check on all the boys, but he'd be back with breakfast before I needed to start work.

Yeah, that totally gave me warm fuzzies, because we'd had an amazing night. We'd talked, and we'd cuddled, and we'd watched shows, and we'd laughed over stories about our work.

And we'd had sex before all that. Like, really amazing sex. And it hadn't been awkward afterwards, and Wilder hadn't treated me any differently, either.

Because, let's face it, I knew I liked things a little... different. I knew there was nothing wrong with that, but just because I liked things one way in bed didn't mean that was how I always wanted things to go outside of bed. I was smart and competent and capable, and I didn't need someone bossing me around or thinking I wasn't worthwhile.

I think I'd let Rick make me question my value, but I was better than that asshole.

Was I trying *really hard* to ignore what else had happened yesterday?

Yes, perhaps I was.

That was shattered when I looked at my other texts, though. Toby had texted. About forty times. Because he was like a manic squirrel, and he'd type one line and send it and then type the next and send it... and why he couldn't just put it all in one text was beyond me.

I scrolled to the end and groaned, because Toby was on his way over. Because of course he was.

I texted him to just come in and went to hop in the shower. I needed to be a lot more awake to deal with Toby's energy.

By the time I was dressed and came out of the bathroom, I felt more human, and Toby was wandering around the living room, looking at my Lego sets.

"I remember you used to love doing these. I thought maybe you lost interest," he said.

I grabbed a cup of coffee and started setting my computer up for the day. "Do you ever really outgrow your interests? I just got busy for a while."

Toby gave me a stare, because we both knew that wasn't really the whole story.

"So..." Toby trailed off, smiling gleefully.

I rolled my eyes. "Yes, Toby?"

"Ohmygod! You and Wilder! And omg that's so fantastic! Because he's totally hot in a dad vibe kind of way, even though Dexter is hotter, of course. And did you know they're literally hot, too, because of the hellhound thing? And you thought I was being figurative when I said Dexter set the sheets on fire, but he actually set the sheets on fire, and oh my god, have you had Wilder's knot yet?" It all came out in a rush, and then Toby stared at me expectantly.

"Ugh..." Shit. I knew I was turning red, because I didn't really talk about sex.

Toby kept going. "Yep! A knot! You thought it was some new dildo for research purposes, and I totally did use it for research purposes, and my sex scenes have gotten a million times hotter since I got together with Dexter, but of course I'm not just using him for his knot or tail or the fantastic sex."

"Tail?" I murmured, feeling a little dazed.

"Mmmhmmm. And it's totally sexy. Not like a furry dog tail, but like a demon tail, apparently? Think like tentacle sex, only tail sex, although maybe you haven't read much tentacle porn. Which you should totally do, because tentacles are *hot*. Of course, I'm not complaining that Dexter doesn't have tentacles, because knots and tails are even hotter. And don't worry about the whole torture basement thing, either."

"Torture basement?" I asked, not really wanting an answer.

I looked longingly at the bedroom. Could I still be dreaming? Could I go back in there and put the covers over my head?

Toby didn't seem to notice my distress, adding, "Well, plural, I guess, because there are multiple torture basements, but there's not one in my house, don't worry, and I'm sure there isn't one in the cabin, either, because I don't see a foundation that could have a basement, unless they hid it somehow. Oh, maybe they did. I'll have to ask. That would be so cool if you had a secret torture chamber in the cabin!"

Thank god, Wilder walked in at that moment. If he'd knocked, I hadn't heard, and it kind of made me feel warm to think we were close enough that he'd just walk in. It was their cabin, of course, but all the other guys knocked.

I just looked towards him with an imploring expression.

"Toby, there's no secret torture chamber beneath the cabin," he answered, placing a coffee holder with two cups and a bag on the counter.

"Aww, bummer. I think it would make a great plot idea, though," he said, and he started looking around. I knew where this was headed, and I was not giving Toby a pen and paper, because then he'd never leave. I had work, and I really wanted to have breakfast with Wilder.

"It's okay, you can go jot down notes. We'll catch up later," I told him.

He looked at me. "You sure?"

"Totally. I promise. After work. I still do have work today," I added.

"Oh, yeah! Of course! I have to write a chapter as well, and now

I'm thinking about a hidden torture chamber. Maybe underground, maybe not. I wonder how hard it would be to add one to an already existing structure?" Toby muttered, half talking to himself.

"Ask Dexter. He's done construction. He'll be able to help," Wilder told him. He looked amused by the whole exchange.

Toby left with a distracted wave, still sort of muttering about construction. Wilder looked after him fondly, like he was staring at a little kid who'd just done something cute. Then he turned to me, and his expression changed to one of concern.

"I'm okay," I answered, even though he hadn't asked.

He came over and kissed me, and I opened my mouth to him without thinking. He wrapped his arms around me, and I just grabbed on as he led the kiss. His mouth was firm and demanding, and I knew I was making little moaning noises, but I didn't care. He bit my bottom lip, and the sting had my dick jerking. He gentled the kiss after that, though, eventually just wrapping me in his arms and holding me tight while I leaned against him.

As much as my dick might've been on board, now was not the time for sex. I hoped maybe later, but I had work soon, and there was still all that other... stuff. Which I was trying really hard not to think about, but of course Toby had shattered the hope that it had all been some kind of crazy dream.

Wilder hugged me tighter, as if he sensed my distress. How could someone's arms already feel so comfortable? So much like home? I didn't want to think about Rick any more, but he popped into my head, and I realized we rarely ever hugged.

"What are you thinking, Mei Ume?" Wilder asked.

"Rick and I never really hugged or cuddled," I said.

I cringed a bit. Wilder was my new boyfriend, and it was a new relationship—hello, you did not bring up your ex and talk about him. I wanted to smack myself in the head, but Wilder just squeezed me again.

"That's Rick's loss, then, because you're perfect to hug." Wilder paused, then he added, "You know that none of that is your fault, right?"

I sighed. "Yeah, I know. I'm going to see Aiden's therapist—did I tell you that? I already talked to her, and she seems really nice. I promise I won't always be thinking about what happened, and I'll try not to bring it up."

Wilder pulled back and looked me in the eyes. "Mei Ume, you bring up whatever you need to as often as you need to. I don't mind when you talk about what happened. You're working through all of it, and I would rather you talk to me than keep it bottled up. I want to know everything that you're thinking, okay?"

I shrugged, and Wilder kissed my forehead.

"I mean it. Everything that you're thinking." He looked into my eyes again, giving me a moment. Then he added, "Do you want to talk about—"

"Nope," I cut in.

It was Wilder's turn to sigh, although he had a fond smile on his face. "Mei Ume..."

I leaned my head into his chest. "No, I don't want to talk about all the super insane stuff that happened last night, because I have work today. And I really just want to sit down and have a nice breakfast with my boyfriend."

I blushed at the last part, glad Wilder couldn't see my face since I was cuddled into his shirt. It felt weird but really good to call him my boyfriend, and I hoped that he was okay with it.

He gave me a squeeze—that seemed to be his way to reassure me, and it really did work—and kissed the top of my head. "Ok. Let's have breakfast, then."

So we did. More of Aiden's baked goods, and coffee that was made just the way I liked it. We chatted about our plans for the day, and Wilder actually seemed interested in hearing about my work, which was definitely a first. Seb and Toby always listened to me talk about what I did, but I knew their eyes sort of glazed over. And Rick... Well, he used to cut me off when I started talking about work.

But Wilder listened, asked questions, and laughed when I told him about the client who didn't realize there was a difference between paying sales tax and state and federal taxes. The guy had been shocked, and more than a little confused, when I tried explaining it all to him. Some people had great products and were fantastic at customer service, but they were financially clueless. You kind of needed to be savvy in everything to run a small business, or you needed to hire someone to fill in the gaps. Which was where I came in.

"You help people," Wilder stated as we cleaned up breakfast. "You allow them to achieve their dreams with less stress in their lives."

I laughed a little. "I don't know if I would go that far. I'm just a finance guy."

Wilder walked over and put his hand on mine. "Don't sell yourself short, Josh. You're smart and capable, and people depend on you. Some of these small businesses wouldn't have survived without your help. You help people live their dreams. Don't ever underestimate that."

I mumbled a bit, but Wilder swooped in and kissed me, cutting off any protest to what he'd said. The kiss was scorching and passionate, and Wilder completely took control of my mouth, licking and nibbling and turning me into jelly in his arms.

He gentled it, though, bringing me down easily. It was amazing how he knew how to do that. He ended with a light peck to my lips.

"You're beautiful, Mei Ume. Never underestimate your worth. I'll bring dinner over later? Or would you like to go out?" he asked.

"Do you want me to cook?" I asked. "I'm not bad in the kitchen, and I'd like to cook for you."

Wilder smiled. "Perfect. I look forward to it."

With that, he kissed me again and took his leave. I sat down at my computer, ready to log in to work on some client's books.

For the first time in a long time, I couldn't wait until the work day was over.

CHAPTER 18

WILDER

I headed over to Liam's place after leaving Josh. It was tempting to just hang out and watch him work, but I wasn't sure of his comfort level. I would've moved in with him, except yesterday's conversation over rent made me think that he would've thought it was "too soon."

If I stayed every night but kept my things somewhere else, that didn't count as moving in, right?

I wasn't sure why it was too soon. We'd been courting since Josh broke up with Rick, and we were obviously compatible in all ways, from dealing with my pack of rowdy boys to conversations to sex. Josh knew all about hellhounds now, as well.

Well, that might've been a bit of an issue. I wasn't sure how much he had really processed all of that. Giving him time with it was the least I could do. I didn't think he really had an issue with the fact that I was a hellhound. I think his issue came more out of the fact that supernatural things existed in the first place.

I pondered that as I walked into Liam's house, heading to his office. Quinton was at work, so it was just Liam, and he was, as usual, sitting in front of his monitors.

"We might have a problem," Liam commented, not even looking up.

I sat in the vacant seat next to him and raised my eyebrows. I hoped it wasn't too technical of a problem—when Liam got started on computer talk, he tended to lose me completely. His affinity for technology was amazing.

"So... Rick is causing a bit of trouble," Liam muttered.

I crossed my arms. "Hmm. How interesting. Just a guess here, but perhaps it has something to do with two hellhounds who went over and threatened him."

"Yeah, I know. We shouldn't have done that. But Quinton was all fired up, and Atlas suggested it, and it seemed like a good idea at the time." Liam shrugged.

"What's Rick doing?" I asked.

"Posting about supernatural creatures all over the freaking place. All his socials had a description of what happened, but I was able to take those down pretty quickly for 'violating community standards.'" Liam snorted. It was apparently very easy to disrupt someone's social media posting.

"Did he mention names?" I asked.

"Josh's, but not ours." Liam cut off my growl by saying, "Everyone knew they were dating, though. Most people who know Rick treated it like a joke, and then it got taken down. The problem is that he went deep after that, posting in chat rooms and finding all sorts of message boards and sites to post on. Most of them are full of conspiracy theorists who have no real sway."

"But..." I said, because there was always a "but."

"But, he might have gotten the attention of the Order of Astrophagia," Liam admitted.

"You have got to be fucking kidding me," I said, throwing my head back and looking up at the ceiling. "How in hells would that happen?"

"They've been looking into this area, and Rick posted some

weird shit. If I were looking for info, I'd start off with trying to find anything out of the ordinary on socials and in groups. Rick has no common sense and has been throwing the name of the town around." Liam looked at his screens again, scrolling through chats and messages.

"Can you shut it down?" I asked.

"I deleted his posts, but they'd already gotten a contact number out to him. I didn't think to have him that closely monitored, which is my fault, and I'm sorry."

"No apologies, Liam. We wouldn't even know about it if it weren't for you," I assured him.

"He wouldn't be a problem if it weren't for us," Liam countered.

He had a point, but... "I have a feeling Rick wasn't going to give up easily. We couldn't have predicted it would go this way, but I don't think it would have been simple for Josh no matter what."

Liam hummed in agreement. "When I looked into Rick's finances, I found out Josh was his meal ticket, so that doesn't help things. I don't think he'll give up on their relationship easily—he hasn't even told anyone on his socials that they broke up. A lot of his posts and chats had to do with getting his boyfriend away from the 'cult' that kidnapped him."

"How ironic," I muttered. Of course two problems would combine into one bigger one, and in claiming Josh was kidnapped by a cult, Rick would end up in league with a cult. It was all rather absurd.

"Yeah, and usually I wouldn't even worry. Who trusts some random stranger on the internet with their information?" Liam rolled his eyes. "But Rick is not the brightest flame in the fire, and I think he's working with a faulty hard drive at this point."

"Any more word on Aiden's grandfather or the money?" I asked, since those were tied into the cult.

"Nope. The grandfather is definitely involved with the cult, but they're doing all his dirty work now. He's kind of dropped off the radar, and I'm not sure if I should be worried or not that the cult has taken over."

I hummed in agreement. Cults were unpredictable at the best of times. You never knew what kind of insane schemes they would come up with.

"As for the money," Liam continued, "it's pretty tied up. I can't even hack my way into stealing it, so I doubt any of their resources will be successful either. They need Aiden's brother or a dead body, and neither one is available."

"So we're still on guard for the cult—that hasn't changed. Rick is added to our list of people to keep a very close eye on. Any idea where he is now?" I asked.

Liam shrugged. "He left Paradise Falls and went back to his friend's house. I'm guessing from his lack of activity that he stopped using his phone, which means he's probably using a burner phone or a friend's phone. I'll do what I can, but his phone was how I was tracking him. I have tabs on his job if he stops showing up, and most of us have his scent in case he tries coming around here."

I nodded and stood, giving Liam a pat on the shoulder. "Good work. You'll do what you can, and we'll deal with trouble if it comes. Cults are nasty, but hopefully their main concern is money. If we or Aiden can't be of assistance in getting the funds, then we can hope they won't venture into our territory."

Liam grunted, and I didn't blame him. They wouldn't be after Aiden, but that didn't mean they wouldn't still stir up trouble in the area while looking for his very dead older brother.

We said our goodbyes, and I went and checked in with the other boys. Everyone was home, and I chatted with each of them. Dexter would need to hunt soon, and I assured him that we would look out for Toby. Jude had brought home a hellbound soul to torture, so I helped him a bit with that, and I coordinated with Atlas on clearing a roadway to the cabin.

All in all, the morning went by quickly, and I dropped off a sandwich for Josh in the early afternoon. He was on the phone with someone discussing LLCs, EINs, and S Corps—it sounded like a foreign language—but he smiled broadly when I came in. I dropped off his food and gave him a quick kiss on the cheek, letting myself back out.

Thea texted me as I was walking back from the cabin. She was quick and to the point—*I'm coming. I'll text when I get into town.*

If she was on her way, I needed to tell the boys about her. The human packmates were all working, but I texted all the boys that we needed to meet. I would've liked to have included all the pack in the meeting, but I had no idea when Thea would be getting into town. I could sense a general direction from her, but I couldn't tell the distance. I wasn't sure how well Thea would deal with other hellhounds, so the boys needed a warning to treat her less like a hellhound and more like a human.

Not that they really knew how to treat humans, either, but it was a start.

I did think of my talk with Atlas and Corbin again—mates shared their problems and helped each other. Josh was working, and I didn't want to disturb him, but I also wanted to treat him like a partner. I pulled out my phone and stared at it for a moment before sending him a text letting him know Thea was on the way and I needed to tell the boys.

My heart warmed when he responded right away—*Give me two minutes to finish up my call and I'll head over if you want.*

I breathed a sigh of relief, glad he was coming. I let him know we'd be meeting at Jude and Corbin's house. I supposed it was my house, too, but I was rather hoping that the cabin would be my place with Josh sooner rather than later.

Humans—they had such short lives, but they still wanted to

take their time about things. I understood the frustration my boys had faced in courting mortal mates.

All the boys were making their way toward the house, and I decided to go meet Josh at the cabin and walk with him. He was coming out the door as I walked up, and his smile lit up the afternoon. He came straight to me and let me wrap him in a hug, and he melted into my arms. I knew Josh could be hesitant about physical proximity after what had happened to him, but I could also sense he was touch-starved, and I was glad he trusted me.

He sighed and pulled away, and we started walking. I grabbed his hand to hold onto, and he sent me another beautiful smile.

"Why the family meeting? Do you think they won't be accepting for some reason?" Josh asked.

I hummed thoughtfully. "It isn't that, exactly. She's just a bit more of a wild card than the boys are used to, and they might need to exercise a little tact in dealing with her."

Josh snorted at that, and I tended to agree with him. Tact was not a strong point for my boys.

We made it to the house and everyone sat in the living room. I think Josh would have distanced himself, but I pulled him down to sit close to me. I told the boys about Thea—that she was human-raised and hadn't changed forms until recently, that she thought she was a sociopath who killed bad people, and that she wasn't trusting. I also told them that the messenger angel and his demon apprentice had given me the message that I ought to find her, so some afterlifer had an invested interest in her. The boys let me talk, and they were silent for a moment when I finished.

Of course, that didn't last.

"Wait, since when does the archangel Gabriel have a demon apprentice for delivering messages? I thought angels and demons didn't fraternize that often," Liam commented.

"Dude—focus," Jude cut in. "Who cares about afterlifers? I

wanna know how come I never knew there were female hellhounds."

"Where do you think I came from, idiot?" Dexter asked, rolling his eyes.

"A hellhound dad and human mum, just like the rest of us," Jude answered.

"My mother wasn't human," Corbin cut in.

"Yeah, but she wasn't a hellhound, either," Liam reasoned. "I thought there were only a handful of first gen female hellhounds, but that all second gen hellhounds were born male."

Jude motioned to Liam. "Yeah. What he said."

Everyone looked at me, but I wasn't sure what to answer. I hated not having all the answers. Josh reached over and took my hand. I gave him a squeeze in return.

"I have never known of a second gen female hellhound, and many of the first gen hellhounds would identify as nonbinary. It isn't unusual to have no knowledge of a female hellhound. That makes Thea all the more extraordinary, and all the more alone in the world, as well," I answered.

The boys all looked at me, and I don't think they knew what to make of that. Luckily, Josh took over.

"That means that you have to be *nice*. Maybe treat her like another human for a while until you figure out what she's comfortable talking about or seeing." Josh looked at Atlas. "And no turning into a flamy dog in front of her. Or being naked."

"Was just being helpful," Atlas grumbled.

Josh just shot him a look, then gave each of the boys a stare in response. "That means being on good behavior. Be *nice*."

They all nodded their heads in agreement.

"Let our human packmates know. We'll have to figure out a place for her to stay, too," I added.

"She can stay with me," Josh answered.

Everyone turned to stare at him.

"What? I'm pretty normal and very human, and there are two bedrooms in the cabin. She seemed nice on the phone, and she might not be comfortable staying with you guys—no offense."

"It's not a bad idea," I mused, "but I'm not sure you should be staying with a relatively unknown hellhound."

"Wilder can stay at the cabin, too," Corbin volunteered.

Josh turned a little pink at that and gripped my hand more tightly. I didn't sense distress or disagreement from him, but it never hurt to check.

"As long as Josh doesn't mind, I would love to stay with him," I said, looking over at him.

"Umm, yeah, sure, if you don't mind..." Josh sort of trailed off.

"All set, then," Corbin said, getting up and going out the back door.

Atlas followed him. Dexter at least said goodbye before he headed back to Toby's, and Jude wandered into the kitchen area to scrounge for food. Liam was the only one left staring at us.

"I'll look into her background," he said. "It'll be useful to know about her life so far."

"Not yet," I answered. "Trust is a fragile thing."

Liam snorted. "I knew there was a reason you didn't give us a last name." He paused before raising his eyebrows and looking in Josh's direction.

I nodded. Yes, Josh should be filled in on his ex.

Liam proceeded to do just that, giving Josh all the details we had so far, including the issue with Aiden's grandfather.

Josh seemed to absorb it all, nodding at the right parts, but I could tell he was a bit shaken. He smiled at Liam and thanked him, and then asked if I was coming back to the cabin. I definitely was—Josh was unsettled, and I would be there for whatever he needed.

He'd been pacing across the living room for ten minutes. Josh had logged out of his computer and sent off a text message to his boss, and then the pacing had begun. He hadn't asked me to leave, but he wasn't talking to me, either.

"Mei Ume, what can I do for you?" I asked.

He shook his head. "I don't know. It's just... I don't know."

"It's a lot," I answered.

Josh stopped, running his hands over his face. "Yes. Yes, it's a lot. Because naked men and flamy dogs and a sexy older guy wasn't enough for me to deal with. Now there's some immortal guy who's related to Aiden and a cult, and my ex-boyfriend somehow ended up in cahoots with them."

I couldn't help smiling at the sexy older guy part, and Josh caught the look on my face.

"No smiling! Because cults and immortal bad guys and... And some woman who's gonna be family is coming here, and she's coming into a freaking disaster!" Josh started pacing again. "How are we gonna make her feel comfortable if we have to be on the lookout for a cult?" he asked, stopping and staring at me.

"I..." I started, but Josh kept on talking.

"And Rick! What a stupid, idiotic, *dumb* asshole! Who gets involved with a cult?! Who is *that* stupid? Do you know how many times I told him he can't believe everything he reads online? He used to say it was snarky and annoying to fact check people's social media posts, but really, you can't just repost fake news like it's real!"

I smiled again, because I could picture Josh going through and telling people their posts had incorrect factual information. He wouldn't do it to be mean, though. He'd do it because he cared about people.

"And yes, he's a total jerk, and yes, I stayed with him too long, but... I don't want him killed as a human sacrifice by some cult because of me! I don't want to be responsible for anyone's death!" Josh finished ranting and started pacing again.

My Mei Ume was all wound up, and he needed a way to unwind.

I stood up, walked over to him, and grabbed him in my arms, pulling him close and holding him tightly. I breathed deeply, and I felt him take a few deep breaths against me.

"Mei Ume, you're obviously overwhelmed. Anyone would be. Will you let me take your mind off things and settle your thoughts?" I asked him.

In case he had any doubts about what I meant, I leaned down and bit the corner of his neck and his shoulder.

He gasped at the sensation, and I felt his breathing pick up.

"But we don't know when Thea will get here," he protested.

"I can sense her, and she isn't close yet. I'll know when she is. I'll have a good twenty minutes' warning," I answered. I continued to nibble at his neck, squeezing him tightly. "Will you let me take care of you? Will you let me make you feel good?"

Josh whined deep in his throat, his breath catching. "But I want to make you feel good. I want to please you."

"Oh, you will, Mei Ume. You will," I answered. "It will pleasure me immensely to use you and take you out of your head. Will you let me do that?"

"Yes," Josh whimpered, pulling away.

He went to sink to his knees, but I caught him.

"Stop means stop, and I'll know if you're not enjoying yourself. I'll be very upset with you if you aren't enjoying something and you don't tell me. Understand?" I asked, looking into his eyes.

His pupils were blown wide, his face tinged pink, his breathing heavy. He was exquisite. I waited, not letting his arms go.

He licked his lips. "Yes, I understand."

CHAPTER 19

JOSH

My brain had been chasing around itself, the anxiety building, until I felt like my mind was a broken record and I was going to need to crawl out of my skin to make it stop. It was too much to process, and I was stuck on it.

Then Wilder bit my neck, and my mind came to a screeching halt. Yes, please—I wanted out of my head. I wanted to bring Wilder pleasure. I wanted to make him feel good, and suddenly more than anything, I wanted his hard dick in my mouth. I wanted to suck on him until he was panting and groaning.

He had stopped me from falling to my knees, and he wanted to make sure I was enjoying myself. I told him I understood. Didn't he understand that giving him pleasure would make me feel good?

"Good," he said, still holding my shoulders tightly. "I'll tell you exactly what you need to do to please me, Mei Ume. Do you like that idea? I'll give you directions for everything, so you don't have to think about it."

I nodded my head. Yes, I loved that idea.

He let me go, and I couldn't help the little whine that escaped me.

"Go into the bedroom and strip off all your clothes," he said.

I turned and headed straight to the bedroom, pulling off clothes as I went. I could hear him following, stripping his own clothes. By the time I made it into the bedroom, I was stripping off my boxers.

"So beautiful. Turn around and let me see you," he commanded.

I had the barest moment to feel self-conscious—I was not built like Wilder and the guys—but his growl of approval was enough to set me at ease, and then I was distracted by his hard cock jutting out in front of him.

"Mmm. You like what you see? Come and show me how much," he growled.

I dropped to my knees in front of him, and he grabbed onto my hair. I moaned at the sensation, and he tilted my head up.

"So beautiful," he murmured, and he brought my face close to his cock.

He smelled like musky forest, like man and winter and sex, and I breathed him in. He brought me closer, and I opened my mouth, sticking my tongue out. I wanted to taste.

He pushed his dick into my mouth, and my eyes rolled back in bliss. He didn't go too deep. There was precum on his cock—it was both salty and sweet—and his hard length in my mouth was a warm, full presence.

He held me tightly by the hair, moaning, and some part of my brain registered that I was moaning as well. I worked my tongue against him, pressing my lips tightly around him, moving the tiniest bit because that was all I could do with his hand in my hair.

I got lost in the sensation of sucking him. The taste, the smell, the hard length in my mouth. I worked my lips and my tongue, my dick growing harder with each groan from his mouth, each whispered word of how good or beautiful I was. His hand was tight in my hair, and sometimes I pulled harder against him, moaning at the sting.

I looked up at him, my mouth full of cock, and the look in his eyes—I was making him so happy, and my cock jerked at the bliss on his face.

All too soon he pulled me off, and I whined at the loss. I could have sucked on him forever.

"I want to come inside you, Mei Ume. Would you like that?" he asked.

"Yes. Please," I answered.

"Go lay on the bed on your back," he commanded.

I rushed to obey him. As soon as I was laying down, he crawled on top of my legs.

"Put your arms up and hold onto the bed frame, Mei Ume. Can you do that for me?"

I moaned and grabbed onto the bed frame behind me. When he leaned down over my cock, breathing me in, I gripped tighter, pulling against the frame. He smiled up at me.

"Good boy, doing what I say. I'm going to taste you now, because I want to."

His mouth was on me in the next second, and I tried hard to keep my hips still, but it was exquisite heat and pressure against my cock, and it felt so fucking good. I whined, throwing my head back. He came off my cock and bit my thigh, hard, and my entire body shuddered, a gasp leaving my mouth.

"I'm going to mark you up so everyone knows you're mine," Wilder growled.

I nodded my head, pulling against the bed frame and mewling in my throat, and he bit the other thigh. It was a bright spark of pain for a half a second, and then it was all pleasure, like the bite was connected to my dick and my nipples. Everything was warm, and I couldn't help the thrust of my hips, my cock looking for some friction. He licked at the spot on my thigh, and my body tensed, waiting for another bite.

Wilder chuckled low in his throat, the sound sending goosebumps across my skin. "Do you like that, Mei Ume? Do you like that I'm going to mark you up?"

"Yes, Wilder. Please. God, please," I whined, and then his teeth were sinking into my hip. The pain was exquisite, my entire body pulsing, the sharpness grounding me in every sensation. Wilder's chest pressed into my legs, one arm held my hips down, and everywhere he touched felt sensitive and warm.

I could barely keep my eyes open, but I looked down at him, and he was smiling, so amazingly sexy. He reached up, his hand skating across my chest, heading right toward my nipple.

Oh god, oh god, I wanted him to make it hurt so good. I wanted him to twist and pull and—

I gasped, panting, fire shooting from my nipple through my chest, my cock jerking, my entire body shuddering, as he pulled hard, twisting the tiniest bit. My hips pushed up, and my cock rubbed against Wilder's chest as he slid up my body a bit more.

"So beautiful. So perfect. Such a good boy for me," he murmured.

His words sent sparks through me, and then his hand was on the other nipple, twisting and pulling and sending fire through me. I was panting and thrusting, twisting in his grasp. I felt like a bundle of exposed nerves, and I wanted the pressure to stop and to never stop at the same time.

He chuckled gruffly. "I bet you'd like something clamped on those nipples, wouldn't you, Mei Ume? A constant pressure to remind you that you're mine?"

I groaned, and his finger pinched and twisted again. I pulled myself up the bed, my hands gripped tightly around the bed frame, which pulled my nipple more, because Wilder didn't move his hand with my body.

"Oh my god, Wilder," I cried out.

"So pretty," he murmured, and then he let go and lifted his weight from my body. I groaned in protest, and I heard him opening the bedside drawer. He climbed back onto me, only he was facing my legs, and he positioned himself so his dick was in front of my face, like we were about to sixty-nine.

"Suck on me, Mei Ume, while I play with you," he growled.

I leaned up, pulling him into my mouth, my hands gripping his hips. Warmth flowed through me at the groan that erupted from his mouth. I lost myself in sucking on him, listening to every sound he made, lapping and tasting. Each time a burst of precum hit my mouth, I moaned, thrilled at my reward.

Wilder groaned and told me how good I was, how beautiful—so many pretty words, and it all became hazy with my mouth full and his words floating through me.

I registered his finger at my hole, slick and warm, and I whined loudly against his cock as he entered me, slow but steady. There was a burn, but it was like Wilder knew that I loved that feeling. He wiggled his finger, making my body twitch. He pulled out, and two fingers were at my entrance. I whined, frantically sucking at his cock, my body strung tight in anticipation of those thick fingers filling me up.

"Relax, Mei Ume. Relax and let me in," he murmured.

His fingers slid in, and I was so full. My hips jerked, and I could barely concentrate on the cock in my mouth, but Wilder was moaning in appreciation anyway.

His fingers found my prostate, and he pressed against it. I sucked his cock down into my throat, cutting off the scream that wanted to erupt. I grabbed tightly onto his hips and ass with my hands, holding myself on his dick.

"Oh, yes, Mei Ume. Beautiful. You like that, don't you? Your throat feels so good around me," he rumbled.

His fingers were relentless, pushing in and out, hitting that spot inside me. At some point he went to three fingers, and I could barely process all the sensation. I was so filled up—everywhere was full with Wilder, his cock in my mouth and his fingers in my ass, and each word of praise sent me higher and higher.

He seemed to know when I was on the edge, because he slowed down, his fingers avoiding that spot that sent electricity through my body. Eventually he pulled out, and I groaned as his hips lifted at the same moment.

He turned around, coming chest to chest with me, and his mouth devoured mine as his hand snaked down to pull and tweak my nipple. I threw my head back, gasping, and his teeth nibbled at my neck.

"Wilder! Please!" I cried out, not even sure what I was asking for.

"So beautiful for me. You make me feel so good," he murmured.

His hand switched to the other nipple, and at the same moment, his dick pressed against my hole. I tried to push down—I wanted him inside me, but he only chuckled, pulling harder at my nipple.

It was exquisite torture. When I moved down, the pull against my nipple became bright and painful in a pleasurable way, and I started thrusting against his dick, up and down, the pressure increasing and then letting up against my nipple.

"So beautiful," he whispered, and he pushed inside me in one solid thrust.

Stars exploded behind my eyelids as he thrust into my prostate over and over and over. He twisted and squeezed my nipple while he filled me up. I cried out, my orgasm crashing through me, each thrust feeling like it was making more cum shoot from my cock.

Wilder didn't slow down—he kept going, making my orgasm last. It was too much. I groaned and panted. His hips stuttered, and holy fucking shit, it felt like he was getting bigger inside me. Like his dick was expanding.

I cried out, so full, my entire body shuddering and rocking.

"So beautiful," Wilder murmured again, and then his teeth were sinking into my neck, the pain bright. It was like there was a wire between my neck and my dick and my ass, because everything just became pleasure again, and a second orgasm swept through me, taking me out of myself, making tears leak from my eyes at the intensity of it. Too much. Too good.

⸻ ⁕ ⸻

Wilder was still inside me, his body pressed against mine, not moving. He wasn't so impossibly big anymore, and as he gently slid out, I made a noise of protest.

"Shhh. I know, Mei Ume," he murmured, and he rolled off me and left the bed.

I closed my eyes and rolled onto my side, facing the wall. I felt... I wasn't sure what I felt. I took a deep breath in through my mouth, and then let it out quietly. I'd just had really good, really fulfilling sex, and I was going to enjoy this moment and look forward to more like it.

I heard Wilder come back, and then his arm reached around, and I felt a warm cloth gently cleaning up my cum before he moved to wipe my hole. I made a little sound of protest, though I tried to hold it in.

Yeah, I had liked the idea of Wilder's cum still being inside me and on me.

"Next time, Mei Ume," Wilder whispered, like he knew what I was thinking.

Then he was gone again, but only for a second before I felt him come back and lay down behind me.

He pulled me closer and shifted me until I was facing him and nestled into his chest, his arms wrapped around me, one hand gently caressing my back.

Shit. I was gonna start getting all emotional. I had the sudden, overwhelming urge to cry. It was idiotic that I felt this way. No one liked when someone just randomly cried after sex. Talk about killing the mood. Rick had always hated it when I got emotional after sex, and it was easiest if he just didn't even know about it. I was pretty good at holding it together for a few minutes until I got privacy.

I tried to pull away, mumbling, "I'm just gonna go shower," but my voice sounded a little wobbly.

Wilder only held me tighter.

"I'm fine. I just need a minute." I pulled again, but his hold didn't loosen, and I realized that I probably sounded awful, like the sex hadn't been good or something. I added, "You were perfect. That was probably the most amazing sex I've ever had."

"Mmm, on that we agree." His hand came up to cup the back of my head, and the totally gentle, caring gesture made my eyes fill up.

Fuck. I was not going to be able to hold my tears in. Nothing like crying after sex to chase someone out of bed and ensure there wasn't a repeat.

I lifted my hand up to wipe at my eyes, hopefully discreetly, and I patted Wilder's chest afterwards, like that was my aim all along. My fingers threaded through his chest hair and reached up until I got to his beard.

"Did he never hold you after sex?" Wilder asked.

I froze, unsure what to say. All I could do was shake my head no.

Wilder's arms squeezed so tightly I could only get a shallow breath in. I rested my face against his chest, the tears falling freely now. Maybe he wouldn't notice if I was quiet enough.

"I will always hold you. You are strong and resilient, but the tree does not weather the storm alone. The earth keeps it in place, cushioning and nourishing its roots. Let me be the ground for your roots, Mei Ume. Let me hold you safe."

The tears came faster, and I couldn't help the sniffles that came along with them. I kept my head buried in Wilder's chest, and he held me against him, softly rumbling.

"I don't know why I'm crying," I finally muttered. "It really was perfect. Everything. I'm just being silly."

"Experiencing your emotions is never being silly, Josh. Sometimes we just... feel too much, and our bodies need a way to get it out."

"Yeah, but most guys don't cry when they feel too much," I mumbled, still sniffing.

Wilder made a contemplative sound, then said, "Some get angry. They might scream or shout, or they might lash out at those around them. I've seen overwhelmed people say some very hurtful things. Some people withdraw into themselves, unable to communicate. Some cry, even if they hide their tears from others. You feel passionately, and that comes out in tears."

I huffed, but my tears were slowing down. I was running my hand through Wilder's beard, marveling at how soft it was.

"What do you do?" I asked.

"I suppose it depends. If I'm angry, I hunt. I know that we can all be fiery, and although age has taught me how to control myself, I do still get angry on occasion. When I'm worried or happy, I suppose I seek out those I love. I like physical contact. That's one of the things that grounds me." As if to prove his point, Wilder ran his hand through my hair again.

We lay there quietly for a few moments, and I felt more peaceful because of it. Wilder kept up a soft, low grumble that I wasn't going to ask about, and I kept petting his beard while he caressed my back and occasionally ran his fingers through my hair.

It was soothing, and I felt my thoughts drift to the last few weeks. It felt like it was a year ago when I'd stood in that kitchen with Rick yelling at me.

"Sometimes I just feel like I'm an emotional wreck," I muttered. "Like I can't get my bearings on everything."

"You've had to deal with a lot, and this latest news only adds to that. Are you sure having Thea here won't be too much?" he asked. "There are plenty of places for her to stay."

"No, I want her here. I don't know why, but I do." I paused, pulling back. Wilder let me this time, and I looked into his eyes. "I want you here, too."

His eyes lit up, quite literally, and I blinked. He leaned down to kiss me, and we gently explored each other's mouths, our hands wandering over each other's body. Before the kiss could get too heated, Wilder pulled back. He gave me light kisses on the corner of my mouth and squeezed my ass with his hands.

Eventually he sighed, pulling back. "She's nearby, I think. Still plenty of time, but not *that* much time."

"Well, then, let's get ready to welcome our guest." I grabbed hold of his beard and pulled him in for one final firm press of our lips.

He gave my ass a squeeze and then smacked it lightly, and I groaned in response. He smiled against my lips, and I couldn't help the smile that lit up my own face.

I could do this. I could do anything I needed to. Hellhounds, asshole exes, cults, immortal bad guys—I could just go with the flow. I could bend with the wind, because Wilder would be there to hold onto me. I didn't know why I had so much faith in him already, but I did.

He wouldn't let me go.

Chapter 20

Wilder

When Thea was within a mile of us, I could firmly sense her presence, so Josh and I went out to meet her. The boys, thankfully, stayed out of sight for the moment. I was sure she would get along with them, but she didn't need to be overwhelmed by them right off the bat.

I didn't think she was sold on the idea of a pack.

Some part of me wondered if she was meant to be a permanent addition. I'd been instructed to find her, and I could sense her, but there wasn't that bone deep connection I'd had with the boys. Her hesitation shouldn't have mattered; not all the boys had been sold on the idea of a pack, either, but I still knew they were mine.

Thea felt like someone I needed to guide and help, like her pack was supposed to run next to but not within my own pack. Which made no sense, because she had no pack.

I could sense Josh's surprise the moment she opened her car door. He had probably expected the female version of the boys—someone muscular, menacing, and tall.

Thea was none of those things. She was short, well under six feet in height, and she was curvy. I knew she was strong, but she didn't exactly look it. She was easily underestimated. She looked rather sweet, but that impression was dispelled easily enough once you got to know her.

"This town smells fucking weird, Wilder," she said, stopping about five feet away from Josh and me.

She looked Josh up and down and sniffed, barely glancing at me. I hated to admit it, but I was rather at a loss as to what to do to set her at ease.

Josh stepped forward and held out his hand. "Hi, I'm Josh, and this is Wilder, which I'm sure you know already. We're... umm... dating?"

I didn't like the hesitance with which he said the last word, so I stepped forward and placed my hand along the back of his neck. "We're partners and mates," I clarified. I didn't know if it would mean much to either of them, but I had to say it anyway. Josh was so much more than just someone to date.

"Athena," she answered, "but call me Thea."

To my surprise, she reached forward and shook Josh's hand.

"What particular afterlifers did you detect? Did you sense a cult on the way in?" I asked.

Both Thea and Josh turned to stare at me. I looked back and blinked, unsure what the issue was. Thea had brought up the smell of the town, not me.

Josh turned back to Thea. "Yeah, so we apparently have a little cult problem. My asshole ex-boyfriend couldn't take no for an answer, and the idiot apparently got involved with some cult with the immortal son of Cain or something really weird. So, you know, that's fun."

Thea was frowning. "Couldn't take no for an answer?" she asked.

Josh stilled, but he still answered. "I'm sure you'll hear soon enough. He sprained my wrist and gave me a few bruises, and then he didn't take it well when I broke things off after that."

I could hear a subvocal growl come from Thea, but she got herself under control very quickly, which was impressive.

Josh was staring at her. "You been there?" he asked.

I wasn't sure what he meant, but Thea understood. She shook her head, adding, "No, a close friend."

Josh nodded, she nodded, and then Josh started walking toward the cabin, and Thea followed.

"I'll show you my cabin, and you can decide if you want to crash in the spare room there. There's a house as well, but I'm not sure if you want to stay with the guys just yet. They can be... a lot. Not in a bad way, but sort of in a teenage boy way, if you know what I mean."

Thea laughed at that, and they both walked toward the cabin. I trailed along after them, listening as Josh told Thea who lived where. He managed to describe the guys and make them all seem rather harmless, and Thea laughed more than once at his stories.

He glanced back occasionally, and I smiled reassuringly at him. Josh may have wanted me to take charge in the bedroom, but he was obviously very good at taking charge in other areas, and I was pleased that he'd taken to Thea. I was also thrilled that she seemed comfortable with him. She'd never let her guard down so much in my presence.

We got to the cabin, and Josh showed Thea around. By the time we were sitting down to coffee, it was like they were old friends. When there was a lull in the conversation, I couldn't help asking the question that had been plaguing me since her phone call.

"Why now? What made you decide to trust me?" I asked her.

Thea sipped her drink, looking at me. "I didn't." She nodded her head at Josh. "He's good, though. Really good. I trust him."

Ah, I thought I understood. Hellhounds could sense hellbound souls; we could smell the level of rot on people. But afterlifers didn't have the same scent. I would have smelled like something different to her, but she wouldn't have known how to judge that odor.

"I understand. You can meet our other human packmates, as well. You'll see they're all good souls," I told her.

"I don't need a pack," Thea stated. "I don't plan to stay here; I rented a room in town, and I don't know how long I'll be in the area. I'm sorry if that's not what you were hoping for."

I wasn't sure what to say to that, so I took another drink. I was supposed to find Thea, and I had, but what was my purpose beyond that? I wasn't shocked that she wasn't going to join us permanently, but I had to admit to being a little disappointed. I felt protective of her.

Josh broke the silence. "You kept in contact with Wilder, though, even though you weren't sure if you could trust him. You don't have to stay here forever, but we can still be family."

Thea took a sip of her coffee before answering. "I've never met anyone else like me. Wilder was the first, and he had a lot of interesting stories. Just because he's the same kind of... person that I am doesn't mean he's good. Or honest. But you, Josh"—she gestured her mug at him—"you're honest. And I wanna know more about what I can and can't do. It was weird as fuck turning into a fire dog, and I have a feeling I need to know more."

I stilled, looking at her. "What type of feeling?"

She shrugged. "I don't know. It's hard to explain. It's like when you know it's going to rain, so you get everything ready for the storm. I feel like a storm is coming, and I don't want to be caught unawares."

Interesting. I didn't have the same feeling, but I recognized what she was saying. Perhaps my goal with Thea was to teach her and train her, and then send her on her way. That made me a little sad to think about.

Josh seemed to sense my mood, because he took my hand and squeezed it. "Of course, Wilder will help you, and so will the guys.

But you can't just up and disappear in the night or anything. You're family now, and family stays in touch, even if we're like the weird cousins that everyone gossips about. Okay?"

Thea eyed him. "Is that a condition of my living here and being taught?"

"Yup," Josh answered. "And once you meet the rest of us regular people, you'll realize no one will leave you alone for long, even if you don't stay. Get ready for texts and phone calls. This group is like barnacles—once they latch onto you, there's no getting rid of them."

Thea laughed again, and I thought her body loosened a bit at Josh's words. Perhaps she needed more than just training. Perhaps she needed friends and family, too.

We talked some more and eventually ordered some food, and over the course of the evening the entire pack made their way to Josh's at some point or another. Thea was definitely friendlier with the human packmates, and they all seemed to set her at ease.

I hadn't realized how much she distrusted hellhounds, but I should have. Our intentions and our level of good couldn't be judged like human souls could. I imagined all afterlifers would make her wary. She had grown up with humans, and she had learned to trust her senses. She had nothing to go on when it came to afterlifers.

Eventually it got late enough that Thea said she was heading to her room in town. We agreed to meet tomorrow morning in town to talk more and so I could show her around. I figured I could introduce her to the other types of afterlifers and how to sense them.

"Will you be there too, Josh?" she asked.

Josh looked at me, and I gave a slight shrug. I was fine whether he wanted to come or not. I wasn't totally sure he wanted to know all the ins and outs of being a hellhound, but I would love to have him with me.

"Umm, I should probably stop by my office in the morning. Even though it's the weekend, some people will be in. But you and Wilder could do some hellhound stuff or whatever, and then we could meet for lunch," he answered.

She nodded, we all said goodbye, and she made her way out, which left Josh and I sitting on the couch. He was suddenly filled with nervous energy, and I wasn't sure why.

"Are you disappointed she isn't staying here with you?" I asked him, putting my hand on the back of his neck and gently squeezing.

"Um, yeah, maybe," he answered. He was still all squirmy.

"What is it, Mei Ume?"

Josh took a deep breath. "You're, umm, still welcome to stay here. Tonight. Overnight. If you want to. You know, in case you planned to because you thought Thea would be here. Or whatever."

I smiled. "I would love to stay here with you, but not because I thought Thea would be here. I would love to have you in my arms all night long."

Josh turned to look at me, and I gazed into his eyes. I wanted to tell him I'd stay with him every night, that I'd marked him without even thinking about it, that he was my mate. I wasn't sure if that was wise yet, though. Josh was shy about me spending the night. He probably needed to be eased into spending eternity together.

Eventually he nodded, and we got up to get ready for bed, cleaning up from the evening, washing up, and getting changed. It didn't take more than half an hour, and Josh got into bed first while I finished in the bathroom. When I crawled into bed beside him, he was scrunched up on one side of the bed, looking stiff and uncomfortable.

Without words, I hauled him over and pulled him into my arms, turning him so he was facing me and tangling my legs with his. He gave a soft sigh and melted into me, and I smiled as I kissed the top of his head.

His breathing evened out, and I let my eyes close, enjoying his warmth next to me.

⚜

"Can you sense what's inside?" I asked Thea.

We were standing outside an old house, and there were three demons inside and one human. We'd been walking around town most of the morning, discussing what different smells meant to hellhounds. She understood humans very well—she was exceptional at reading their souls. She still wasn't quite sure what to make of afterlifers, though.

"Three demons? And one human, a very bright soul," she answered.

I nodded in approval.

"Should we do something? To get the human out of there?" she asked.

I looked at her, raising my eyebrows. "Why would we do that?"

She rolled her eyes at me. "Demons, Wilder. You gonna leave a nice, bright person with a bunch of demons?"

Ah. I don't suppose I'd explained afterlife politics to her very well. I looked up at the building thoughtfully. She followed my gaze.

"Focus on them," I told her. "You can't smell or sense them the same as humans, but focus on what you can sense. How do you feel about them?"

She frowned, looking at the building and breathing in. Then she looked at me and shrugged.

"Do you feel nervous? Disgusted? Any of the things you feel around rotten souls or people on their way to being rotten?" I asked.

"No... They smell... I don't know, kind of like camping in the fall."

I laughed at that, and Thea shot me a dirty look.

"So, what, you're saying they're not evil? But they're demons," she answered.

"And just like angels, they have a job to do. Everyone in the afterlife has a job, and they're created to do that job. That doesn't make them good or evil. Hellhounds originated in hell, and our job is to rid the earth of hellbound souls. I wouldn't call us evil. Would you?"

She started walking, and I followed her. I explained, as best I could, what I remembered of afterlifers and the politics of it all. I was so far removed from it that I remembered very little.

"So afterlifers are just like people in some ways. How will I know if an afterlifer is evil?" she asked.

Huh. I'd never thought of afterlifers being evil. "I suppose they won't smell right, just like humans. Dexter did talk about an afterlifer gone wrong in town, and he did smell a rot from it. Although I believe that sort of thing is very rare. On the whole, we avoid afterlifers. They tend to be a pain in the ass, and they have their own agendas that do not coincide with ours. The afterlifers in this town seem to be a genuinely good bunch, though."

"Do they typically all gather in one place?" she asked.

"No, not at all. That's another thing that makes Paradise Falls rather unique. We have quite a collection of beings here, and you don't usually see that."

We walked on, and Thea was able to identify demons as we traversed the town. There were a few around. By noon, I figured it was time to take her to the coffee shop. Hopefully, the angel would be there, and she'd get to sense the other side of the afterlife.

When we walked in, I grabbed us a table before we went up to order. Thea was looking toward the front of the shop, frowning. Quinton was looking grumpy behind the counter, as usual, but I figured it was Kushiel that was puzzling her. He was sitting at a table right next to the counter, drinking coffee.

"Sort of a demon, but not?" she asked.

"That's an angel. He's a good sort. Usually they're rather insufferable. You sense the slight difference between them?" I asked.

She nodded, then turned her attention to Cassius. "He's human. But... he's something else, too. I can see his soul, but there's... I don't know how to explain it. There's something extra there."

"Very good," I praised her. "Cassius is human, but he's an oracle and can speak to ghosts. There are a variety of humans out there that have a little something extra, as you call it. It doesn't make them good or evil—you'll be able to sense that in their souls —but if you ever go up against one who has something extra and is evil, take care."

She nodded, and we chatted for a few minutes about the people in the shop and what she sensed from them. I was once again impressed with her ability to read people—she was exceptional.

She was in the middle of a sentence when I felt it—that vague itch under my skin. Thea trailed off, perhaps sensing my distraction. The itch quickly turned to a burn, and I had only one thought in my head.

Josh.

Chapter 21

I finished chatting with Barb and headed out to meet Thea and Wilder at the coffee shop for lunch. I was glad I'd gone into the office, but I also missed Wilder.

Was that weird? Maybe. I didn't know. This was all so fast, but things had never felt so right for me before. Wilder seemed to know what I needed before I did half the time. He was kind, patient, caring, and he was sexy as hell. He showed me respect and gave me affection.

Part of me was waiting for something bad to happen. Could things really be this good? Was I going into this with blinders on and ignoring red flags, like I had with Rick? Not that Wilder had red flags like Rick; I never had to make excuses for his behavior towards me.

There had to be something wrong with him. Or maybe it was that something was wrong with me. I was kind of screwed up, after all. I had an appointment with the therapist in the afternoon, and I guessed maybe this was something I could talk to her about. Was I moving too fast? Was I on the rebound? Was I missing red flags? No one could be this perfect, right?

I snorted a little at myself. Well, Wilder was actually a supernatural being that killed people, so maybe he wasn't *totally* perfect. I mean, some people would say those were some pretty big red flags. Was I kind of ignoring that part of things? Yeah, maybe I was. But he was still Wilder, the guy who held me while I cried and took care of his family. Sure, he killed people, but only really bad people.

Was that making excuses for him?

I sighed. I didn't know. All I knew was that he treated me like I was special and important, and I wanted to see him. Although I was fine all morning, I was feeling a little out of sorts now, and I knew Wilder's presence would make me feel better. Was that codependent?

I was lost in my thoughts, and when the hand grabbed me and pulled me into the alley between stores, I didn't quite process what happened right away. I fell backwards, landing hard on my ass with an oomph. My brain felt like it rattled in my head, and maybe that's why I didn't panic—I just felt confused.

"I've been waiting for you!" Rick hissed.

I looked up at him, shaking my head a bit. "Rick?" I asked stupidly.

Obviously it was Rick, and he was blocking my exit out to the street. He also looked... rough. He was disheveled and dirty, I could smell him from where I was sitting on the ground, and his eyes were darting around. He reminded me of a junkie, and my heart sank. What the hell had happened to him?

"It's okay, baby, I'm here to help. I'll get you away from them," he said, turning away from me to look out at the street.

"Get me away from who, Rick?" I asked carefully, sliding backwards a tiny bit to get further away from him.

"The demons." He turned to look at me, his eyes wild. "I know all about them, Josh, and we can help you. I know people. They'll get rid of the demons for us, and everything will go back to normal."

"Who's 'we,' Rick?" I asked.

He focused on me then, smiling maniacally. "The angels, Josh. I found the angels, and they want to help us. They want to cleanse the world of the demonic scourge."

He kneeled down in front of me, grabbing onto my knee, and I tried to slide backward, but his grip was strong. He was still smiling, and it wasn't right.

"They're so powerful, Josh. So majestic, and they'll help us. And if we do what they say, we can be like them one day. Don't you want that, baby? Money and power and immortality."

I tried to slide out of his grasp, but Rick grabbed my other knee with his other hand, frowning at me.

"You shouldn't do that, baby," he said, and his grip tightened to the point of pain.

His face twisted, and there was the Rick I knew, the temper I knew. I couldn't help the cringe backward. He lifted one hand up off my knee, and without even thinking, I kicked my foot out, catching him in the head. He fell backward with a cry, and I jumped up, racing around him to get out of the alley. His hand caught my foot, and I would've fallen, but strong hands gripped me before I could.

I looked up into Wilder's eyes, and Rick yelled out, but his hand let go of my foot. Wilder pulled me out of the alley and onto the street, wrapping me up in his arms. I could hear running footsteps in the alley.

"Wilder," I gasped out, suddenly breathless, holding tightly onto him.

"Did he hurt you, Mei Ume?" Wilder asked, pushing me back a bit so he could look me over, his hands gripping me tightly.

I shook my head, still feeling shell-shocked. He looked me over again, fire in his eyes. I stared at them, like I was under a spell, and I was only jerked back to reality when Thea jogged up.

"Trouble?" she asked, not even out of breath.

Wilder nodded toward the alley, and Thea ran down it.

"Did he hurt you?" Wilder asked again.

I just shook my head no. "I'm okay. He surprised me, but I'm okay."

Wilder pulled me back into his arms, and his deep breaths helped to calm my racing heart. I don't know how long we stood there, but Thea eventually came back.

"I got a license plate, but I didn't pursue the car. I didn't want to be conspicuous. He wasn't hellbound, either. Certainly not a good person, but not ruined," she said.

I felt Wilder nod his head against me. "Let's get Josh some food and sugar. He's a little shocked."

I didn't argue, and Wilder held onto me and guided me as we started walking.

"Do you need to be carried, Mei Ume?" he asked me.

I snorted at that, imagining Wilder carrying me down Main Street in front of everyone. I knew he would too, and it made walking a little easier.

I wasn't paying attention to much, and before long we were inside the coffee shop and Wilder was sitting down and guiding me onto his lap. I didn't complain.

"What the fuck!" I heard Q say, and he was suddenly in front of me.

I took a deep breath and looked around, taking in my surroundings. The shop was thankfully not that full, and most people weren't paying us any attention.

"Do I look that awful?" I asked, sitting up and trying to straighten myself out.

"You're beautiful," Wilder whispered in my ear.

Q just snorted. "You're all wrinkled and you've got dirt on your clothes. Very un-Josh-like."

"Can you get him some coffee and something sweet?" Wilder asked.

Q nodded and headed back to the counter. Thea was sitting across from us, looking pissed off.

"You okay?" I asked her.

"I should've been quicker," she muttered, shaking her head. "Wilder was just up and out the door without a word"—she gave Wilder the side eye—"and I took too long to follow. I thought he saw you or smelled you or whatever and was just going to greet you, but when he didn't come back in, I went out and followed his scent."

Wilder grunted, and it might have been an apology. I leaned my head back against him, thinking about what had happened. I wasn't sure what they would have done if they'd caught Rick, and maybe a part of me was glad they hadn't. I was done with him, and maybe I would be happy if karma made him miserable for quite awhile, but I didn't want him killed because of me.

"There was something wrong with him," I murmured, thinking back to the crazed look in his eyes.

Wilder hugged me more tightly. "It's okay, Mei Ume. You're safe now. I won't let you out of my sight again."

"I mean, there was *really* something wrong with him. He looked strung out or something. He was ranting about getting me away from demons and how the angels were going to help and how powerful they were. It was... it wasn't anything like Rick. He doesn't believe in supernatural stuff. He has a temper, but he isn't delusional."

Thea raised her eyebrows, looking at Wilder. "You said angels and demons don't always get along. Could he be working with actual angels?"

I sat up and turned to look at Wilder. Q came over with coffee and some muffins, setting them on the table and staring at us.

"I'm okay, Q. I ran into Rick, but he didn't hurt me, and I'm fine. I was just shocked," I told him.

"That amoeba-brained, shit-sucking pile of puke. Where is he? I'll fucking kill him myself," Q seethed.

I raised my eyebrows. That was pretty creative, even for Q. Usually it was just cursing.

He saw my look and grimaced. "Toby has a character who swears in creative ways. He keeps asking my opinion on them. They're kind of fun to use." He shrugged.

I laughed, and Q cracked a little smile, heading back to the counter when one of the other employees called him. A line was building up, but Q still took his time.

We drank our coffee and ate the muffins, and Wilder must have sensed I needed some normality, because he talked about the layout of the town, the nearby cities, and the rural areas with Thea. They chatted easily, and the coffee and muffin made me feel less shaky.

By the time there were only crumbs left, Thea and Wilder were both quiet. Thea got up first.

"I'm going to continue exploring, maybe see if I can scent anything. He wasn't hellbound, and he was just human, but there was some scent clinging to him... I don't know." She shook her head, and then headed out the door without a goodbye.

Ok then. I guess she was as fond of social niceties as the rest of the guys.

"Ready to head out, Mei Ume?" Wilder asked, and I nodded.

He helped me up, and we made our way to his car. He opened my door and even buckled me in, and I didn't complain, although I did blush. He drove with one hand on my knee, and he kept looking over at me. It made me feel warm inside.

With everything that had happened, I'd totally forgotten about my appointment with Helene, but Wilder obviously hadn't, because we pulled up in front of a brick building.

"Shit. I forgot," I muttered.

"If you want to put it off, I'm sure she'll understand," Wilder reassured me.

I sighed. "No. It's good. I'm just not sure how I'll explain all of this without talking about all the hellhound stuff."

"Oh, well, Helene is a fury, so she knows all about us," Wilder said.

I turned and stared at him. She was a what now? I had the urge to check and see if my ears were clogged or something. Did I have a concussion?

Wilder must have sensed something in my look, because he looked apologetic. "Ah, sorry? I thought Aiden had told you that. I'm sure she's ok—the guys have vetted her—but I still planned to walk you up and check her for myself. If that's okay, of course."

I just continued staring at Wilder.

"So, ah, you ready to go meet her?" he finally asked, fidgeting a bit.

I opened the car door and got out, and Wilder followed behind. Was I ready to meet the really nice lady I'd talked to on the phone, who was also apparently a fury? Sure. Why not? My day certainly couldn't get any more fucked up than it already was.

<hr>

Helene was... nice. Normal. Sweet, but also with a take-no-shit kind of attitude. I liked her, and I felt better talking to her. She and Wilder had stared each other down when we first got in, but she apparently passed whatever test he had, because he told me he'd wait in the car.

I'd given her some background over the phone about Rick and our relationship, so jumping straight into the explanation of what happened that afternoon was easy. That led into talking about Wilder and my feelings for him, and expressing all my concerns about moving too quickly.

"Your mind tells you it's too quickly, but what does your heart say, Josh?" she asked.

I tilted my head at her, unsure how to answer that question.

"How would you feel if he was gone from your life?" she asked.

I rubbed my chest, which was suddenly tight and aching. I blinked my eyes, because they felt watery. "Wilder wouldn't leave me," I answered hoarsely, and as I said it, I knew it was true.

"Of course he wouldn't," she answered, easing something in me. "What about if you left him, though?"

"I wouldn't leave him!" I said, outraged at the thought. "Wilder is kind, and good, and he deserves to be happy, too. I wouldn't *ever* cause him pain."

Helene leaned back in her chair and smiled. "Well, I think you have your answer, then, don't you? Logical Josh may have reservations, but your heart knows what it wants."

I nodded my head. I supposed she was right. "It just... It all feels kind of crazy."

She nodded back at me. "You're judging things based on regular society, but Wilder isn't part of regular society. Things may be done a little differently, but you're adaptable and strong, Josh—you've proven that."

"What if I can't be enough for him?" I asked, voicing the fear I hadn't even admitted to myself. "Wilder is amazing. He takes care of everyone—he takes care of *me*—and he handles everything, and I don't want to be a burden to him."

"Perhaps you should talk to him about that, Josh. I'm sure you aren't a burden, and I'm sure that you lighten his burden in many ways, but you won't believe it until you speak to him about it."

She was right, and I knew that, but ugh, I didn't want to have that conversation.

"Is there anything else you want to talk about today?" she asked, and I knew our time was pretty much up.

"No, I'm good, unless you know how to deal with a troublesome cult," I joked.

Helene sat up, though, suddenly very alert and slightly intimidating.

"What cult?" she asked, and her voice was a little rougher.

"I... I don't know? Wilder knows," I answered, feeling nervous for the first time.

Her head turned in the direction of the door, and as if I had conjured him, Wilder opened it up a minute later.

"Mei Ume?" he asked. I instantly relaxed when I saw him.

"I'm okay," I answered, looking over at Helene.

"My apologies, Josh. I didn't mean to make you nervous. I was just upset by the news of a cult," she explained.

Wilder eyed her, and he finally nodded. "The Order of Asterphagia. I know they're trouble."

She looked pensive for a moment, her gaze staring off into the distance. "Yes, trouble is an understatement. I thought the last of the leaders had been dealt with decades ago, and I'm quite sorry to hear that isn't the case. I'm assuming they have Cain's descendent?"

Wilder looked surprised. "How did you know they were working together?"

"It is one of the few reasons I can think of for them to make themselves known. They would have been looking for him," she answered.

Wilder walked over and pulled me into a hug, then he turned back to Helene. "Why would they look for him? He can't give them his immortality."

"No," she said, looking at us both. Her face twisted, as if she smelled something foul. "They don't want his immortality. They want his seed."

Well, wasn't that just creepy as hell. Definitely not what I expected to hear. Wilder seemed surprised as well, but Helene had no more information than that. She cautioned us to be careful, and then it was back to business, scheduling my next appointment.

It was all rather odd, but I supposed that was my life now. A little on the odd side.

"What do you say to an afternoon of Legos and documentaries?" Wilder asked when we got in the car.

"Sounds fantastic," I answered.

Perhaps I could convince him to have an evening of sex as well, and I shifted a little in my seat thinking about it. As if he knew what I was thinking, he winked at me before he started driving.

My morning had been a little shitty, but I had faith my afternoon was going to improve. After all, I was going to get to spend time with Wilder.

Chapter 22

The next week passed quickly. Josh seemed more sad and surprised than traumatized by seeing his ex. We cuddled that evening, and although I was determined not to rush him, he initiated sex. Josh was so beautiful when he gave himself over to pleasure and let me take control, and I accepted it for the gift that it was. He was so intent on pleasing me, and his reactions and joy at doing so only increased my own pleasure.

It was amazing, and I enjoyed exploring his reactions and what he liked over the course of the week. I couldn't help knotting him whenever we had penetrative sex, but we also explored each other with hands and mouths and tongues.

It wasn't all sex and cuddles, though, most unfortunately. Liam and Quinton dropped off some financial files for Josh to go through, and we finally cleared a road back to the cabin so cars could drive to it. I continued training Thea, as well, and each of the guys took some time with her, showing her their areas of expertise. She was feisty and took no shit from them, and the boys seemed amused whenever she told them off.

Had I stayed at Josh's every night? Well, he hadn't asked me to leave. I knew he was perfectly capable of telling someone to get out of his space, as he'd done so to the boys numerous times. He'd also ushered me out more than once when he was on work calls or needed to focus on data, so I knew he was comfortable with me.

So, yes, I had pretty much moved in. I could tell him it was for his protection, but if he asked, I'd probably blurt out that he was my mate. At some point I needed to have that conversation with him, but I knew he thought things were happening quickly, and I didn't want to panic him.

As for the Order of Asterphagia—things were deceptively quiet. There had been no sign of Rick after he grabbed Josh in the alley, and he didn't show up at work all week. The boys had checked Josh's old place, and he hadn't been there. Jude had taken a ride out to Rick's friend's house one night, and he'd said the friend was there, but Rick wasn't.

So Rick was missing, the descendent of Cain was missing, and we had no idea where the cult was, either.

None of it was very comforting to me, and I found myself more and more on edge as time passed with nothing happening. By Friday, I knew that Josh sensed my restlessness. I should have gone out to hunt, but a part of me rebelled at the thought of leaving Josh alone. I knew he felt my anxious energy by the wary looks he gave me as the day wore on, though, and by dinnertime, I was pacing around and feeling indecisive and itchy.

Josh had retreated to the corner of the couch to finish up his work, and I felt like he was huddled up there. The last thing I wanted was for Josh to be afraid of me. I kept my distance, staying across the room, and Josh closed his computer, staring at me.

"Wilder..." he said, and I turned toward him, but he didn't say anything else.

"Do you want me to go?" I asked, the thought suddenly occurring to me. I was making Josh uncomfortable, and that wasn't what I wanted. Perhaps he needed space from me when I was feeling this itchy.

He stared at me, finally asking, "Do you want to be somewhere else?"

His eyes were piercing, and I probably should have said yes. There were no lies between us, though, so I simply shook my head no.

He stood up slowly and walked toward me, almost like I was a wild dog about to bite. I kept very still, not wanting to spook him. I knew I was already setting him on edge.

"You're... agitated. Talk to me, Wilder. What is it?" he asked, placing a hand gently on my arm.

I shrugged, but he just continued staring, waiting.

I blew out a breath. "I just feel... itchy. Unsettled. Nothing is happening, and it's making me anxious. I can go train with the boys, though, and get out of your hair."

His hand gripped my arm tighter. "But you don't want to train with the boys, or you would have done it already."

I shrugged at him. He wasn't wrong. "I don't... I don't want to make you uncomfortable or nervous," I finally admitted.

His hand released me. Maybe it was best I go until I could settle myself down. I turned to leave, but his voice stopped me.

"Don't you dare walk out that door, Wilder."

I turned back at him, surprised. He looked determined.

"Josh—" I started, but he came over, grabbing my hand and pulling me into the bedroom.

I was still trying to figure out what was going on as he started stripping off my shirt. "Josh—" I said again, but he shushed me.

"You're going to lay down, and I'm going to massage the tension out of you. If you still need to go wrestle with the guys after, that's fine, but let me do this first." He looked up at me, and his eyes were soft and pleading. "Please, Wilder."

How could I say no to him?

I let him strip me and lead me to the bed, where he motioned for me to lay face down. I heard the rustling of clothing behind me and Josh leaving the room and then coming back a moment later. He must have grabbed massage oil, because I smelled a faint, soothing aroma and then felt a smooth warmth across my skin wherever he touched.

His hands were firm as he rubbed across my shoulders, down my back, and then down my legs. He brushed his hands on my skin in a rhythmic motion, and I felt myself sinking into the mattress a bit. When he started kneading my back, I couldn't help the groan that escaped. His hands were finding every knot and sore point and working away at them, and he took his time rubbing everywhere, from my shoulders down to the small of my back.

"You have such a beautiful back, Wilder," he murmured. "Relax and let me make you feel good."

I hummed in response, and his hands moved to my arms, rubbing my biceps and squeezing them. His touch wasn't tentative—it was sure and possessive, and it made me melt. He moved down each arm and massaged each hand, even rubbing every finger. I had no idea my fingers even needed to be massaged, but I felt the tension sliding out of me the longer he worked on me.

By the time he was kneading my thighs, my dick was hard. I couldn't help it—Josh's touch was magical, and his scent surrounded me. I tried not to think about it and focused on Josh's touch. When he reached the tops of my thighs, he didn't stop. He went on to knead my ass, and a groan escaped me again.

"I love taking care of you," Josh said softly. "Roll over for me, Wilder."

I opened my eyes, barely aware that I'd shut them. "Umm..." I muttered.

"It isn't anything I haven't seen before," Josh said, and I could hear the smile in his voice.

I did as he asked and rolled over, my dick hard and flushed. I looked at Josh's face, but he only had a soft smile for me, like he was perfectly fine with my very turned on state.

"Close your eyes and just enjoy, Wilder," he murmured, taking a foot in his hand and beginning to rub it.

I did as he asked, letting my eyes drift shut and just feeling. He lavished attention on each foot, pressing into the soles and rubbing the arches. He firmly rubbed and kneaded each leg, then massaged each arm. By the time he reached my chest, I was turned on and yet also incredibly relaxed. His hands remained firm as he rubbed each pec, brushing over each nipple. I was breathing deeply and softly moaning with his touches.

I almost shot off the bed when I felt his oil slick hand on my cock. My eyes flew open and my hands went up, but Josh stopped what he was doing.

"Shh. Close your eyes and relax. Enjoy your massage, Wilder," he ordered.

"You're gonna kill me, Mei Ume," I said, but he only shushed me again.

I smiled and did as he asked, closing my eyes and trying to relax again. I was rewarded with his hand on my dick again. He gently massaged me, his hands soft and warm as they slid up and down my shaft, focusing on the head and rubbing at the underside. It was slow and easy, and somehow despite how totally turned on I was, it was also relaxing. One hand gently caressed my balls, giving them their own massage.

"Mei Ume, let me…" I started.

"Shhh. I'm giving you a massage. All you need to do is lay there and feel. No moving, Wilder."

Josh was in no rush, and I didn't think his aim was to make me come. He never sped up, he just gently caressed me, making appreciative noises and moans every so often. A hand would occasionally caress up my leg, onto my chest, rubbing against my nipple, then it would travel back down to my balls, all while his other hand worked me.

I descended into a sort of haze, like I was floating on a gentle wave, the pleasure ebbing and flowing. My body felt like it was detached from me except in the places that Josh was touching. Thoughts left my head, and all I could do was feel.

I don't know how long Josh touched me, but at some point, the pleasure took a turn, and I felt the peak coming.

"Mei Ume," I whispered.

Josh hummed, and then both hands were working me, rubbing and pumping, and my orgasm washed over me like a gentle breeze. It seemed to go on and on, yet it was soft and easy. I panted through it, feeling like I was being drained in every way.

Josh leaned down and nuzzled at my thigh, giving me small kisses, and I could hear his heavy breathing. I felt like I could barely move, but I wanted Josh to feel good, too. "Mei Ume, let me—" I began, but Josh moaned, long and low, his teeth sinking gently into my thigh. I felt my dick twitch valiantly, because it was sexy as hell to have Josh mark me.

After a moment, he crawled up my body, laying next to me, naked, and I felt his soft, wet cock against my thigh. He'd been so turned on from pleasing me that it hadn't taken much for him to come. I wondered if he'd used my own cum to jerk himself off, and a thrill went through me at the thought. He reached over and grabbed tissues to clean us up, and then he wrapped his arms around me and nuzzled into my side.

I felt myself drifting in a sea of calm. We didn't speak for a bit. Josh's breath tickled the hairs on my chest, and his fingers gently caressed me. I ran my hand gently up and down his arm, smiling when goosebumps rose at my actions. I leaned down and kissed him on the head.

"Thank you, Mei Ume. I'll reciprocate the favor."

Josh looked up at me. "I wanted to take care of you. You're always looking out for my pleasure, even when taking your own. I wanted this to be about you. You needed to relax, and I wanted to help you do that." He smiled at me. "Not that I'll ever complain, but you don't *always* have to be in charge."

I laughed lightly, leaning down and kissing his lips. "I enjoy being in charge of your pleasure. That brings me pleasure. But you were right that I needed to just relax. That was a gift. Thank you."

Josh was glowing at the praise, and I wondered how I was so lucky to have such a giving, beautiful man by my side.

Which made me realize that perhaps it was the time for honesty. Not that I'd been dishonest, exactly, but I hadn't told Josh I'd marked and mated him. I ran my fingers along his neck where I'd bitten him.

"We need to talk, Mei Ume," I said.

He frowned. "Nope. Unless you're breaking up with me, do *not* start a conversation with that serious face and that phrase."

I laughed. "I am most definitely not 'breaking up with you.'"

"Then how about you tell me about earlier and why you thought you should leave," he stated.

Ah, well, this was not where I had seen the conversation going, but Josh deserved an answer. And an apology.

"I was full of nervous energy."

Josh snorted, because I supposed that had been obvious. I gave his side a little pinch, and he giggled a bit.

"So, as I was saying, I was full of nervous energy. An itch under my skin. I get that sometimes when something is wrong. When someone needs me. There's too much that's up in the air, and while it's been quiet, I don't think that will last."

Josh hummed, then asked, "Is that a part of being a hellhound? Knowing things ahead of time?"

"I'm an original hellhound, created in the underworld before I came topside. I have forgotten more than I remember from those early days. It's the only way to live on the mortal plane. Did I have foresight at some point? I don't know. Even if I did, foresight is complicated, because people have free will, so things can be changed."

Josh hummed in agreement and went back to softly petting my chest. It was comforting.

"That itch, though—I think it means something has already been set in motion. Something is already happening. It can be… frustrating," I admitted.

"Why did you think you should leave?" Josh asked.

"Mei Ume, you aren't going to let me get away with it, are you?" I asked.

"Nope," he said. "Tell me."

I sighed. "I didn't want you to be afraid of me. I didn't want to trigger you with my nervous energy."

Josh leaned up on my chest and looked in my eyes. "You know that I trust you, right?" he asked.

"Of course I know that, but—" I began.

"No. No buts. I know that no matter how upset or anxious you get, you wouldn't hurt me. Might I occasionally flinch or curl up when someone is mad? Yeah, sometimes I find myself doing it," Josh admitted. "My brain doesn't even process it; my body reacts first. Do you think less of me for that?"

"Mei Ume, I could never think less of you. You are strong and resilient, and a flinch does not change that."

"Ok," Josh said. "So if it doesn't change who I am, then it definitely doesn't change who I know you are. It's just my body reacting, but my brain *knows* you wouldn't hurt me. My body knows that, too, and if given the option, I'll curl up in your arms at every opportunity. You make me feel safe and cared for, Wilder."

"I understand, Josh. Thank you," I said, leaning up to kiss his lips.

He gave me a peck and then backed up. "Do you? Because if the option is having you here or not having you here, no matter how angry or upset you are, I will *always* choose having you with me. I would help you through your anger or nerves, just like you've helped me. You can lean on me, just like I know I can lean on you."

I rubbed my hands against Josh's arms and stared into his beautiful eyes. He *was* strong and resilient, and it was part of what I loved about him. He was right, though. By thinking to hide my pain from him, I had done him a disservice.

"Forgive me, Mei Ume. You're right. You are my partner, my helpmate, and I know you can bear my burdens with me, just as I can bear yours with you."

"It's not just that I *can*, Wilder. I *want* to bear your burdens with you. I love you." He stared down at me, his eyes searching mine as he said those words.

"I love you, too, Josh," I answered. "More than you can possibly imagine."

Our mouths eased together, and we kissed leisurely, our tongues tracing each other's lips, our hands gently touching wherever they could reach. Josh was resting on top of me, and his weight was a warm, comforting presence, his smell surrounding me and entering into my very soul.

I eased him away eventually, because I still had more to tell him.

"Josh, you are my mate," I finally said.

He looked down at me, his head tilted slightly to the side.

"Like Dexter and Toby? And Liam and Q? And Aiden and Atlas?" he asked.

"Yes. Hellhounds mate for life, and there are some... perks. You'll live as long as I do, and you won't need to worry about illness or disease. I should have asked you first, but I claimed you when I bit you. I acted without your permission, and I apologize for that."

Josh leaned down, and before I knew what he was going to do, he bit into the space between my shoulder and my neck. I gasped, and despite the pain, I felt myself rubbing up against him and growing hard.

He pulled away, looking at me seriously. "There. Now we're even. I claimed you too, Wilder, and don't you forget it."

I tugged him down into my arms and hugged him tightly, tears coming to my eyes. "Thank you, Josh. You are a gift."

We basked in silence for a few more minutes, and then I heard Josh give a small sigh. He had smelled of happiness and joy, but now there was a slight tinge to it.

"What is it, Mei Ume?" I asked.

"Don't tell Q," he mumbled grumpily. "I am *not* having the rent conversation again."

I couldn't help the bark of laughter that escaped me, and then Josh was giggling as well.

We laid together until our stomachs were growling, and then we finally got up, ready to argue over who got to feed who that evening.

Josh was right. I loved taking care of him and seeing to his pleasure, but he was my partner, and he knew sometimes I needed to be taken care of, too. I was blessed to have someone so perfect in my life.

CHAPTER 23

JOSH

I woke up to Wilder's hands running gently up and down my back. When I blinked my eyes open, he smiled and gave me a gentle kiss on the forehead. He'd figured out pretty early that I was a little shy about tongue kissing in the morning. Because, you know, morning breath. Not that Wilder ever seemed to have morning breath, but I was sure I did, and then I would get in my head about it, and it's hard to enjoy kissing if you're busy thinking about your breath.

I wondered if after a dozen years I would still care. Even if you lived forever, you still had to worry about morning breath. I chuckled a little to myself at the thought.

"What has you laughing, Mei Ume?" Wilder asked, smiling at me.

"I was just thinking that we have, like, I don't know how long together, and I wondered if I'll still be worrying about morning breath in ten or twenty years."

"I hope not, because I love your breath in the morning. I love all your smells," Wilder murmured.

I laughed again, because it was such a Wilder thing to say.

Wilder loved me, and we were mated. I still wasn't sure I had my brain wrapped around that. It seemed too good to be true.

"I love you, Wilder." It felt good to say it.

He gave me a hug. "I love you, too, Mei Ume. You are my world."

We lay tangled up together for a few minutes, just enjoying each other, before Wilder gave a sigh, announcing, "Thea is on her way."

I gave his bare chest a peck and then rolled out of bed. "Let me make you guys breakfast, then. I'll hop in the shower and then start cooking. And don't you make food without me," I ordered him. "I like cooking for you."

Wilder held up his hands and smiled. He was sitting up in bed, the blankets pooled around his waist. He was so unbelievably sexy, and I had the urge to climb right back into bed and get my hands all over him. He winked at me, like he knew exactly what I was thinking, and I sashayed out of the bedroom and into the bathroom.

I don't think I'd ever sashayed before, but knowing that Wilder was looking at me and appreciating my body gave me that extra swagger.

I hopped into the shower, soaping up and thinking about yesterday. I felt... really good. Yeah, I still had trauma to work through. I might flinch when people got mad or moody. I might sometimes fall back into trying to fix things when nothing was wrong, or I might apologize too much when things weren't my fault.

But Wilder *saw* me, and he knew I was more than those things. I wasn't perfect, but he wasn't perfect either. The important thing was that we listened to each other. The fact that Wilder had apologized was kind of amazing, too. I knew I wasn't the only one in a relationship who could say "I'm sorry," but I'd kind of forgotten that with Rick.

I rinsed off the soap and turned the shower off, drying myself and then wrapping the towel around my waist to go throw some clothes on. Wilder wasn't in the bedroom, and I hoped he hadn't tried starting the coffee maker.

Wilder and coffee makers did not get along.

I chuckled to myself as I got dressed. I loved that he wasn't perfect. I loved that he couldn't seem to work the coffee maker.

When I walked out of the bedroom, I grabbed him and kissed him, and his lips were soft and pliant against mine. He let me take charge of our quick kiss, although he gave my butt a little smack when I pulled away. It made me smile and feel sexy and appreciated.

Agh, I loved this man so much. I felt near to bursting with happiness, like I was just gonna float out of my skin.

We chatted about the day ahead as I started on breakfast, and it was only about five minutes before Thea was knocking at the door. Wilder hollered for her to come in, and she did, throwing a bag on a chair and then plopping down at the table. She stared at me cooking breakfast for a moment, her gaze assessing.

"Well, looks like someone was well-fucked," she said.

"Thea!" Wilder reproached, but I laughed.

"What?" she asked, motioning toward me. "He's practically glowing."

"Jealous?" I joked.

"Fuck, yes," she responded right back. "Everyone here is all paired up and has this content, satiated look about them most of the time. It's infuriating."

"I don't know—I wouldn't describe Q as looking content and satiated," I said, placing some eggs and bacon on the table.

"Yeah, well, Q looks like he's about to eviscerate someone most of the time. And Liam just gazes dopily at him like it's the cutest thing he's ever seen," she said, spooning some food onto her plate.

I laughed again, because that was a totally accurate description.

"Ok, old man, what wisdom are you imparting to me today?" Thea said between bites, looking at Wilder.

Wilder didn't rise to her bait; I guessed he was used to attitude and snark. We finished up breakfast while they went over Thea's knowledge of weaponry. Apparently the bag was full of guns and knives and other things I didn't really care to think about, so when my phone rang and I saw it was Sebbie, I excused myself to take the call.

"On the way to work or on the way home?" I asked after our greetings.

"Ugh, on the way home. I worked an overnight shift at the hospital, and I'm exhausted. It seems like people always die at night, and every nurse and doctor seems to call me in for the final moments," Sebbie grumbled.

He did sound tired, but he wasn't really in a bad mood. Then again, Sebbie was never really in a bad mood.

"They know you aren't afraid of death and that you're really good with patients," I answered.

"Well, yeah. There's nothing scary about death. It's just a transition, and people deserve to feel safe and comforted in their final moments here. I'm honored to give that to them. It's really a beautiful thing," Sebbie stated.

Sebbie wasn't religious, per se, but he definitely believed that death was not an ending, as he always told us. He was probably the only person I knew who seemed totally comfortable with the thought of dying.

"Well, I'm glad you could help people, but I'm sorry it was a long night," I answered. "Hopefully you have tonight off? Because it's really late to be getting off your shift."

"Yeah, I stayed with a patient for a bit after my shift ended. I have the next few days off, so I plan to head home and sleep for like fifteen hours," Sebbie joked.

He did sound drained, despite his cheery tone.

"You okay driving? If you need a ride..." I trailed off, ready to get someone to pick him up if necessary.

"Yeah, I'm okay. I'm tired, which is why I decided to talk on the phone. So distract me with details about the sexy silver fox staying in your cabin," Sebbie said.

I blushed, but I did just that, gushing about Wilder a bit to Sebbie. He knew that we were seeing each other, but I got to fill him in on the "I love you" exchange. I left the whole mate thing out, though, because Sebbie didn't know about hellhounds. Honestly, even if he did, I kind of preferred to ignore the whole supernatural aspect of things.

Sebbie let me gush, but I made sure to ask him questions and keep him talking, too, so he stayed awake. He yawned a few times, but he sounded alert enough that I wasn't worried about him falling asleep while driving.

"Thanks, Josh. I'm pulling in at home now..." Sebbie trailed off. "What the hell?" he mumbled.

"What's up?" I asked. "Did Toby order you sex toys to get delivered again or something?" I joked.

Sebbie didn't laugh, though, and I heard the car door open and shut. "Rick? Is that you?" he said.

My heart froze. I had walked outside to chat, but I hustled my way back inside. "Sebbie! Don't go near him!" I insisted, Wilder and Thea looking up as I rushed in the door.

"Josh, he's hurt. I think... Oh, Rick," he murmured, and I could hear movement and rustling, then the sound of birds through the phone.

"Sebbie is home and Rick is apparently outside his place," I told Thea and Wilder, and they both stood up from their chairs.

"Let's go," Wilder said.

I turned my attention back to the phone, following Thea and Wilder outside. "Sebbie, don't go near him, okay?" I said.

Thea's car was in front of the house, and she opened the

passenger door and motioned me in as Wilder got in the driver's side.

"Sebbie?" I asked. I could hear groaning and rustling, and there was still the sound of birds cawing in the background, but Sebbie hadn't answered me.

"It's okay, Rick. You'll be okay now. I'm here to help you," Sebbie murmured, his voice soft and gentle. I thought the moaning was coming from Rick, and I wondered if maybe it wasn't just a ploy to get to me. Maybe Rick was actually hurt.

"Sebbie, what's happening?" I asked.

Thea climbed into the back, and Wilder started the car.

"He's badly hurt, but he won't die," Sebbie said, and his voice was gentle.

My stomach flipped nervously. I still felt like this was some kind of ploy. Wilder started driving, but I was only vaguely aware of what we were doing.

I heard Sebbie gasp, and I croaked out, "Sebbie?"

"Who are you?" he said, his voice strong, and I knew he wasn't talking to me.

"Who's there with you?" I asked, and I could feel Wilder's eyes on me. Thea reached up from the back seat and rested her hand on my shoulder.

"Death," I heard a voice say, the bird sounds getting louder for a minute, and then there was silence.

"Sebbie? Sebbie??" I cried out, but the line was dead.

Wilder slammed on the brakes, and I was glad that someone—Thea, maybe?—had put my seat belt on, because I jerked forward in my seat. I looked up, dazed, and Corbin and Jude were standing in the middle of the road. We were out of the woods and near the main houses.

They both rushed over and got in the back seat, and there was a crow on Corbin's shoulder. It got in the car, too, and just cawed once at me.

"Let's go," Corbin stated, and Wilder started driving again.

I felt like I had fallen down some weird rabbit hole and was in an alternate dimension. There were hellhounds and a crow in the car, and Rick was hurt and someone was at Sebbie's who had called themselves Death. Would they hurt him? Would they kill him?

Wilder's hand grabbed onto my thigh, squeezing. I hadn't realized I was shaking until that moment. Thea's hand was still a solid weight on my shoulder, too.

"We'll get there in time," Wilder said, but he couldn't really know, could he?

Sebbie didn't live far away, but the fifteen minute drive felt like it took an hour. He had a small house on the other side of town. It was somewhat private, with thick trees separating him from neighbors on both sides. Sebbie always said he loved the privacy of his place, but I was cursing it right now. If it was less private maybe his neighbors would have seen or heard something and intervened.

My thoughts were a jumbled mess, and finally we were pulling up the driveway to Sebbie's house. We barely came to a stop behind Sebbie's car before we were all piling out. Jude and Thea stopped at the bottom of the stairs to his small front porch, where Rick was laying in a heap.

I kept going, calling out Sebbie's name as I ran up the steps and threw open the front door. I ran through the house, checking the living room, kitchen, and small bathroom downstairs, then I was pounding up the stairs, still calling out for Sebbie. I ran into both bedrooms and the bathroom upstairs, but they were all empty.

"Sebbie!" I yelled again, turning around and bumping into Wilder. He grabbed onto my arms, holding me steady, his eyes soft as he looked at me.

"No, no, no, no," I mumbled.

"He's not here, Mei Ume. I'm sorry. We can find him, though," Wilder said.

Wilder led me down the stairs and out the front door. Thea

and Jude were still hovering over Rick, and Corbin was standing in the middle of the yard, crows surrounding him.

He looked up when we came out. "They'll lead us," he stated. I don't think I'd ever seen Corbin anything but completely calm, but he looked anxious. It only made me more nervous for Sebbie. Did he know something?

"Is Sebbie okay?" I asked, although I don't know why Corbin would know that.

Corbin nodded his head once, and then he went to the car, getting in the driver's seat. Wilder led me towards the car as well. Thea and Jude were talking quietly, but Thea got up and headed toward the car too, getting in the passenger seat.

"Jude?" Wilder asked.

"He'll be okay with human intervention. I'll stay here and call for an ambulance. It's more important that you get to Sebbie than worry about this asshole," Jude answered.

Wilder gave a nod and opened the back door, ushering me in and climbing in next to me. Corbin had already started the car, and there was a crow on his shoulder. His window was open, and I had the crazy thought that the crow would escape. But it wasn't exactly a pet anyway—at least I didn't think so?

Corbin made a K turn in the driveway and started out toward the road, pausing at the end of the long driveway. His crow ruffled up its feathers and gave a soft caw, and Corbin turned left. Wilder reached out and pulled me in close, and I pressed my face into his chest, letting his scent comfort me.

"We'll find him, Mei Ume," Wilder promised.

"I know you will," I answered, my voice muffled by his shirt.

I kept my face pressed into Wilder, breathing in and trying to calm my racing heart. The car occasionally slowed, and then we'd turn or pick up speed again. The cawing of crows was a constant sound outside in the trees, but I didn't ask. I didn't care, as long as we got to Sebbie.

I trusted Wilder. We would find Sebbie.
I just hoped we found him in time.

CHAPTER 24

WILDER

The crows guided Corbin, and I was never more thankful that he had an affinity with them. Josh stayed pressed against my chest, and I rubbed his back, occasionally murmuring to him.

I thought I could sense Sebbie, but I wasn't sure. He seemed to be slightly connected to the pack, but the tether was barely there. I knew we were headed in the right direction, however, and there *was* still a faint link, so I knew he was alive. I could only hope he stayed that way.

I thought the cult had probably taken him in order to get to Josh, and maybe through him to us, but it all seemed very convoluted. We didn't have access to Aiden's grandfather's stolen money. I couldn't understand their motives, and that made them unpredictable.

Then there was Sebbie's... otherness. I hadn't delved too deeply into what he was, because I could sense the humanity in him, and his soul was good. There was something there, though, that I could almost remember. Something familiar from long, long ago, but I hadn't really tried to place it. I cursed myself now for that, because it was just one more level of the unknown added to an already fucked up situation.

We eventually left the main highway and drove onto gravel and then dirt roads, the car bumping along and our speed slowing down quite a bit. Josh roused himself from against me and looked out the windows.

"We're close," Corbin said, still focusing on driving.

The road was getting narrower, with only room for one car. There was a clearing in the trees ahead, and we pulled up and saw an old house.

"Oh, lovely. This looks like it belongs in a horror movie," Thea grumbled.

I wasn't sure why she said that, since it didn't look particularly scary. It was a rather large Victorian home, and it seemed well-maintained, although deserted. I didn't watch horror movies, though, and Josh must have agreed, because he gave a little sound of distress as we pulled to a stop.

Thea turned around to look at him, reaching into the backseat to pat his hand. "Don't worry, Josh—we're the monsters in this horror movie. We'll save your friend and end these fuckers."

"Wilder?" Corbin asked, and I could hear the concern in his voice as he stared at the house.

"I know," I answered.

It smelled of rotten souls, but it also smelled of something else. I would have said afterlifers, but that wasn't quite right. It was a stench like burnt food. The smell of angels and demons was sort of there, but it was like their essence had been tainted somehow.

It was unsettling.

"Not too many people in there," Thea said, staring at the house. "Less than ten? It's hard to tell for some reason."

We all opened our doors and got out of the car. I grabbed onto Josh's hand and held on. Technically, I had marked and mated him, so he was as immortal as I was. I still worried, though.

The front door creaked open, yet no one was there.

Thea sighed. "Definitely horror movie shit. So trite, though." With that, she led the way, walking up the steps and into the house.

I don't know what I was expecting, but the inside of the house was well-kept, if sparsely furnished. There was a hallway and then a door at the end of it, which was an odd set-up. Thea took the lead, opening the door at the end of the hallway. She wasn't attacked, and I could see past her to a large room that was currently empty. She walked in, and we all followed.

The door shut behind us, the lights went off, and Thea scoffed as a door across the room opened up and people filed through it. They were all wearing robes and carrying candles.

"Oh, brother. Not even original," Thea mumbled under her breath.

Josh stifled a slightly hysterical giggle. They were all mostly human, and they were all rotten. That slightly burnt flavor existed on all of them, but it was a faint trace.

"Behold Death, majestic in her beauty, triumphant in—" a man's voice started, but Thea cut him off.

"Yeah, yeah, we get it. Can we get this show on the road, please?" she complained.

What appeared to be an angel came in through the door, her wings flaring out behind her. She wasn't an angel, though. She was... wrong.

She wore an all black robe, her hair was long and dark, and two small grey horns protruded from her forehead. Her wings were a beautiful white color, fully feathered, but there was something off about them that I couldn't quite place. It was almost like it was a costume, because it didn't look totally real. I had seen angels, and I had seen demons, and she didn't quite look right for either. The burnt smell emanated most strongly from her—she smelled of angel, demon, and rotten soul.

She stepped up onto a dais, which made Thea snort. She bared her teeth at that, and they were all pointed and sharp.

"Oh my god, did you seriously file your teeth?" Thea asked. "Because that's just so 2010, girlfriend. And the horns are cute, but the wings need some work, don't they?"

The woman hissed at that, and I noticed it then. Her wings were real, but most of the feathers were not. I thought without the artificial additions, her wings would be a patchy mess.

"Nephilim," I said, the realization suddenly coming to me. That was the underlying odor, but it was so distorted it had been hard to place.

Corbin and Thea both looked at me, confused. I didn't blame them. They were both relatively young, and the only Nephilim they had seen looked just like people. Nephilim of today might have some extra abilities, but their appearance was all mortal.

In the beginning, though, Nephilim had not always looked like humans. But that had been centuries ago, and although Nephilim had longer lives, they were *not* immortal.

"How?" I asked.

The woman—I refused to call her Death, even in my head— smiled at me.

"We have been here since the beginning, even though we were cast out and forgotten. We have cultivated our powers, being careful to keep our bloodlines pure and hidden from those like you. We have flourished in the darkness, in secret, but our time is near," the woman said.

"For fuck's sake," Thea said, and I could literally hear the eye roll in her voice. "You sound like every other cult out there. Let me guess—you're all going to off yourselves and take over the afterlife or some other crazy shit like that."

The woman laughed, a high, tinkling sound that grated. "What use do we have for the afterlife? They all betrayed us. They left us here on Earth, and then they took away our dominion of this place."

"Oh my god, really? World domination? That's just so predictable," Thea mocked.

"Human, your sharp tongue grows tiring. Perhaps my acolytes will cut it out so I'm not subjected to any more of your impertinence," the woman hissed.

I reached over and gently touched Thea's elbow, hoping she understood. They didn't know she was a hellhound. That could work in our favor, and I didn't want her correcting the Nephilim.

"You're all Nephilim," I stated, attempting to draw attention away from Thea. "But I've had encounters with the Order before, and there were no Nephilim then."

"You think we do not have humans who worship us and do our bidding? We didn't have the means to deal with you then, so we stayed in the shadows," she snarled.

Josh gripped me more tightly, and I understood his fear. Her words implied that she *did* have the ability to "deal with us" now. I couldn't imagine what that meant, though.

"Where's Sebbie?" Josh asked.

She turned her attention to him, which made my hackles rise. I couldn't suppress my growl, but Josh just leaned into me.

"Your friend is safe—for now. A shame you didn't bring the rest of your pack with you, although I imagine they'll come along eventually." She smiled then, and Josh shivered at her pointy teeth.

Thea was slightly ahead of us, and one of the men grabbed her and pulled her forward, a knife to her throat. I put my hand up slightly, cautioning Thea to remain compliant. I wanted them to continue believing she was human. I didn't understand what they wanted, and it frustrated me. We needed every advantage we could get.

"What is it that you seek?" I asked. "We only want our friend returned safely. We have no access to the son of Cain's money and fortune, if that's what you search for."

The Nephilim laughed gleefully. "Oh, no, we do not seek his fortune, although we wouldn't turn it down. The real prize was the son of Cain."

"We have no interest in him. Give us back those that belong to us, and we shall part ways," I answered.

"You want your friend? Follow me, and I'll bring you to him. I warn you that your hellfire cannot harm me, but it would be detrimental to the building and all those in it, including your mortals." She motioned her head toward Thea, who was standing calmly with a knife at her neck, looking bored.

The Nephilim walked through the door, expecting us to follow, and I turned to look at Thea again. She actually rolled her eyes at me and made a slight gesture with her hand, telling us to go ahead. I didn't like leaving her behind, but if they thought she was mortal, perhaps they wouldn't hurt her. I turned and followed the Nephilim, hoping I was making the right decision. I heard Thea mumbling softly to her captor as Corbin, Josh, and I made our way through the doorway.

Some of the other robed figures followed behind us, but I focused on the woman in front of us. Her burnt, wrong smell was the strongest of any of them. She led us through the house and to a padlocked door, which she opened, leading us down a flight of steps. Once down in the basement, there was another door. I wished Thea were there to make some quip about horror movies, because this would have amused her for sure.

"It really is kind of cliched," Josh murmured, like he knew exactly what I was thinking.

I moved my hand to the back of his neck, giving him a squeeze. We went down another set of stairs, which ended in another door. She opened it, and I could see a large round stone chamber inside.

She walked through, but Corbin, Josh, and I stopped in front of the doorway.

I suddenly realized why she smelled so wrong, and why she had both demonic and angelic features. "Inbreeding," I murmured.

She turned and looked at me. "Selective breeding," she corrected. "The original Nephilim started the order, and they made sure to keep the bloodlines as pure as possible. It has kept us powerful, although some lines have flourished more than others."

We stepped into the room, and Josh gasped as he saw Sebbie chained to the stone wall, sitting with his back against it, legs stretched out in front of him. He looked okay as he glanced up at us, but the old man who was unchained and laying in his lap did *not* look okay. He was skeletal, most of his hair was gone, and his skin was gray and wrinkled. It was like he had been mummified, but I saw his chest rising and falling, so I knew he was breathing.

I took a sharp inhale as I realized who I was looking at.

"Yes. As you can see, you won't have to worry about the Son of Cain anymore," the woman said.

"This is evil work," Corbin stated, and I heard the anger underlying his words.

"He is an evil man," she answered calmly.

"What does that make you?" Corbin asked, tilting his head at her.

The other Nephilim had crowded behind us, blocking the doorway. I had no doubt that we could fight our way through them all, but I wasn't sure if we could do it before Sebbie was injured.

Hellfire would have been the practical solution, and although I wasn't sure she was telling the truth about being immune to it, there was too great a possibility she, and some of the others, actually were. They were Nephilim, after all, and if they had strong demonic ancestry, an immunity to hellfire was likely. I couldn't chance them retaliating and hurting Sebbie.

The Nephilim woman finally answered Corbin's question. "It makes us a necessary evil. We know about the afterlife. How wrong things have gone. How the universe is breaking apart. The original Nephilim wanted the destruction of the universe, but in later centuries, we realized that goal was shortsighted."

"World domination for the win," Thea said from behind me, and the man who was holding her brought her through the others and into the room, going over to stand next to Sebbie.

The Nephilim woman bared her teeth at him, but he seemed unfazed. "They won't attack with both their humans here," he responded.

I had known they thought Thea was a human, but I hadn't realized they thought Josh was a hellhound. If they knew he was human, I had no doubt they would have tried to take him away from us as well, and then I would have had no choice but to act.

"You think too small, little girl," the woman hissed. "We want what was rightfully ours and was denied to us."

"Immortality," I said, looking at the husk of the old man in Sebbie's lap.

Somehow, they were draining the descendant of Cain and stealing his immortality. I didn't know how they were doing it, and I wouldn't have thought it possible if the evidence wasn't in front of me. The man's very life force was sucked dry, his soul just a small sliver in his body.

Corbin hadn't said a word, which was beginning to concern me. He seemed... mesmerized. He was staring at Sebbie, who was looking down at the old man in his lap. Corbin moved to sit down on the floor, crossing his legs. The Nephilim glanced at him, but she did nothing, probably because he seemed less of a threat now than before.

She turned her attention back to Josh and I. "Immortality... and control of the universe. Why destroy what we can instead control?"

"You're insane," Josh whispered hoarsely.

"No, I'm afraid not, hellhound. Although perhaps you'll wish I was," she answered.

From the folds of her cloak, she pulled a dagger. It was a plain-looking thing, the hilt and the blade both made of the same metal. It was silver in color, slightly tarnished looking, and if I hadn't felt the power emanating from it, I might have mistaken it for a regular weapon.

It was not, however, simply a weapon. At least not a mortal one.

We were fucked.

CHAPTER 25

I had the distinct feeling shit had gone sideways.

I admitted to being worried when the creepy, sharp-toothed, winged, and horned woman had come onto the scene.

I might also have freaked out a bit when we'd been led into this weird underground stone room, although I'd also had the idea that Toby would have loved to have been in my place, because this would've given him so many ideas.

Then Corbin had gone all weirdly catatonic-like and was sitting on the floor staring at Sebbie, and Sebbie was sitting on the floor staring at the dying old man in his lap. Then Thea had come in, and that was good, right? The more the merrier! Which I knew was a slightly hysterical thought, but I'd *still* been mostly okay, because Wilder totally had things under control.

But when psycho lady pulled out the dagger, Wilder got really still beside me, and I knew something majorly fucked up was happening.

Wilder was *scared*. I could feel it, somehow, and if Wilder was scared, then I was fucking terrified, because it meant he could be hurt by that dagger.

I couldn't let that happen.

The door behind us clanged shut, and I turned to look. The room was empty, all the other robed psychos having shut us in, apparently. There was just the psycho lady across the room, and her psycho friend holding Thea by the arm. That should have made me feel better, but she was holding that dagger, and Wilder wasn't moving. He was just staring at it.

Thea looked at him, then looked at Corbin, then looked at me and raised her eyebrows. I gave a little half shrug. I had no fucking clue what was going on.

"Um, would you mind filling in the mortals in the room, Lady Macbeth?" Thea said.

I resisted the urge to say, "Out, damned spot!" to Thea's nickname for psycho lady. Not that I was sure that nickname fit, because from what I remembered of that play in high school, Lady Macbeth felt guilty, and the psycho lady in front of us didn't look the teeniest bit remorseful.

"You are an insolent little beast," she said to Thea, her attention turning toward the female hellhound.

"She's going to keep us alive," Corbin said, his voice low and melodic. Everyone stopped what they were doing and looked at him. His voice was like a song, weaving around us. Even Sebbie looked up from the dying old guy, gazing into Corbin's eyes.

"She's going to keep us alive, and she's going to drain us with that dagger. There will be no peace, only pain. Never-ending pain." Corbin was staring at Sebbie. "She is not death, little reaper. Do you know why?" Corbin asked

I saw Thea moving so fast she was almost a blur. The man holding her did nothing to stop her, and with one single move she grabbed the woman's hand holding the dagger and plunged the blade into the woman's chest.

The woman looked shocked, but she didn't fall, and her hand

still held the blade. Thea backed away, toward Wilder and I, muttering, "Fuck," under her breath.

"There's no blood," I whispered. "There should be blood, right? That's what happens when you kill evil people. Blood. Wilder, why isn't there blood?"

"I will not let her harm you, Mei Ume," Wilder promised, and I didn't like the sound of his voice when he said it.

"Fuck that. I'm not gonna let her harm you, because obviously that dagger is some kind of weird... thing... or whatever," I said, motioning toward where it was still embedded in the woman's chest. The woman who was still not bleeding.

Shit.

"You are not mortal," the woman said, her shock evident.

"Thanks, Captain Obvious," Thea said, turning to look at us. "Well, this took an unexpected turn. A little guidance would be good right about now, Wilder."

"It's a blade created by and for afterlifers. It's one of the few weapons which can cause their destruction," Wilder said softly, gripping my hand tightly.

Throughout all of this, Corbin and Sebbie were still having their weird stare-off moment; I had no idea what was going on there.

"She is not death," Corbin said again, still staring. "Why not, little reaper?"

Sebbie's eyes were staring into Corbin's, unblinking, and his one hand was gripping the old man.

"Why is he calling him that?" I whispered to Wilder, but he just shook his head at me, staring down at Corbin and holding onto me.

The woman was slowly drawing the blade from her chest, like it was a show she was putting on. She was smiling the whole time, and when it was withdrawn, she looked at her fellow Nephilim, who was staring at her, wide-eyed.

"Your betrayal will not be forgotten," she said, and then she sliced his face with the dagger.

The man screamed and fell to the floor, writhing about, his hand covering his face. We all watched as his struggles slowed. He was facing away from us and toward Sebbie, and I heard my friend gasp. He didn't sound shocked, though—he sounded angry.

"Why not, little reaper?" Corbin said again, urgency in his voice.

Sebbie looked over at him, and I saw the anger in his face. Sebbie was never angry, but he was now, and it was odd to see.

"Because death is not an ending," Sebbie spat out, and it was like I could feel his anger.

Corbin nodded his head. "Give them a new beginning, little reaper," he whispered.

The woman seemed to understand that something important was happening, because she focused her attention on Sebbie, the blade still in her hand.

I felt like I knew what was going to happen next, like everything was slowing down. Wilder's hand had a death grip on mine, and Thea looked pissed off and ready to kick some ass. The woman was bringing her hand with the blade in it up, ready to slash at Sebbie, but Corbin's voice interrupted everyone, that melodic tone making everything stop, like a pause button had been pressed.

"Do what must be done, ferryman," Corbin said. He smiled, though it looked sad.

With that strange statement, the world went dark around me, all the air rushing out of my lungs. I could feel Wilder's hand still in mine, but we were falling, and then there was nothing.

———— ❧ ————

It was dark, but I still felt Wilder's hand in mine. Something heavy was laying across my legs. "Am I dead?" I asked, shifting my feet and trying to dislodge the weight.

"Ow. What the fuck, Josh?" Thea's voice said.

"Are you dead, too?" I asked, because I couldn't see anything, but that was definitely Thea's voice. The weight moved off my legs, and I heard rustling from that direction.

"Mei Ume," Wilder's voice said, and his hand squeezed mine, then I felt his other arm drag me in by the shoulder until we were touching, his hand releasing mine to feel along my body. "Are you hurt?"

"Um, no. I don't think so. I think we're all dead, though," I answered, which made no sense, but also made perfect sense in this fucked up situation.

Thea snorted. "Typical fucking horror movie. Kill off all the heroes," she muttered. "I did not sign up for this kind of ending."

"We aren't dead," Wilder said, but his voice didn't sound sure.

"Corbin?" Thea asked, and I heard a moan come from the other side of Wilder, where Corbin had been standing when we were in that room. He sounded hurt, but also alive. Or dead. Or whatever we currently were.

I was with Wilder, and although I couldn't see him, I could feel him, so I figured it couldn't be all bad. I could smell him, too—the scent of tree sap and evergreens, along with cold winter air and a match blown out.

It made me think of the first time he'd held me. It seemed so long ago now, although it had only been about a month. I looked back at the Josh who had cried into his shirt, who had found comfort in his smell, and I wanted to tell him that it would be okay. That it would all turn out for the best in the end. I had gone through something terrible, and I had thought parts of me were broken because of it, but that wasn't true. I had found myself again, and I appreciated things in a way I never had before.

I felt like everything that had happened after that moment in the apartment was like a dream. Maybe Rick had hit me on the head and I'd hallucinated it all. Maybe there were no hellhounds and angel-demon women and creepy cults. Maybe I really was dead.

But I was calm, despite that thought. Because I had Wilder. He was with me, and my time with him had been some of the best moments I'd had. He'd shown me what it meant to be cared for, and he let me care for him in return. He appreciated me. He *saw* me.

"Even if I'm dead, you're worth it," I whispered to Wilder, nuzzling into him.

"Oh, Mei Ume. You are worth more than you could ever imagine to me. I would risk death a million times to save you. But I'm selfish, too, because my heart is at ease that you're here with me," he murmured.

"Yeah, yeah, that's lovely and all, you two," Thea grumbled, "but where *the fuck* are we?"

I heard Corbin moan again, and then I heard the cawing of a crow.

"So, definitely not in that shitty underground room," Thea muttered, and I could hear rustling, like she was feeling around.

"Thea!" I said, fear suddenly washing through me. "Stay here!"

Thea sighed dramatically, but the rustling stopped.

"Corbin?" Wilder asked, and one hand left me. I figured he was feeling around for Corbin, and I heard a sigh of relief, so he must have touched him.

"Sebbie?" I called out, because he had been in that room, too, and I hadn't heard his voice. "Are you dead, too?" I asked stupidly.

I heard a caw again, and the flapping of wings. It sounded like more than one crow now, though. It sounded like a million of them.

"What do you call a group of crows?" Thea asked, her voice

slightly hysterical. "A murder!" she answered before any of us could.

"I'm not dead," Sebbie said, but I wasn't sure where his voice was coming from. "You aren't dead, either. We're all fine."

The flapping got louder, the sound overwhelming, and everything drifted away once more.

"Mei Ume?" Wilder's voice was frantic, and I managed to blink my eyes open. He breathed out a sigh of relief, leaning down to kiss me.

"Fuuuuck," I heard Thea mumble, and Wilder's lips left mine as we both looked over at her.

Because we could see. It was dark, but not pitch black. I sat up and looked around. I had been laying in Wilder's lap, because we were all somehow on the floor in the creepy stone room. Wilder was sitting up next to me, Corbin was sprawled out on his other side, and Thea was sitting on my other side, moaning.

The psycho woman was laying across the floor, her hand extended, the dagger a few inches away from her. Her psycho helper wasn't moving—he was curled up on the floor where we'd last seen him, and Sebbie was still sitting on the ground, leaning against the wall.

His arms weren't chained anymore, and the old guy was next to him as opposed to on his lap. I didn't think the old guy was breathing, but Sebbie was awake and looking around. His gaze rested on me, and he looked confused, but not scared.

"You guys took care of them?" he asked, looking at the bodies. "I don't think they were very good people, Josh," he added, almost like he was reassuring me. "They hurt Rick, and they were hurting that old guy, although I don't think he was a very good person either."

I opened my mouth, and then I shut it, because I had absolutely no idea what to say.

Corbin groaned next to Wilder, and I saw Sebbie look at him and blush.

"Of course," Thea muttered, using the wall to support herself as she stood up.

Wilder stood up next, putting his hand down to help me up. My legs were shaky, but I managed to keep my feet once I was standing. Wilder knelt down, rumbling softly, until Corbin blinked his eyes open.

Wilder put a hand out, cupping his face. "You always see so much. I'm so proud of you, and I love you, son."

With that, he stood, reaching down to help Corbin do the same.

I looked over at Sebbie, but he'd managed to get up on his own.

"Do you think we need to, like, call the police or something?" he asked. "I mean there are three dead bodies in here. The old guy was just, well, old, and then the crazy lady stabbed the young guy and stabbed herself, so we're obviously in the clear."

As if his words had manifested it, I noticed that the woman did indeed have blood pooling underneath her, exactly where she'd been stabbed in the chest. The curled up guy also had a pool of blood seeping out from beneath where his head lay.

Sebbie stepped over the bloodstains, walking to the door behind us. We all just stared at him as he hauled it open. No one was behind it.

"What about all the others?" Thea asked, and I felt as confused as she sounded.

Sebbie looked back at us from the doorway, raising his eyebrows. "Others? Just the lady and her partner kidnapped me. I think she was part of that cult Josh told me about, but I never saw anyone else here."

He walked up the stairs, and we all followed behind him

silently. We made our way outside, and I could hear sirens in the distance.

"Oh, good, you guys called the police already. I hope they're quick, because I'm starving. Anyone wanna go for some food after this?" Sebbie asked.

I started giggling. I couldn't help it. It was probably more than a little hysterical, and everyone turned to stare at me, concern on their faces.

"Sure, Sebbie, I'd love to go for food. Maybe ice cream," I answered, and some imperceptible tension that I'd barely noticed seemed to ease in him. His smile was bright and blinding, and I couldn't help smiling back.

The sound of sirens drew closer. "It's Jude." Wilder sighed, adding, "And the sheriff."

"I swear to god, if he stole the police car with the sheriff in it, we're grounding him for like a year," I muttered.

Thea barked a laugh next to me, and the crows cawed in the trees as the car came into sight.

Jude was not in the driver's seat—the sheriff was. However, the frown on the sheriff's face and Jude's gleeful expression made me think that there was still going to be something to yell at Jude for.

I crossed my arms and put on my sternest expression, and Wilder stood next to me, his arm resting on my shoulder.

Whatever Jude had done, we'd deal with it together. Anything at all seemed manageable with Wilder by my side. Even death, apparently.

I stifled another hysterical giggle and made my face stern as the car doors on the police car opened, Jude and the sheriff stepping out.

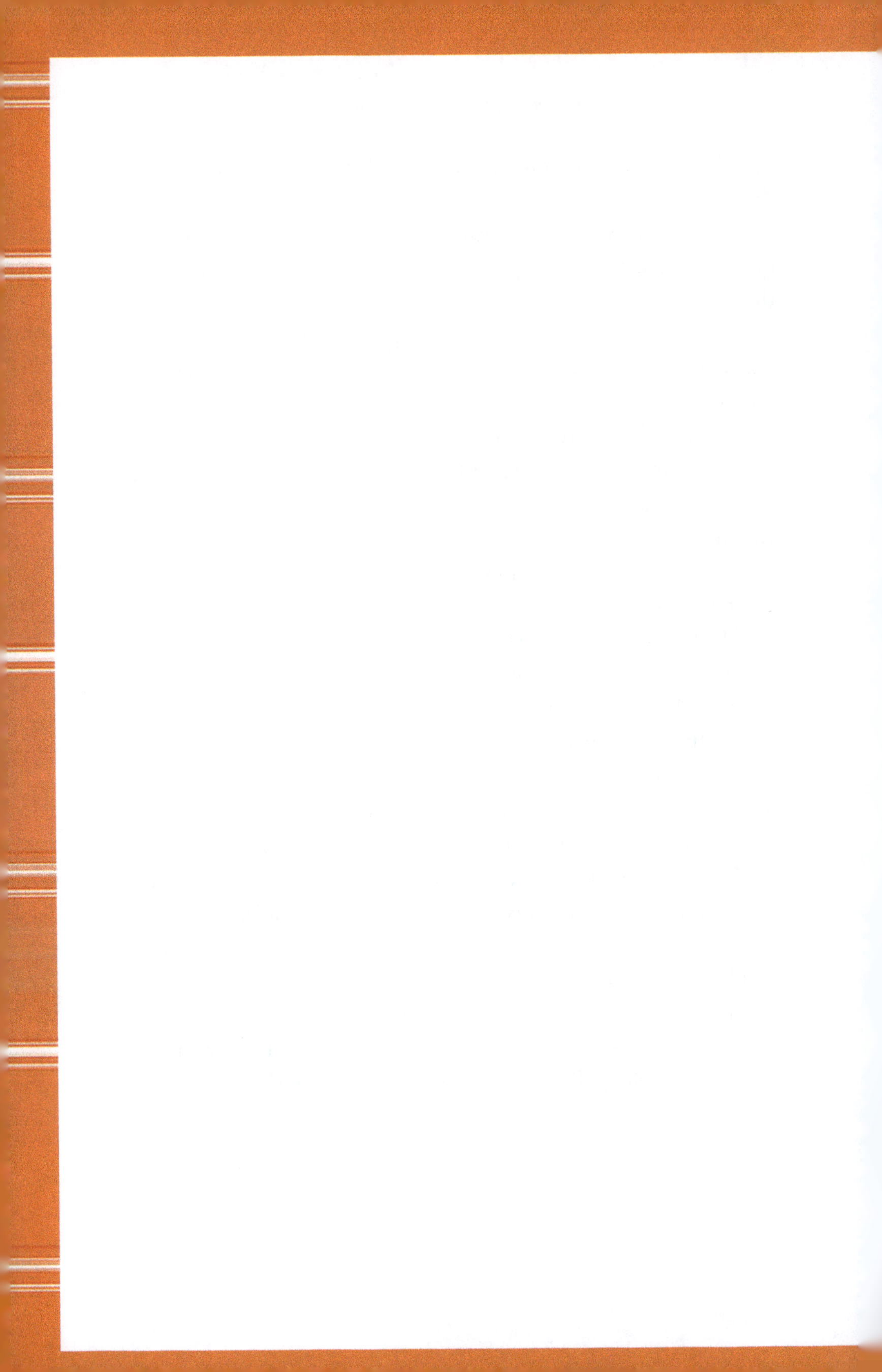

CHAPTER 26

WILDER

"So then the lady slashed the guy across the face," Sebbie said, licking a bit of ice cream off his spoon before continuing. "He fell to the ground, and then she stabbed herself in the chest. I don't know what kind of weird mojo she had going on, because there was a sort of earthquake or something, and everything went dark. Then a second later the creepy lightbulb hanging from the ceiling came back on, and everyone was on the ground."

Sebbie shrugged, unfazed as he finished his story and continued to eat his ice cream. Toby was frantically taking notes and making sounds of interest.

"Are you sure I can't..." Toby started, but the sheriff, Dexter, Josh and I all said, "NO!" at the same time.

The sheriff sighed, staring at us all. Dexter, Toby, Aiden, and Fluffy had joined us at the Victorian house, and a crew of police officers and the coroner were all on the scene. We'd all been separated as soon as the sheriff heard about the dead bodies, although I wouldn't let Josh out of my line of sight. The sheriff seemed understanding, and police officers had taken statements from each of us.

The rest of the guys had shown up with food and ice cream not too long after the coroner. Josh had insisted on the ice cream, although I wasn't sure why. He seemed to find the entire thing slightly amusing, which I supposed was good.

Liam and Quinton had stayed behind to do some computer shit that would cover any tracks that needed covering, although I really didn't think there were many. Sebbie's story took care of all the details. Everything was exactly as he said it was.

The old man was old, and their biggest suspicion was that he had been dead for longer than we all said. The young guy had a slash across his face that was very deep, and he'd apparently bled out from the wound. The woman's fingerprints were on the dagger, and it seemed apparent from the angle that she had indeed stabbed herself in the chest.

No one mentioned Thea helping her along with that.

If I wasn't as old as I was, if I hadn't seen as much of the world as I had, I might start to doubt my own memory. Sebbie's story was just so believable, after all. So practical. He was such a shining soul, and he obviously believed it himself.

I could see him shooting glances at Corbin, though, his face blushing slightly each time. Josh was talking now, and Toby was still taking notes, so I walked over to Corbin, who was sitting against a tree.

Corbin was staring at the group, quiet and thoughtful. A crow cawed in the tree above him, but they stayed away with all the other humans nearby.

"He really doesn't know, does he?" Corbin finally asked.

I hummed in agreement. I didn't think he did.

"He's such a shining soul, so bright. I'm not sure I would have known, except I saw it when he looked at the old man. I saw the shape of him," Corbin said quietly.

"Were you frightened?" I asked.

Corbin looked at me sharply. "He isn't frightening."

"No, not usually," I agreed easily.

"I didn't think they were real," Corbin added.

We both watched as a crow flew down, landing near Sebbie. Without pausing in the conversation, he grabbed a berry from on top of his ice cream and threw it to the bird, who caught it with a slight flap of wings.

"I had forgotten about them," I admitted. "I've never seen one topside. Not ever, and certainly not in a human form. Even in the underworld, they were thought a myth—shadow and wraith, a tale that demons and hellhounds told each other as a scary story."

Corbin looked at me, saying again, "He isn't scary."

"No," I agreed, looking over at Sebbie. "But everyone in that room was immortal, Corbin. Yet three of them are now dead."

"The Nephilim weren't immortal," he insisted. "Nephilim die. And the descendent of Cain... Something went wrong. That's all."

"The descendent of Cain was immortal, although the blade was draining that from him. I'm not sure how many other immortals they'd used that blade on, but the woman had attained immortality, and whatever she did with the blade would have prevented the man's death. I could feel it, and so could you," I said, letting my hand rest on his back.

"He wouldn't hurt us," Corbin insisted, his gaze focused on Sebbie again.

"Not on purpose, no. Of course not. He proved that down in that room, because you and I both know what happened in there. We both know what you were willing to sacrifice for him to live." There was no judgment in my voice; Corbin had done what was necessary.

"Not just for him to live," Corbin replied quietly. "I would have spared you all the pain of what I saw in that blade."

"You did good down there," I said, reassuring him. "And you were right. Apparently even for immortals, death is not an ending."

He looked at me sharply, and I patted his shoulder. I looked back over at the group; Josh was looking toward me, his eyebrows raising slightly. Did I need help? Did Corbin need us? I knew exactly what he was asking, and I loved him all the more for it. I smiled at him in response, letting him know it was okay.

After all, I wasn't sure if Josh was ready to deal with the fact that one of his best friends was a grim reaper and death ferryman.

⁓⁓⁓

It was dark by the time we left the scene. We probably could have left earlier, but the sheriff kept coming back with questions, and it was honestly kind of amusing to watch Jude's juvenile attempts at flirting.

The sheriff was also kind enough to give us updates. Rick was alive, and he would recover from his injuries. I might have been mildly disappointed, but I also didn't want Josh thinking he had somehow led to someone's death, so I supposed it was all for the best.

There was evidence that other people had been in the house, and tire tracks and grooves from other vehicles were clear in the back of the property, so the other cult members were not something that we had imagined. Why they'd left was unclear, but I didn't think we were lucky enough for them to be dead.

I hadn't sensed that same strong, burnt smell on any of them, so I doubted they were immortal. I also felt like we hadn't heard the last of the Order of Asterphagia. If they had been using "selective breeding" to keep Nephilim characteristics strong, there was a good chance that the woman we had met was not the only one with power out there. I also worried that they had other weapons at their disposal. It was something we would need to alert all the other hellhound packs about. Perhaps we even needed to get a message to the other afterlifers, but I would worry about that later. I hated dealing with angels and demons.

Cults were such a pain in the ass.

The dagger, at least, was no longer in their possession. It was, unfortunately, in the possession of the police, but I was sure we could fix that. The problem would be making sure Jude wasn't the one to get it. I had very little faith that he wouldn't *accidentally* get caught by the sheriff. Although, I was beginning to get a sense of where the sheriff was, so perhaps I didn't need to worry about their very strange way of flirting. It seemed the sheriff was on the periphery of our pack, and I didn't mind that at all. He was a good man.

We'd taken two cars back, and Thea, Jude, and Corbin rode with us. Thea had elected to stay at the main house with Jude and Corbin. Sebbie was riding back with Toby and the others, and Toby had insisted that he stay over. It eased something in me to know that everyone was staying close by.

Once we got into town, we all opened our windows, and the air was fresh and clean—no smell of rotten souls. No burnt stench in the air. Paradise Falls remained our safe haven, but that didn't mean that evil couldn't sneak in and do harm. The Nephilim had, after all, gotten onto Sebbie's land and taken him. It didn't help that he was on the outskirts of town, and I hoped that would be rectified soon.

Not that Sebbie couldn't take care of himself, although I wasn't sure if he knew that. But that was also a problem for another day. Right now, I just needed to reassure myself that my mate was safe. Even though I knew that he was, I needed physical closeness to affirm it in my heart.

We dropped off Thea, Jude, and Corbin, then drove back to the cabin and parked. When we got out of the car, Josh reached his arms up to stretch, and I gazed at him, thankful that we'd made it back here, thankful that he was my mate.

He caught my staring and blushed, but he didn't put his arms down. A small sliver of skin was visible where his shirt had ridden up, and I wanted a taste.

"You are so beautiful," I rumbled, and I was pleased to see Josh blush again.

I walked over and wrapped my arms around him, and he snuggled into me. I could smell the faint tinge of his arousal, but he seemed content to just stand and cuddle for a moment, and I certainly wasn't going to complain.

Eventually, he pulled back and looked up at me. "Wilder, were we..." he trailed off, like he didn't want to speak the words.

"I don't know," I answered truthfully. Had we been dead? Or had we been in an in-between place? I wasn't sure.

"I meant it, you know," Josh said, gazing up at me. "You're worth it."

"As did I, Mei Ume. You are worth everything. I love you." I leaned down and kissed him.

We started gently, our lips brushing against each other, teasing, licking, and nipping. It didn't take long for Josh to melt into me, opening his mouth in invitation. I grabbed onto his hair, and he moaned as I teased his tongue with mine, licking into his mouth and biting his bottom lip.

"Wilder!" he gasped as I pulled away.

"Inside," I said, giving him a pat on the ass as he turned around to follow my directions.

We both went in, and Josh looked at me expectantly, waiting for me to tell him what to do. I rumbled in pleasure at the sight. I walked over and circled him, the smell of his arousal growing stronger as I did so.

"What do you want, Mei Ume?" I whispered in his ear.

"Whatever you want," he answered, goosebumps rising on his flesh at the sound of my voice.

I chuckled, coming around to stand in front of him again.

"You think I'll let you off that easily, my beautiful mate?" I took his chin in my hand, meeting his eyes. "Tell me what you want to give me, Mei Ume."

Josh shuddered, but he met my gaze. "Everything," he breathed. "I want you to take your pleasure, use my mouth and my ass, and tell me what to do. I want to please you, Wilder."

I looked into his eyes. "You do, my mate, you do please me. Always." I let go of his chin and ordered, "Bedroom. Naked."

He walked into the bedroom and turned to face me. He watched me as he slowly took his clothes off, doing a sexy little strip tease for me.

"Mmm, such a beautiful body," I said, enjoying the show.

I took my own shirt off, and I kicked off my shoes and socks as I watched Josh, but I left my pants on. When he was totally naked, I stared for a moment at his cock, flushed dark red and jutting out.

"So beautiful," I murmured again, cupping myself inside my pants. His eyes followed my hand, and he licked his lips. "Do you want to come taste?" I asked.

He nodded his head, his eyes still on my hand cupping myself.

I slowly eased my zipper down, pushing my pants down around my hips. "Come show me," I told him.

He wasted no time coming over and falling to his knees in front of me, cupping my balls in one hand and gripping my shaft with the other. Tasting is exactly what he did, giving little licks along my length, savoring my cock like it was a treat.

I put my hand in his hair, brushing it gently back. He liked it a little rougher, and we would have time for that. I needed to cherish him first. I needed him to see how much he meant to me.

"So good to me. Such a good boy, worshipping my cock."

He groaned at my words, pushing his body closer to mine so that I could feel his dick rubbing against my leg.

"Take my pants off, Mei Ume, and then you can suck me into that hot, wet mouth," I ordered, caressing his hair with my hand.

He moved to strip my pants off, and then his hands and mouth were back on me, engulfing me in warm, wet pleasure. I groaned, and he groaned in response, his hips jutting forward so his cock rubbed against my leg again.

I put my hand in his hair, tugging him back so he looked up at me. "Do you want me to use your mouth? Is that what you want?" I asked, my voice husky with arousal.

He nodded frantically, the tip of my cock still in his mouth.

"You'll tap my thigh if it's too much, understand? I will be very upset if you don't tap when you need air, Mei Ume," I ordered.

He nodded frantically, moaning around me.

"Oh, you like that, don't you? You like the idea of holding me in your throat?" I asked.

Josh thrust his dick into my leg again, moaning, and I knew that he would enjoy some pressure against his dick.

I took his head in my hands, looking down into his eyes. "So beautiful, my mate. So very perfect."

I began to thrust into his mouth, and he grabbed onto my hips to hold on, but he was very careful not to tap. I almost laughed, but the pleasure was too good, and it became a moan.

I let my demon tail uncurl outward as I used Josh's mouth. He was gripping onto me tightly, his hard dick, slick with precum, rubbing my leg.

I murmured praise to him while I used his mouth, and my tail curled in front of me and grabbed onto Josh's dick. He jerked in surprise, but I made my tail tighten its hold on the base of his cock, and he moaned at the pulling sensation.

I chuckled then, pulling him off my dick and looking at his face. His mouth was red and covered in spit, and his eyes were watery, but his expression was totally blissed out. He squeezed my legs and tried to move his mouth back onto my cock as soon as he was off of it.

"Look at me, Mei Ume. Look at me," I ordered, and his eyes met mine. "You are so beautiful. So perfect."

I let my tail wind around his dick, and he gasped out my name.

"That's my demonic tail, mate. Do you like the feel of it around you? Do you like it when I pull on your cock with my tail?" I asked.

"Please, Wilder," Josh moaned, his hips thrusting.

"You want my dick back in your mouth?" I asked, and Josh moaned and nodded again.

I kept a hand tight in his hair because I knew he liked the sting, but I let him take control of sucking on me again. I moaned and showered him with more praise, his mouth and tongue working me over, one hand coming back to my balls to gently hold them and give little pulls.

When my tail was slick with Josh's precum, I pulled off his dick. He groaned, but he didn't stop what he was doing, continuing to suck on me.

"Good boy," I said. "So good for me. Look at me, Mei Ume," I commanded.

He looked up, his mouth full of my dick, and I put both my hands on his face. My tail snuck around to Josh's ass, slipping in between his cheeks, and I saw his eyes widen as I found his hole. He moaned around me again as I rubbed against it, getting it wet with his precum.

"Do you want me inside you everywhere, my mate?" I asked.

Josh was moaning and nodding and trying to sink down on my cock, and I held his gaze as I slipped my tail into his ass, feeling the heat of him surrounding the tip. I pulled him down onto my cock, so every bit of me was inside his mouth, inside his throat. He gagged a bit, but he only held my thighs more tightly, moaning, and my tail found that bundle of nerves in his ass and rubbed against it.

Josh's eyes closed, and his hands went slack against me. His throat was swallowing around my dick, massaging it, and he was steadily groaning. I pulled him back just a bit so I could feel little puffs of air coming out his nose. "So perfect. So beautiful. And all mine," I murmured.

Josh's eyes opened, his gaze fuzzy and dazed, and I pulled him off my cock, chuckling at his sound of protest.

"Don't worry, Mei Ume. I'm not done with you," I told him. "I need to be inside you. I'm going to fill you up with my knot."

CHAPTER 27

JOSH

I was floating in sensation, everything fuzzy with pleasure and Wilder's voice. I mewled in protest when he pulled me off his dick—I wanted him in my mouth, needed to taste him, and he laughed, a sexy, throaty sound that made my cock jerk.

His tail was still in my ass, but it was just filling me up now, no longer pressing and undulating against my prostate.

"Do you want me inside you, Mei Ume?" Wilder asked, and I had the sense that it wasn't the first time he'd asked me. My head was nodding, but he wanted words.

Words were hard; I felt too good. But I wanted to please Wilder.

"Yes. Please," I murmured, leaning back toward his dick.

He held me steady, though, then lifted me up by my shoulders. I rose shakily, and somehow he kept his tail steady in my ass, making me moan. My legs could barely support me, and I leaned into him when I was standing. He rumbled steadily, caressing my skin and holding me up. I floated on a sea of pleasure as he leaned down to kiss me, taking control of my mouth.

I let him lead, staying soft and compliant because I could be nothing else. I was Wilder's. All Wilder's. I wanted him to use me in whatever way he wanted to.

He led me toward the bed and eased me down, face up, still giving me kisses and occasional nips that sent zings through my body.

And his tail... holy shit, his tail. It stayed inside me, keeping me filled up, but he barely moved it. It was a steady pressure that felt amazing and kept me floating in my sea of pleasure.

When he had me splayed out under him, he began to work over my nipples. I groaned and thrust my hips against his tail, fucking myself on him. His teeth and lips were exquisite torture on one nipple while his fingers tweaked, pinched, and lightly twisted the other. I couldn't keep still, each spark of light pain sending pleasure to my dick.

"Wilder!" I cried out as he sucked on one nipple steadily, a constant, aching pressure that felt amazing.

"Yes, Mei Ume?" he asked, pulling off, his voice husky. "What do you want, my mate?"

"You inside me," I panted.

His tail thrust against my prostate, making my hips rise off the bed. I moaned uncontrollably as he began thrusting in and out, hitting my spot with each thrust.

"Oh god, Wilder!"

"So beautiful. You are my treasure. Such a good boy for me," he murmured.

"Wilder, please!" I begged.

"What, Mei Ume? What do you want?" he asked again.

"Your knot, Wilder. I want you to knot me and fill me up," I groaned.

He kissed me, his mouth devouring mine. His tail went deeper, and I arched up, gasping. He leaned down and bit my neck, and my hands gripped him, my nails digging into his back.

"So perfect. Mark me up, just like I'm going to mark you up," Wilder murmured in my ear before giving the lobe a bite.

I felt raw, like every nerve ending was exposed, and each bite was a bright spark that lit up my whole body. Wilder's tail slid out of me, and I whined in protest.

"I know, Mei Ume, I know," he murmured.

I could feel him lining himself up to enter me. His dick was slick, and I had no idea when he'd gotten lube and didn't much care if he didn't use it. I wanted the burn and the pressure. I wanted the spark of pain that slid into endless pleasure when he filled me up.

He teased at my entrance, and when the head slid in, I thrust my hips down, taking him all in and crying out at the sensation. Wilder groaned in my ear as my body spasmed around him.

"Yes, mate, take me in. Take what you need from me," he murmured.

He flipped us over, putting me on top, and I sank even further onto his dick, the burn and fullness taking all my attention.

"So beautiful," Wilder said again, holding gently onto my hips.

I took a moment to adjust, reveling in the feel of him inside me. Then I began to move, sliding myself up and down as we both moaned in pleasure. I rested my hands on his chest to get better leverage. He shifted his hips a bit, and with that, he hit my prostate, making me gasp.

He smiled at my gasp, his eyes hooded, his face lax with pleasure, and I felt so good that I was making him feel that way. I was bringing him that pleasure. He used his hands on my hips to help guide me, thrusting up to meet my down thrusts, and I was lost in the sensations.

His body was hot and firm beneath me, my cock was bobbing up and down, hard and aching, and my ass was full of Wilder. I couldn't stop the little noises coming out of me, and Wilder hummed in appreciation, murmuring how beautiful I was, how perfect I was, how good I was.

I wanted the moment to last forever, because it was all bliss. His tail came around and wrapped around my dick. I cried out; I wasn't going to last. His tail wound around me, squeezing my cock and gently pulling on it. The pressure in my hole, the steady thrust against my prostate, and the squeezing of my cock sent me over the edge.

I came with a shout, my whole body going lax on top of Wilder. He thrust up into me as I continued to come, my entire body shaking with the intensity of my orgasm. His tail milked the last of my orgasm from me, and then he effortlessly flipped us so I was underneath him, lifting my hips with one hand so we were angled together.

I groaned as his tail loosened around me, but it held onto my cock lightly. I was still somehow hard, and the pleasure was on the verge of being too much. Every nerve felt like it was exposed, and the line between pleasure and pain blurred. I wanted to pull away and yet I never wanted it to stop.

Wilder thrust into me, chasing his own pleasure, and I grabbed onto his back, my nails digging in and urging him on. His head rested against my shoulder, and I leaned up and bit his neck, hard, just like he had done to me. He moaned out, and I felt his cock growing thicker.

"Please, Wilder," I moaned. "Knot me."

He groaned again, and his movements slowed as he got thicker and thicker inside me. I thrust my hips against him, moaning.

"I'm so full, Wilder, so full of you. Feels so good."

"Yes, Mei Ume, you take me so well. Such a good boy, taking everything, giving me so much pleasure. You feel so good around me," he murmured.

His words sent arcs of pleasure through my whole body, and when he bit down on my neck, I felt another orgasm wash over me, my body shaking with it. It went on and on, like a soft wave washing through my entire body.

Eventually he stilled, his cock still full and heavy inside me, and he rolled us so I was on top again. I groaned in protest—I had enjoyed his weight on top of me. I felt like I might fly apart if he wasn't there to press me down.

He seemed to know, because he wrapped his arms around me, holding me tightly against him. I relaxed against his chest, pressing little kisses and licks on his skin, tasting the smoky, salty essence of him.

He kissed the top of my head, his hands rubbing down my back, pressing me into him, soothing me. He continued to mutter words of praise, and I floated for a while, sated and warm and still full of Wilder.

Eventually the pressure eased, Wilder's knot going down. At some point his tail had let my cock go. I gave a sound of protest as his softening cock slid free and I felt a trickle of cum leaking out. He hugged me tighter, and his tail slid into my hole, making me hum in happiness.

"Do you like that, Mei Ume? Keeping me inside you?" he whispered.

"Mmmhmmm," I moaned, incapable of more words.

He chuckled, continuing to run his hands on my skin and softly kiss my head. He murmured more soft words to me, and I floated in a haze of pleasure. I felt myself drifting off, my eyes and body heavy.

"I love you," I murmured against his chest.

"And I love you, Mei Ume," he murmured back.

I let his hands and his voice soothe me into sleep.

I drank my coffee, which I had made for both of us—Wilder and the coffee maker were still not friends—and stared at the computer in front of me. Wilder had gone out and checked on everyone while I'd been busy, but he was back now, sitting across the table from me and staring at me.

"What?" I muttered.

"You're adorable when you're deep in numbers," Wilder commented.

I blushed but didn't look up. I was not going to be distracted, and looking at Wilder's sexy form sprawled in the chair was definitely a distraction. I clicked back into the spreadsheet that had the notes Q and Liam had made about the missing money. There was something niggling at me, and I hummed in frustration.

"You really don't need to worry about that, Mei Ume," Wilder stated.

I looked up at him. "It's a fortune, and it's missing. I totally do need to worry about it. It's really rightfully Aiden's now, anyway."

"He won't care about the money," Wilder answered.

I hummed, because that was probably true.

"Besides, we already have a fortune," he said casually.

I did look up then, raising my eyebrows.

Wilder shrugged, looking slightly embarrassed. "I forget sometimes. I've been around since time began."

I snorted. "Gives a new meaning to age gap," I mumbled.

Wilder winked at me. "You want to call me Daddy?"

"More like great, great, great, great granddaddy," I answered, laughing.

Wilder laughed with me, and when our chuckles faded he added, "I mean it, though. We don't need the money. We have more than we know what to do with. We periodically give it away to charities to offload funds. Too much money draws attention, and we don't want that."

I looked back at my computer, the thought still niggling in my brain. "Yeah, well, then you could give this money to charity. Better that than some cult getting a hold of it," I answered.

I picked up my phone and called Q, that thought continuing to niggle. He answered on the second ring.

"What?" Q asked. Typical Q, no greeting, just a snarky "What."

"Do you have the guy's cell phone?" I asked.

"Sure, but we broke into his password service where he kept the passwords of literally everything, and the stupid bank passwords were not there," Q answered.

"Can you bring it over?" I asked.

Q sighed dramatically, like I wasn't a quick walk from him, and muttered that he was on his way.

I looked back at the computer, finding the banks that the accounts were in. I had IBAN numbers for the accounts—there were five of them in total, so I had the names of the banks and the account numbers, but that didn't get me into their secure servers to transfer funds. We wouldn't want to close the accounts, just slowly drain them to insignificant amounts.

Honestly, if we could donate it to charities, that would be even better. Funds sent to a lot of different charities wouldn't lead back to us in any way if it did catch anyone's attention, and people with large funds donated money all the time for the tax write-offs.

Q, Liam, Aiden, and Fluffy showed up about twenty minutes later.

I gave Fluffy a look as he walked in. "No flames," I insisted.

Fluffy panted in reply, and Liam snorted. I shot him a look and he sobered up, trying to look like he hadn't just been mocking his brother. I continued to glare until he held out the phone like a peace offering, smiling at me.

"Mmmhmmm. You all can sit down and relax or leave, but there will be no fighting," I declared.

I could see Wilder's smile behind his coffee cup, but I ignored it as everyone sat around the living room and started chatting. Wilder went to join them, giving me a kiss on the head as he walked by.

Predictably, they all started chatting about yesterday's events, and apparently they wanted more details on exactly what had happened. Sebbie had told a great story to the police, but we'd all seen Thea stab the woman in that basement. There was no way Sebbie could have missed it.

Of course, she also hadn't bled, and then there was some other freaky supernatural stuff that happened, but I was choosing to remain blissfully ignorant on all that. They were hellhounds, they did hellhound stuff, and we were all fine. That was all that mattered.

I tuned out their chatter and looked at the phone, scrolling through the apps. I didn't think this guy had ever cleaned out his cell phone. I went into each folder full of apps, and I scrolled through the google drive as well. There were a lot of docs and spreadsheets to go through, and I'd come back to them if I needed to. Before that, I tried the notes app.

I snorted. Yup, there were a few notes saved, but the most recent one was a mess, to put it lightly. It was like a hallway closet that you shoved everything imaginable into so it was out of sight when guests came over.

There were random log-ins, half of what looked like a packing list, a list of movie recommendations, notes that made little sense out of context, two drafts of emails, dates and appointments, a list of hotels... it just went on and on. I scrolled and scrolled and scrolled, amazed that he could find anything in the chaos.

Eventually, near the bottom, there were five twelve digit numbers. Beneath that, there were two words and a string of numbers with no spaces.

If the guy weren't dead, I would have to have a serious talk with him. Did he seriously use the same password for all five bank accounts, and then write it in his notes app? I guess I shouldn't have been surprised, because people were idiots about protecting their online finances, but still...

I went into each bank based on the account numbers, and I used his first and last name as username and the password he had written down. That didn't work, so I tried his first and last name with the number one after it.

Jackpot.

I went through each account, and the sign-in and passwords were all the same. I snorted in amusement, and I heard silence. I looked over at the living room, and everyone was staring at me.

"So, Aiden, what do you plan to do with your millions of dollars?" I asked.

EPILOGUE

WILDER

As I'd predicted, Aiden did not want the money. We had a family dinner that night at Toby's, and everyone, including Thea and Sebbie, came. Corbin and Jude cooked, because that wasn't Toby's area of expertise, and we all sat around and chatted.

It was noisy, loud, and rambunctious, and I knew Josh was slightly overwhelmed but also very happy. He yelled at each of the boys at least once, and they just smiled and gave him sheepish looks. I almost thought to tell Josh that they were going out of their way to do something to get reprimanded for, but I thought he might have already realized it. It was kind of cute in an adolescent sort of way. I think all the boys wanted to feel accepted by Josh, and reprimanding was his love language. The boys knew it and were pleased each time they got told not to do something. In return, they jokingly called him step-dad or dad, and Josh blushed adorably each time they did.

He smiled and muttered about "kids" at one point when Jude and Dexter were poking each other, and I chose not to remind him that they were all way, way older than him. My mate preferred to ignore most of the supernatural elements, and I could respect that.

Josh liked things neat and orderly, and I was happy not to disrupt that.

"Tell me again, in detail, how you got access to the money," Toby told Josh when we were done with dinner. He, of course, had a notepad out.

Josh sighed but did exactly as he was asked. Toby hummed and asked questions, scribbling down things as he did.

"You know, I tried to google how to transfer money from an offshore account that didn't belong to you, and would you believe that the stupid AI answer that pops up at the top told me that I was searching something that was illegal, and then it gave me other search suggestions?" Toby grumbled.

Josh looked slightly alarmed at that, and he looked over at Liam.

"Yeah, I'll clear his browser history and make sure he doesn't end up on any watchlists," Liam promised.

Toby seemed not to notice, and Dexter just looked pleased with his mate, regardless of any possible trouble he might have gotten into.

Everyone praised Josh extensively on how he'd managed to get access to the funds, and my Mei Ume just blushed and brushed it off, but I could tell he was pleased.

"Now there's no way you're *ever* paying rent," Q declared at one point, looking smug.

I knew Josh was about to argue, and we didn't need those two butting heads again, so I murmured to Josh, "You really did an amazing job, Mei Ume," then I kissed him.

Eventually, we all started discussing the money. We made a list of charities that we planned to distribute the funds to, and Liam insisted on being the one to actually do it so that Josh didn't break the law. It was kind of sweet, although Josh reminded him that he'd already signed into the accounts from his computer. Liam said he'd take care of that, and then we were back to finding places to donate to.

Josh told everyone that we needed to make sure to spread the wealth over different charities but also over different locations, so that we didn't leave a heavier donation zone by where we lived. Everyone praised him again for being so smart, and Josh just blushed, saying it probably wasn't necessary since the account holder wasn't alive. It was still good thinking, and I gave Josh a smile and murmured my appreciation.

Eventually, Josh and I found ourselves in relative privacy in the kitchen area, cleaning up the counters while everyone else chatted in the living room. I think Josh just needed a moment away from all the attention.

"You did good, Mei Ume," I said, putting my hand on the back of his neck and pulling him in for a quick kiss.

He kissed me back, moaning softly into my mouth.

"I'm so lucky to have found you," I murmured.

"I'm the lucky one," Josh answered. "You really see me, Wilder, and you give me everything I need. You let me take care of you, too. I love you."

"You are my plum blossom, and I'm glad to be the ground that holds your roots. You keep me steady and give me shade in return, and I love you," I answered. I felt a little silly with my metaphor, but Josh only beamed at me. He really was perfect for me in every way, and I would never grow tired of telling him that.

Eventually talk in the living room turned to the cult and the investigation, and Josh and I leaned against the counter and listened.

"We'll need to get the dagger back, obviously," Dexter stated.

Jude started to speak up, but before Josh or I could say a word, everyone else in the living room said, "NO!"

Josh snorted next to me, and I smiled as well. Somehow I thought it probably *would* be Jude going to get the dagger from police lockup, but I trusted he wouldn't get into *too* much trouble. After all, I could sense the sheriff in my mind, a faint pulsing beacon in the distance.

Thea remained a faint pulse as well, but Sebbie was brighter and more connected to the pack. He was his usual cheerful self, although he kept sneaking glances at Corbin. Corbin stared at him more openly, and Sebbie just blushed and looked away each time he noticed.

"I think we're going to have a new romance in our midst," Josh joked, looking at Corbin and Sebbie.

I hummed in agreement. "Yes, those two have some things to figure out, though."

Josh shrugged. "Yeah, Corbin is a bit quiet and mysterious. Sebbie is like a ray of sunshine, though, and I'm sure he'll figure Corbin out."

I chuckled at that, because I rather thought that Corbin was the one who would need to figure Sebbie out, but I wasn't quite sure my mate was ready to hear about his friend's gifts. Besides, I didn't think Sebbie even quite knew himself.

Josh motioned over to Thea, who was also giving Sebbie looks every now and then. "You don't think she's interested in Sebbie, too, do you? Because that could get messy."

I chuckled. "No, I don't think she's interested in him like that. I think she's more interested in the story he told the police."

Josh nodded in agreement. "Yeah, that makes sense, because there's no way he missed Thea stabbing that lady. He'll cover for her, though," Josh stated, confident in his friend.

I hummed again, but my guess was that Thea was more interested in what Sebbie was and what exactly had happened after she'd stabbed the woman. I sensed no sexual interest between them, but I thought Thea might be a good friend to Sebbie. Corbin seemed to know it as well, because there was no jealousy when he noticed her staring at Sebbie.

As if thinking about him had drawn his attention to us, Sebbie wandered over to talk to Josh. "I stopped into the hospital this morning and I checked in on... well, you know..." he said, looking awkward.

Josh smiled at his unwillingness to say Rick's name. "It's okay, Sebbie. Rick is an asshole, but I don't want him dead."

Sebbie looked relieved. "Well, he'll be okay. He was stabbed a few times, but no major arteries were hit, and he'll survive. He's still kind of out there mentally, according to the nurses, but apparently his brother from out of state is planning on taking him with him once he's released from the hospital."

Josh nodded his head. "Thanks, Sebbie."

Toby called Sebbie over, probably with another question about being kidnapped, and Sebbie just rolled his eyes and smiled, walking away.

"Do you want to see him before he leaves the state?" I asked Josh. "Do you need closure from everything that happened?"

Josh paused for a moment, and I was glad he was thinking it through. He sighed and looked at me after a minute.

"No, I don't think so. I'm still seeing Helene and processing everything. I know Rick was an asshole, and I know he was abusive. I loved him once, but that love dried up with his actions. Helene says it's okay if I hate him, but I think I left before it got to that point. I don't like him, but I don't want him dead, either. I'm glad he'll live, and I really hope he'll work through his own shit and figure out why he's like that," Josh said.

I wrapped my arms around him and hugged him, kissing the top of his head. "You are kind and forgiving, Mei Ume. You have a beautiful soul."

"Mmm. Maybe. I'm just glad he's gone from my life, and I don't need anything more than that. I don't want to give him the time or energy required to see him. It'll take time for me to fully get over everything that happened, but I *will* get over it. He isn't my problem or my worry anymore, and it's like a weight lifted off of me to know that," Josh confessed.

"If you change your mind, or if you ever need to talk about anything, I'm here for you," I promised him.

He looked up at me and smiled. "I know you are, Wilder."

We leaned in and kissed, our mouths soft and gentle, our arms wrapped around each other.

I admit I probably would have gotten a bit more carried away —my mate was irresistible, after all—but Jude's voice broke into the moment.

"Josh and Wilder, sitting in a tree, K-I-S-S-I-N-G," he sing-songed.

Josh groaned against my lips, tucking his head into my chest, and I heard a pillow getting thrown at Jude. I looked up to see Jude about to throw it back at Dexter, who had apparently been the offending party, and I just raised my eyebrows at him.

He looked a little sheepish but smiled at me. Everyone turned to look toward Josh and I, and I saw the love shining in all my boys' eyes, not just for me, but for Josh as well. If he had been looking up, he probably would have been embarrassed.

As if they all knew it, the chatter started back up, everyone shifting their gaze away. Josh picked his head up and looked out at the group scattered around the living room.

Thea was sitting next to Corbin and Jude, and they were chatting about weapons, although Corbin's eyes mostly stayed on Sebbie. He was talking with Dexter and Toby, with Toby still scribbling away in his notebook as Sebbie described the basement room we'd been in. Aiden was sprawled on the floor petting Fluffy, listening to Q complain about a customer in the shop that morning, and Liam just stared at his snarky mate adoringly.

"You did a good job with your boys, Wilder," Josh whispered, looking up at me.

"Our boys," I corrected, looking down at him. "They're yours now, too."

Josh smiled, looking out at the group. "Family," he murmured. "I guess we're all each others', now."

"Yes, I like the sound of that," I answered, wrapping him in my arms in front of me and resting my chin on top of his head.

We both looked out at our eclectic group, and happiness flowed through me. Yes, there were still troubles to work through, including a rather worrisome cult, and all my boys weren't quite settled yet. Nevertheless, I felt peace looking at them. Whatever troubles lay ahead, Josh would be by my side to help navigate them.

"Our family," Josh said.

All those decades ago, when I had taken in my first son, I had never imagined it would lead to such joy. I'd thought I was fulfilled before, but then I'd met Josh.

"Our family," I agreed, squeezing my mate tightly.

He brought new meaning to my idea of family, and I was blessed with him in my life.

AUTHOR'S NOTE

Dear Reader,

Oh, Josh. I'm so glad you finally got your HEA. Josh experienced an abusive relationship, but I want to make sure to note that everyone's feelings, ways of coping, and journey will be different. Josh is by no means meant to represent everyone who has undergone abuse.

Josh and Wilder were an interesting pairing for me. Josh enjoys a bit of a submissive role in the bedroom, yet he definitely wasn't submissive outside of it. He's a caretaker, and he just wants everyone to be safe and happy. Wilder is also a caretaker, but he had to be sure to treat Josh as an equal and not someone else who just needed care. Their conversations on being partners and the scene where Josh takes care of Wilder were total surprises to me, but Josh insisted on them. He wanted a partner, and Wilder wanted to treat him like one. Their love, and their love for their family, was very special to me. I love them as parents to the rowdy band of hellhounds.

If you didn't read the previous books, you can find Toby and Dexter in <u>How to Flirt with a Hellhound</u>. Liam and Quinton got up to their own trouble in <u>How to Hack a Hellhound</u>. Aiden and Fire Fluffy, aka Atlas, had their story in <u>How to Tame a Hellhound</u>. It was a joy to revisit all these characters, and I don't know how I'll say goodbye when the series is done.

Originally, Jude and the sheriff were supposed to be up next. I even got the cover made! But Corbin is really very insistent that he can't wait, and he's usually very patient, so I have to listen to him this time. Besides, Jude needs to flirt with the sheriff (and hopefully not get arrested) a little more. He's really having too much fun. (The sheriff is, too, although he wouldn't admit it lol.)

If you enjoyed this book, please leave a review. Every time one of my books is recommended or I hear from a fan, it inspires me. None of this would be possible without all of you. Thank you!

Happy Reading!
Shannon Mae

ABOUT THE AUTHOR

Shannon Mae began her journey in the M/M romance world as an avid reader, then a beta reader, and eventually an editor who works with the unparalleled Tammy B. PA from Aspen Tree E.A.S.

When a dear friend suggested she should write her own book, she decided to do just that. She gravitates to writing paranormal romance, since that genre is her first love, and her books tend to be low-angst and filled with happily-ever-afters.

She is an unfailing optimist with a side of snark and sarcasm. When she isn't editing, writing, or working her day job, which she loves, you'll find her on some outdoor adventure or embarking on a hands-on project (that is probably slightly more complex than she thought it was).

She lives in a small, seaside town on the east coast, and she spends her free time with her eye-rolling, sassy teenage daughter and her adorably loving dog.

Life is a place full of mysteries and wonders, and she hopes to capture that joy and fun in her writing. Adding some fun, sexy times makes it all complete.

Shannon Mae loves hearing from readers!

Join <u>Shannon Mae's Menagerie</u> on Facebook for updates and all kinds of fun things!

Visit Shannon's website at <u>shannonmae.com</u> and sign up for her newsletter! You'll get teasers, free chapters, and all the latest updates!

ALSO BY SHANNON MAE

**Demonic Disasters and Afterlife Adventures:
(Paranormal Romance)**
A Beginner's Guide to Death, Demons, and Other Afterlife Disasters
A Beginner's Guide to Mistakenly Summoned Demons and Other Misadventures
A Beginner's Guide to Revenge, Chaos, and Other Absurd Escapades
A Beginner's Guide to Ghosts, Fallen Angels, and Other Afterlifers

Demonic Disasters and Afterlife Adventures Novellas:
A Beginner's Guide to Christmas Miracles (A Holiday Novella)
A Beginner's Guide to the Care and Feeding of Pet Demons (A Novella)
A Beginner's Guide to Demonic Possessions (A Novella)

Collections:
Demonic Disasters and Afterlife Adventures Collection 1

Hellhounds of Paradise Falls: (Paranormal Romance)
How to Flirt with a Hellhound
How to Hack a Hellhound
How to Tame a Hellhound
How to Trust a Hellhound